The Cowboy Who Saved Christmas

The Cowboy Who Saved Christmas

JODI THOMAS
SHARLA LOVELACE
SCARLETT DUNN

KENSINGTON BOOKS
www.kensingtonbooks.com

KENSINGTON BOOKS are published by

Kensington Publishing Corp.
119 West 40th Street
New York, NY 10018

Compilation copyright © 2020 by Kensington Publishing Corp.
"Father Goose" © by Jodi Thomas
"The Mistletoe Promise" © by Sharla Lovelace
"Christmas Road" © by Scarlett Dunn

All Kensington titles, imprints, and distributed lines are available at special quantity discounts for bulk purchases for sales promotion, premiums, fund-raising, educational, or institutional use.

Special book excerpts or customized printings can also be created to fit specific needs. For details, write or phone the office of the Kensington Sales Manager: Kensington Publishing Corp., 119 West 40th Street, New York, NY 10018. Attn. Sales Department. Phone: 1-800-221-2647.

Kensington and the K logo Reg. U.S. Pat. & TM Off.

ISBN-13: 978-1-4967-2550-9 (ebook)
ISBN-10: 1-4967-2550-6 (ebook)
Kensington Electronic Edition: November 2020

ISBN-13: 978-1-4967-2549-3
ISBN-10: 1-4967-2549-2
First Kensington Trade Paperback Printing: November 2020

10 9 8 7 6 5 4 3 2 1

Printed in the United States of America

Contents

Father Goose

JODI THOMAS

Chapter 1

Time: December 1867
Location: Jefferson, Texas

Trapper Hawkins rode into the settlement of Jefferson, Texas, at dusk, just as he had the day before. Late sunshine flickered off Big Cypress Bayou like diamonds on new-formed ice.

The wind was cold, promising rain that might change to snow by midnight. The temperature didn't matter. He'd been cold to the bone so long he wasn't sure he was alive. Now and then he thought if someone cut out his heart, he'd still function.

Memories drifted in his mind like sand on the wind. He'd been seventeen when he'd signed up to fight for his state, Tennessee, in a war he didn't understand between states. But his three big brothers were excited to go, and Trapper didn't want to be left home on the farm with his father.

The old man blamed Trapper for his mother's death. His father never looked at his youngest and left Trapper's raising to his older sons. One of his first memories was being locked out of the cabin for forgetting to do something. He'd been four and the night was cold. He lay on the ground without cover and pretended he didn't feel the cold. Pretending became his first defense.

Trapper grinned to himself. His bad luck might have started at birth, but he chose to remember his childhood as easy, not the hard reality it had been. Maybe that was how he made it through the war. Maybe that was why playing the part of a gambler at night fitted him well. No one knew him, so he could be whoever he wanted to be.

As he moved down the main street of Jefferson, Trapper saw two soldiers walking toward him. The war had been over for two years, yet he still came to full alert when he saw Yankee blue.

He leaned forward, patting Midnight's neck so the soldiers couldn't see his face. "Easy now, boy," he whispered as he had a thousand times during the war. The horse seemed to understand to remain still and not make a sound.

Trapper never wore a uniform in the war. He'd first been assigned as a dispatcher. He rode from camp to camp delivering messages. He was tall and lean at seventeen. Young enough, or maybe dumb enough, to think it fun to tease danger. He'd cross the lines, play the part of a farmer when he was questioned, and set traps so that anyone following him would be sorry.

Often the traps caught game, and as the war lingered on, the fresh meat was much needed. That was when the men began to call him Trapper. By the end of the war, he barely remembered his given name or the life he'd once had.

"Hello, mister," one of the soldiers yelled, drawing Trapper's attention. "Mind telling us why you're out so late? Shouldn't you be home having dinner?"

Trapper had no idea if this town had a curfew. When the soldiers came in after the war, they set all kinds of rules. Jailed people for pretty much any reason. Most of the Yankees were just doing their job, but a few, who came south to make a fortune, liked to cause trouble.

Trapper kept his hat low. Few could identify him from the war, but if someone did, he was a dead man. He'd been a spy many times. He'd traveled through northern states, picking up information. Men who crossed the lines were sometimes called gray shadows. They were the only Southerners not pardoned.

"I ain't got no wife." Trapper made a Southern accent drip from every word. "I'm heading to the saloon for my dinner. Heard it's only two bits."

One soldier moved closer. "Did you serve in the war?"

"I did." Trapper straightened. "I was one of the cooks for General Lee. They call me Trapper 'cause I can trap a rat, roast it with onions and greens, and you'll think you're eating at your mother's table."

Both men laughed. "My mother never cooked rat," one answered.

The other soldier waved him off.

Neither one questioned Trapper's lie. He'd figured out the more elaborate the lie, the easier it was believed.

As he neared the saloon, he smiled. Maybe, if his luck held a few hours, he'd make enough money to buy a ticket on the westbound stage. Following the sun was his only goal.

When he'd gone home two years ago, he'd learned his brothers were dead, the farm had been sold for taxes, and his pa had disappeared. That night he'd slept in the trees near town and realized there was no home to go back to or memories to keep.

Trapper grew up during the war. All he'd learned was to fight, and he'd had enough of that for a lifetime. The only skill he'd developed was passing unnoticed through towns and open country. He could shoot and track any animal or man. He could live off the land, but he didn't know how to live with people.

Ever since the South surrendered, he'd watched people, never getting too close to anyone. You make friends, they get to know your secrets, and then they're not secrets anymore. In his case, one secret could end his life.

Saloons seemed to be the easiest place to find a cheap meal and disappear among strangers. He'd learned to play poker well during the war and followed three rules from the first day he walked into a saloon: One: Never step away from a table broke. Two: Never cheat. Three: Never sleep with one of the soiled doves who leaned on his shoulders from time to time.

They were the only women he met. A respectable woman wouldn't talk to a drifter or a gambler. Which left him with no midnight life, even though he left the tables with money in his pocket.

As the months rolled by, he kept moving west until he finally crossed into Texas. Here, there was less of a stain on the earth from war. The people might be poor, but they were still dreaming, not like most he'd seen. Yankees and Rebels even talked over a drink now and then. Texas had more to worry about than scratching at old wounds. The state was still untamed, with most saloons little more than tents with dirt floors. If the storms and the rivers didn't kill you, outlaws and Apaches would.

Folks said half the men who survived the war were broken, but it seemed the ones in Texas were also downright crazy.

Trapper thought there must be good people in the world—settlers, farmers, traders—but the men he saw at the gaming tables often had dead eyes. They'd given up on life even though they still walked the earth. Others had become hunters looking for their next prey, be it animal or man. But here, in the Lone Star State, he'd found dreamers. And dreamers will always take a chance on the turn of the cards.

He managed to avoid the broken men or those who preyed on the weak as much as he could. Trapper studied people and saw few he wanted to remember.

As the sun set, he tied Midnight to the hitching post in front of the saloon. Be ready to ride had always been his motto. The town might be an important inland port, but Trapper feared trouble could be coming toward him just beyond the bend. A fast horse and lightning action had kept him alive many times.

A wreath of evergreen branches hung in the bar window looked out of place. Three weeks away from Christmas, he thought, and the saloon boiled with unrest. In a few hours the place would be packed with men, angry and drunk. Like most, Trapper didn't care about the holiday. It was just another night.

He took a seat at a corner table near the kitchen. When he signed up for the War Between the States, he soon learned that one meal a day was a luxury. He always saved that one meal until sundown.

The thin cook, looking more kid than woman, brought him a plate of the nightly special. Trapper didn't look up.

"You want anything else?" The shy girl barely raised her head, and the worn hat she wore hid both her hair and her eyes.

"No, I'm good." He never talked to the women in the saloon more than needed, not even the kitchen help. He knew that as soon as this one filled out, she'd double, maybe triple her pay by climbing the stairs a few times a night. One night he'd see her in a fancy, low-cut dress, and not the rags she wore now. She'd be billed as a virgin for a few months, then the new girl for a while, and finally her rate would drop a bit and she'd simply be one of the doves. Her fancy dress would become ragged and her eyes dull from whiskey.

When the kitchen girl came back for his empty plate, he tipped her. She whispered a thank-you and moved away as a few men joined Trapper, ready to play cards.

Here among down-on-their-luck cowboys, outlaws, and river rats, the game was far more than poker. Trapper had to be able to read men. Sore losers, cheats, men looking for a fight, and even a few looking for a way to die.

But until he found work, it was his only way of making

money. He could have just lived off the land, but he liked his bath in a bathhouse and he liked his one meal on a plate.

Trapper played his cards close. He never bragged when he won or complained when he lost. Tonight the game was casual, slow moving. It seemed the men at the table were simply drinking and playing to pass the time.

Trapper was about to call it a night when a barrel-chested teamster sat down at the table. He played with coins for a while, then offered his next hauling job as his ante.

"It's a three-week haul and pays five hundred dollars. Best part is I don't have to come back to Jefferson with the wagon. It's a one-way trip that pays ten times the normal rate. That should be worth money."

The drunks at the table laughed. "Yeah, all you have to do is stay alive between here and Dallas. Outlaws, raiders, storms, and who knows what. I heard this morning that one guy is already thinking about ambushing your wagon thanks to all your bragging. Must be something special if they pay so much."

Another man added in a mumble, "You shouldn't have been crowing so loud, mister. You just may have signed your own death certificate. There are men in this town willing to do anything for money."

The teamster smiled at the men. "But if you win this pot, and make it to Dallas, you'll have more than you made last year in your pocket. All you have to do is transport one wagon full of something priceless."

The big man patted his chest. "I may have got a bit drunk and said too much, but when I win this pot and take all your money, I'll be able to hire help. If one of you wins the pot, the trip will no longer be my problem."

Every man was in on the hand. A year's salary for a few dollars bet would be worth the chance.

Trapper didn't even smile; he simply played his cards.

Ten minutes later all were out but the teamster and Trapper.

The pot was worth more than any since Trapper had been in Texas. If he won, he'd have money and a free ride to Dallas.

The teamster called. Trapper showed his hand. A pair of jacks.

The teamster smiled and laid down a pair of eights. "Looks like you win, stranger."

Trapper raised an eyebrow. The man looked too happy to have just lost.

The teamster leaned closer and whispered, "One thing I need to tell you. The cargo is five little girls. Spoiled and pampered rich kids. You'll need a lady's maid, a few men to ride shotgun, and probably a cannon to get them to Dallas. Every outlaw within a hundred miles has probably heard of the girls coming home and plans to ransom them after they leave you for the buzzards."

The teamster shook his head. "I might still have tried the trip except for one thing. The little girls' daddy has sworn to kill me if his daughters arrive with even a scratch. I figured out tonight that I'd be double dead if I took this job."

Trapper looked in the man's eyes and saw true fear. "Why don't the parents come to meet them?"

"Word is there's a big range war north of Dallas. If he leaves, he stands to lose all the land he's fought for. Some say he tried writing to the school to keep them over the holiday, but the girls were already on their way."

The teamster shrugged. "You'll spend all your money hiring guards and still not have enough." He stood. "Well, I'm heading home fifty dollars richer thanks to the advance they gave me. I'll keep the money left after I bought the wagon and supplies. You can collect the rest if you make it to Dallas. If ..." He walked away whistling.

Trapper didn't argue. It was too late. He'd won the pot. "Where do I find them?" he yelled at the teamster's back.

The man turned around. "They'll be arriving before noon

tomorrow by paddleboat. The nurse with them will turn them over to you and return as soon as the boat is reloaded. A wagon will be waiting for you by the dock. It ain't big, but it's got a cover. I stocked it with enough food and water to last the trip."

"Aren't you going to be there to see us off?"

"No. I'm staying home with my wife. She's been complaining about having to go along since I signed on. She might be happy enough to be nice to me."

Trapper nodded. He'd faced worse odds before, like every night in the war, when he'd crossed enemy lines. Five hundred would give him a real start. So he'd take the job no matter what danger came with it.

Besides, how much trouble could five little girls be? They'd probably look at it as an adventure.

Chapter 2

Emery Adams watched the card game from the door of the kitchen. She usually tried to be invisible once she stepped into the saloon, but she liked serving supper to the tall man called Trapper. Once he'd glanced up at her, and she'd seen kind eyes in a hard face that rarely smiled.

He couldn't be much older than she was, twenty-four maybe, but he looked so confident. Sandy brown hair a bit too long, as most Westerners wore it, and blue eyes as blue as a summer sky.

He wasn't like the other men. He never tried to talk to her or kidded her about being so homely that men wouldn't take her upstairs even if the ride was free.

A few men would try to see if she was developing, but her mother wrapped her breasts every morning before Em slipped on the dress made of rough wool. It hung to her ankles and was hot in the kitchen, but it was the only way her mother would risk her working in the saloon.

If anyone knew she was twenty, she wouldn't be invisible.

So she dressed the part of a girl not grown and shuffled her feet as she stared at the floor.

Eight years ago, when she'd just turned twelve, her father pulled her out of her bed before dawn and said it was time she earned her keep. Two of her sisters had married the year before and the third had run off.

Em was the only one of his worthless daughters left, and her father planned to take advantage of her shy ways. He knew she wouldn't fight him; he'd beat that out her when she was little. She'd do as she was told. Em, the baby, would never run away. She wouldn't have the energy after she learned to work. He'd make sure of that.

Em had to play the role or her father swore he'd turn her out to starve. She was small, but beneath her baggy clothes her body was definitely a woman's. Her mother cut her honey-brown hair blunt to her shoulders with bangs that hung in her eyes. As time passed, she braided it so her mother wouldn't cut it again.

At first she just washed dishes at the saloon where her father tended bar. She hauled supplies for the tiny kitchen, kept the fire going, and helped the old cook. When the cook died two years later, Em did both jobs.

Her father made sure she never saw her pay.

Though she had three sisters, her father swore Em would never leave him. Her hair was usually dull brown from the cook stove's smoke. As it grew longer, she stuffed it in an old hat she'd found left in the bar. Her skin was dull from never seeing the sun, and her body thin. Em's arms were scarred from burns. It had taken her a year to grow strong enough to lift the heavy pots without occasionally bumping her skin.

Her father reminded her now and then that she was worthless. She'd questioned him once about her pay, and he'd bruised the entire left side of her face with one blow. Em stayed, never owning a new dress or even a ribbon for her hair. Six nights a week she cooked, then cleaned at the saloon after midnight.

On the seventh day the saloon was closed. While her parents went to church, Em went in early to clean the upstairs. Half of the rooms were for the doves and their hourly guests. The other half were rented out to travelers. Once a week the sheets were changed and the rooms swept out, no matter how many times the rooms were rented.

The barmaids were nice and often left a quarter on their beds. A traveler once left a dollar. Em kept whatever money was left in the rented rooms hidden away in a rusty tin in the kitchen. It was mostly only change, but someday she might need it.

Long after Trapper's poker game was over and the saloon closed, she cleaned. In the silence she wished she could go on his journey. Even a dangerous adventure would be better than this. She'd grow old here, her days all the same.

When she finished cleaning, she heated one more pot of water and carried it upstairs to a back storage closet. At one time it had been a tiny room, but now the bed was broken, the windows boarded over to prevent a draft.

An old hip tub sat in one corner. Once a week, in the stillness before dawn, Em took a bath and pretended to be a lady. The drab, scratchy dress came off, as did the wrappings to make her look flat-chested. By candlelight she dreamed of more to her life than cooking and cleaning. If she just had a chance, she'd be brave, she told herself as she used the bits of lavender soap the girls tossed out.

In the silence, with warm water surrounding her, she relaxed and fell asleep. The tiny room's door was locked. No one would look for her.

When a noise downstairs jerked her awake, sunlight was coming through the cracks in the boards.

Em jumped out of the tub so fast she splashed water on her

wool dress. Panic gripped her. She'd freeze walking the mile home in wet clothes.

She wrapped herself in a towel one of the barmaids had given her when she left, headed back to New Orleans on one of the paddleboats.

The barmaid had whispered, "Get out of this place, honey. It will rot your soul."

Em knew her parents wouldn't worry about her being late today. She often slept in the corner of the kitchen on the bench where deliveries were dumped. Her father never wanted to wait on her to finish her cleaning, and it never occurred to her that he might come back for her. She'd stayed in the kitchen a few times on Sunday so she could catch up.

As long as she did her work, he didn't care where she slept.

Em paced the tiny room. Over the years it had become a storage room for broken things no one had time to fix and lost luggage no one ever came back to claim.

A dusty black bag in the corner caught her eye. It was worn. The leather had been patched on one side. It had been in the corner for years.

She remembered the day she'd turned twelve and her father said she had to work. He'd almost dragged her into the back of the saloon. He'd showed her around the place and told her she'd have no more birthdays. She couldn't remember how long after that she'd found the forgotten little room. It became her one secret place where she could think and dream.

Now, feeling much like a thief, she loosened the straps on the old bag. Maybe she'd find a shawl or coat she could wear home. Em promised herself she'd return it tomorrow.

One by one she pulled the things from the bag. A black dress, undergarments, a shawl someone had crocheted with great care, and a pair of ladies' boots with heels too high to be practical.

It seemed to be everything she needed. She'd dress like a

lady in the fancy clothes if only for a day. She'd walk through town with her head up. She'd be a woman and no longer pretend to be a girl.

In the bottom of the bag she noticed a thin black ribbon. When she tugged, a false bottom pulled open. Below lay three black boxes. They were made the same size as the bag, so unless someone looked closely, no one would see them.

Em pulled them out as if finding a treasure. The first was a small sewing box, packed full. The second was loaded with creams, a little brush, and a comb set to keep her hair in place. The third box held a Bible with money hidden one bill at a time between the pages. It wasn't much, but it might be enough to buy a ticket on the paddleboat or passage on the stage to the next town.

A gold ring lay in the corner of the third box.

Em slipped on the ring. It was a perfect fit. It was small, thin, the cheapest kind sold at the mercantile, but she'd never worn a ring before, so she felt beautiful wearing it.

Carefully, she began to put on the underthings. They smelled of dust, but they were clean. To her surprise, each fit. She'd seen camisoles in the stores, but she'd never felt one lightly touch her skin. The bodice pushed up her breasts and slimmed her waist.

With each piece she felt like she was shedding her old skin and putting on another. The shoes were a bit too big. The jacket a little too small.

When she stood and looked in the cracked mirror, Em didn't recognize herself. She pulled her damp, clean hair back with the combs and a woman stood before her. A lady in black with a widow's pin over her heart.

A plan shot through her thoughts. This was her chance. If she didn't take it, she'd wish every day for the rest of her life that she had.

Em rolled up the damp wool dress along with the towel and

put them inside the leather bag. Then she circled the shawl over her shoulders, held her head high, and walked through the silent saloon. She quickly crossed to the kitchen and got the rusty tin that held her coins and rushed to the saloon's front door.

As a man entered, he held the door for her and said a polite, "Mornin', ma'am." He didn't realize his daughter was stepping out of his life.

"Goodbye, Father," she whispered when the door closed.

With shaking bravery she walked toward the dock where people were already gathering to welcome the paddleboat's arrival.

Chapter 3

Trapper spent the morning preparing for his new job as if it was an assignment during the war. He studied maps, learned a bit about his employer, the girls' father, Colonel Gunter Chapman. He'd been an officer in the Mexican–American War back in the 1840s. He was ruthless and came home with injuries. But that hadn't stopped him from moving farther west from the protection of even the forts and starting a huge ranch.

Trapper had seen that kind of man many times in the war. A king on his land.

Trapper bought clothes for winter, a new hat and a warm coat from his winnings last night. He'd worn most of his clothes too long for them to be presentable. Now, when he got to Dallas, he'd be dressed more like a cowboy, a Westerner. And, if the raiders killed him along the way, he'd have a fine funeral outfit.

Walking toward the dock, he planned. He'd meet the little ladies, tell them the rules for the trip, and get underway. He decided he needed only three rules. One: Be ready to travel at sunup. Two: Stop at midday for thirty minutes to rest, take care of private needs, and drink water. Three: At sundown make camp. He'd cook a meal of whatever he shot along the way or use the supplies.

When Trapper had checked the wagon, he noticed the teamster hadn't packed but two blankets, so he bought the girls each one. After all, they were little girls, and they'd need comfort.

He also added apples and canned peaches to his load.

Trapper was feeling hopeful about the journey. He'd bought two extra rifles and several boxes of bullets. He'd get these girls home safe and collect his five hundred dollars. Then he'd drive away in his new wagon with Midnight tied to the back.

A man who has a wagon, a horse, and enough money in his pocket to buy land was rich indeed. For the first time since the war he allowed himself to dream. He thought about something besides surviving one more day.

As he waited, he saw a small widow lady sitting on a bench near the dock. Trapper remembered the teamster had told him to hire a woman to travel with him, but surely he could handle five little girls.

There were so many women in black right after the war, it seemed like every woman dressed the same. Strange, he thought; the men wore blue and gray, but all the widows wore black. Mourning had no side, no color.

The paddleboat pulled up to yells and waves from the waiting crowd. As cargo began to roll off the side, passengers walked off the front in a thin line. It wasn't long before he saw a tall woman in a light blue cape marching with five little girls behind her. She had to be the nurse traveling with his cargo. They all wore a uniform of sunny blue and white. They reminded him of a mother goose and her goslings. He guessed he was about to become the father goose.

Trapper had no doubt these were his charges. The first girl was tall, only a head shorter than the nurse. Her blond hair was tied back, as if she was trying to look older. The next two were shorter, with auburn hair. The younger and thinner of the pair wore an old wool cap and seemed to be crying. The fourth girl was probably about five and was round as a goose egg. The last one, and the smallest, seemed to be having trouble staying in line. She weaved back and forth as she kept jumping up and down as if she could see everything if she was two inches higher.

Trapper straightened and removed his wide-brimmed hat. There were several families meeting travelers, but he was the only man standing alone in front of a small covered wagon. Eventually, the nurse would find him.

The tall woman weaved her way around groups of people and the girls followed in a row. Well, all but the last one followed. The littlest one seemed to be having trouble keeping up.

Finally, the lady noticed him and headed his way. She stopped three feet from him and the girls lined up behind her. Except number five, who bumped into four and almost knocked two and three out of line.

"Are you the driver for Colonel Chapman's girls?" The woman's voice was cold and held no hint of a Southern accent.

"I am." Trapper bowed slightly, not sure what to say or do. He decided to keep the poker game quiet. "I'm Trapper Hawkins, ma'am."

"I understood there would be a nurse traveling with you to take care of the girls' needs."

He thought of saying he could handle them, but for the first time he wasn't sure. Number five had lost her shoe and was starting to cry. The tall one, number one in the line, was glaring at him and the chubby one, number four, was laying her head on one shoulder, then the other, as if trying to see if he might look better from another angle.

"Mr. Hawkins, I'm sure you got the instructions. I assure you I will not be releasing my charges to you until you fulfill your part of the bargain. A woman to tend to their needs is essential."

He thought of giving up. Letting the oh-so-proper lady take them back. They'd be safer on the boat, if the rumors were true. "If I don't have a lady with me, you planning to turn around?"

"No. I'm going to file charges on you for breach of contract. Then I'll notify the girls' father and wait here until a proper escort can be arranged. Colonel Chapman will not be happy if his exact orders are not followed."

Trapper didn't even know if there was a crime called breach of contract in Texas. They had too many murders, robbers, and cattle thieves to mess with a breach of anything.

The woman pushed out her chest and made her stand. "If the colonel doesn't have his daughters home by Christmas, there will be hell to pay."

Trapper had no idea what she was talking about. He was starting to look forward to the outlaws on the trail.

"I'm loaded and ready, ma'am. I'll get them to Dallas."

She opened her mouth to fill him in on all the facts when number five started limp-walking on one shoe and fell over her bag. Her foot went through the handle, so now she limped with one leg and dragged the bag with the other.

He just watched her. This last kid had the coordination of a day-old calf.

To no one's surprise, the tiny girl started crying.

The chubby one, number four in line, started to help the littlest one up, but the nurse cleared her throat so loudly several people turned in her direction.

Number four looked like she might cry too, but she let go of number five.

The nurse said to him in her lecture voice, "We don't baby our girls. Not even the littlest one. Understood? These girls are

Texas princesses. Born in this wild state. They'll grow up to be strong women, not crybabies."

Trapper thought of pushing the nurse off the dock and seeing how strong she was, but he figured she'd file charges for that too.

Before anyone could move, a lady in black knelt down and lifted number five off the dock, freed her foot from the bag, and cradled the crying girl in her arms. "Come sit on the back of the wagon, child, and I'll put your shoe back on. It's far too cold a day to go without it."

The nurse glared at the woman for a moment, then seemed to relax. "I see the traveling companion for the girls has finally arrived. She'll be too soft on the girls and we'll have our work cut out for us when they come back to school in February. However, it is good to see you picked a proper lady."

As the widow tied the little girl's shoe, the nurse stepped away to direct the luggage to be loaded into the wagon.

Trapper leaned toward the widow. "Lady, if you have the time, would you act like you're traveling with me? Just till we get out of sight of that woman. I got to get these girls to Dallas and I'm not sure that nurse will let me do my job without a proper lady traveling with us."

"I was going to Dallas also." The widow's voice was low, almost a whisper. "The stage doesn't seem to be running this week. If you'll let me ride along with you, I'll play the part all the way."

Trapper was shocked. "You would?"

She nodded. "I'd be safer with you and five girls than traveling alone. If you prove to be a not-so-honorable man, I have a weapon and will shoot you."

He smiled. Her voice had a bit of the South in it and she could shoot. She had to be a born Texan. They understood each other. If he broke his word, she'd shoot him, no breach of contract needed.

"I'm Mrs. Adams."

Trapper removed his hat. "I'm Trapper Hawkins. You're doing me a great favor, ma'am."

The nurse came back as men finished loading the wagon. "I'd like to introduce my little ladies before I leave them with you."

She started with the oldest. "Catherine Claire, thirteen. Anna Jane, eleven. Elizabeth Rose, ten. Helen Wren five." The nurse pointed to the smallest, still in the widow's arms. "Sophia May is four. Colonel Chapman had three wives. All died in childbirth and none gave him a son. Poor man."

Trapper studied them as the nurse gave instructions to Mrs. Adams and marched back to the boat. The tallest daughter, with her blond hair, would probably be from the first wife. Two and Three from a redheaded wife. And Four and Five from the third wife. He'd guess that wife had brown hair and big brown eyes.

Trapper turned to his charges. "Look, little ladies, I doubt I'll straighten those names out in three weeks, so how about I call you in order by number?" He pointed to the tall blonde, first in line. "One." Then the two auburn-haired girls. "Two and Three." He smiled at the next and couldn't help but laugh as she giggled, waiting for her number. "Four," he said, touching her nose. The tiny one waited for her new name. "You're Five. It's a game we'll play." He glanced at the widow. "A secret game. Like code names."

When he noticed the widow asked no questions, he added, "Only we have to call her Mrs. Adams. She deserves our respect. She lost her man in the war."

All the girls nodded except Five. She was spinning around again like an unbalanced top.

Chapter 4

After a stop at the outhouse behind the church, Trapper headed out smiling. He could almost feel the five hundred dollars in his hand. For once he was planning a future and not running away from a past.

This might work, thanks to the widow. She'd watch over the girls and help with the cooking. She didn't even want to be paid. Just a ride to Dallas. How lucky could he get? She was pretty too, but sad and pale. With no husband she probably thought she had the weight of the world on those little shoulders.

An hour out of town Number One crawled up on the bench with him. She looked as proper as if she was sitting in church. "Mr. Trapper."

"Just Trapper," he corrected.

"Mr. Trapper," she insisted. "I was wondering if I could man the reins."

"You know how to handle a wagon?" He swore her pointed little nose went up two inches. "A four-horse rig."

"I'm Colonel Chapman's daughter, sir. I assure you, I was driving a wagon by the time I was six, riding at four."

Trapper was impressed. He handed her the reins. The road was pointed straight west and dry. How much trouble could she get into?

Ten minutes later he decided she was better than he was at handling the team. "Any time you want to drive just let me know, One."

She smiled. "I'm thirteen years old, sir. I'm almost grown. We will get along fine if you remember that fact."

"Almost," he whispered as he watched the countryside passing. He'd been an "almost" when he'd joined the army. Now, at twenty-four, he felt like an old man. He'd seen enough fighting and dying to last him ten lifetimes.

He smiled. Widow Adams would take care of the girls and One could drive when he circled back to make sure they weren't being followed. This trip was going to be easy.

He heard the girls in the back singing songs. Farms spotted the land, and now and then a farmer waved from the winter fields. This was going to be the easiest money he'd ever make.

An hour later Trapper wasn't so sure. Number Four poked her head out of the canvas cover. "I have to stop to take care of private things, Mr. Tapper."

"Trapper," he corrected.

"I need to take care of private things, Mr. Tapper!"

She wasn't listening to him and he wasn't understanding her.

When Trapper raised his eyebrows, Mrs. Adams whispered, "Chamber pot."

"I didn't bring one." He started wondering if he needed to drive back to get one. He'd never been around women. He'd talked to girls in grade school when his dad let him go, and he'd managed to have a few conversations with ladies over the years, but he'd never asked about how they handled private things. In fact he'd never seen the nude body of a woman except in pictures over a few bars. Even if he'd wanted to court a girl after the war, none would be interested in him.

To his surprise, all the girls looked confused including the little widow.

Number Five helped him out as her little hand patted him on the shoulder. "Please stop and help up us down, Mr. Tapper. We know what to do." The mispronouncing of his name was spreading.

"All of you?"

"Yes," Five answered. "If one goes, we all do. I think it's a rule written down somewhere."

Mrs. Adams took over. "We'll all have to make a circle, Mr. Trapper. It's a lady's way."

"Oh," he said, pulling up the horses though he didn't understand at all.

The girls nodded as he helped each one out of the wagon.

They walked over near a stand of trees and formed a circle, with Number Four in the center. Then they did the strangest thing. They turned their backs to her, held out their skirts, and waited.

One by one, each took her turn in the center, then laughed as they all ran back to the wagon. He climbed down and helped each one up, counting as he loaded.

He noticed when he looked back into the wagon that they'd made their luggage into tiny chairs and tables and the blankets he'd bought were now cushions. Their bonnets were tied to the top of the cover, but Number Three still wore her wool cap, as if it might snow at any moment.

As he lifted Number Five, she leaned close to him and patted his cheek. Trapper couldn't help but smile.

When he looked around for the last girl, he couldn't see her. Number Four, the chubby one, was missing.

Great! He wasn't five miles out of town and he'd already lost one.

He looked around and saw her picking up rocks. "Four!" he yelled.

She paid no attention to him.

He walked toward her. "Four, it's time to go."

She looked up at him, and he saw panic in her eyes.

Trapper knelt to one knee, not wanting to frighten her. "Remember, honey, we're playing a game. You're Four." He told himself to be stern, but he couldn't. She had pretty, brown eyes and curls that bounced.

"I forgot. You want to see my rocks?" she whispered.

"Sure."

Four showed him two rocks. "I love rocks. My teacher said they hold the history of the earth in them."

"They are fine rocks," he said as he offered his hand. "How about we head back to the wagon and you show the others?" Her fingers felt so tiny in his big hand. As he walked, he added, "Do you think you can remember your name is Four for the trip, and that we all have to try to stay together?"

She smiled. "I'll try, Mr. Tapper."

Trapper didn't correct her. He never wanted to see panic in her chestnut eyes again.

After he lifted her in and climbed up on the seat, Trapper found Mrs. Adams sitting beside him. The widow might think he needed company, or maybe she felt she'd been needed as an interpreter.

They rode for a while, listening to the girls talk. Finally, as the afternoon dragged on, the conversations about school stopped.

Mrs. Adams touched his shoulder as she looked back. "They're sleeping," she whispered.

He nodded, still having no idea how to talk to the widow.

"They're sweet little things, aren't they?" she finally broke the silence.

"They are," he managed to say, then asked, "You got family in Dallas?"

"No. I just have to start over and I thought Dallas would be as good a place as any." She straightened. "I think that the war made widows and orphans of us all."

They rode along without talking after that. He didn't want to tell her all he'd lost and he guessed she felt the same. Now and then he did glance at her hands. Her fingers were tightly laced on her lap. Nothing about her seemed relaxed. The band of gold on her left hand reminded him of what she had lost. A husband. The safety of a home, maybe. Any chance of having children.

At sunset they camped by a little stream. The day was warm for December. The girls took off their jackets and ran around, playing a game of tag. Trapper dropped a few fishing poles in the water, hoping to get lucky. Number Two, the shyest one of the girls, said she'd watch them.

By the time Mrs. Adams and Trapper set up camp and got a fire going, Two had caught three fish. The widow cooked a simple supper of fish and potatoes with biscuits.

"Tomorrow we'll be heading into open country." Trapper talked while they ate. "You all have to stay close to the wagon." He looked at Four.

All the girls nodded.

When he came back from taking care of the team and Midnight, he found all the girls asleep in the wagon. Mrs. Adams was wrapping biscuits to save for breakfast.

"Thanks for coming," he said.

"You are welcome. I enjoyed today more than I've enjoyed any day in a long time. It was good to see the farms."

"Me too." He thought it might just be the best day he'd had in years. "I know it's probably not proper for me to ask, but I'd like to know your first name."

She turned away for a moment, and he thought she might not answer. "My mother named me after her family, Emery, but people call me Em."

"What do you like to be called?"

"Emery." She smiled. "No one has ever called me by my full name."

"You think I could, Emery?"

She smiled. "I'd like that."

"How old were you when you married?"

She looked away again. "Can we not talk about the past?"

Trapper watched her carefully, wondering what hardships she'd faced. "Of course." She stood, and so did he. He offered his hand to help her into the wagon. "Good night, Emery."

To his surprise, when she stepped up equal to his height, she leaned and kissed his cheek. "Thank you. You don't know it, but you saved my life today."

Then she disappeared into the crowded wagon.

Chapter 5

Emery sat on the bench watching the days pass and the brown winter land drift by. The wagon of little girls was moving farther away from any civilization. Each mile she calmed knowing there was less chance her father would find her. He'd beat her sister the first time she'd run away. She couldn't walk for days, but as soon as she was strong enough she ran again.

Emery hoped she made it to that better life this time.

Farms and small groups of family homes often gathered in a circle. Trapper said they were often called forts because the group felt safer together. But she spotted homes or barns less and less as the road became more of a trail. Even the weather seemed wild away from all civilization and the wind howled at night like a wild animal.

A comfortable loneliness settled over her. She enjoyed the girls, but they weren't hers. She'd left her family and was surprised how much at peace she was about her choice. Part of her lived inside her memories when all she wanted to do was forget them. To do that, she'd have to make a new life.

Trapper was always polite. He never asked too many questions and when she didn't answer one, he didn't seem to mind.

They talked from time to time, but neither had much to say. He told her he'd been a gambler. When he asked if she'd ever been in a saloon, she knew he truly didn't know she'd been the ragged girl who'd served him dinner many times.

Trapper had no problem finding game, rabbits, wild turkey, and fish. Near the end of the day he'd ride ahead to set up camp. He'd have a fire going and the meat roasting before they arrived.

Number Three, the princess with the old hat for her crown, asked if she could ride Midnight. Trapper said she could if she'd stay close.

Em wasn't surprised when Three knew how to ride.

Emery decided she'd always sit next to Number One when Trapper left to find the next camp. The oldest of the colonel's daughters drove while Emery rested a rifle over her lap. Any sign of trouble and she'd promised to fire a shot. Two, an eleven-year-old and painfully shy, and her sister Three had orders to watch out the back of the wagon. Though they were only a year apart and had the same auburn hair, Two seemed much older. Number Three never took off the hat that looked like she'd found it on the boat. She usually did the talking for them.

All the girls had switched into what they called their Saturday dresses. They were plain but well-made, and much easier to climb around in.

Em had never had a Saturday dress. All of her clothes were hand-me-downs. By the time she was twelve she could sew as well as her mother, but the dresses she made were for her big sisters. Her mother told Em it would be foolish to make anything for herself.

Beneath the cover of the wagon, the girls played games and sang on the journey, but when they camped they wanted to help. Everyone gathered firewood, fearing that Trapper might get cold outside. Number One liked to help him with the horses and Two always helped Emery with the meal.

Chubby Four and tiny Five took on the job of washing the dishes and packing everything away. Five wanted to help fish, but after she fell in the stream twice, Emery appointed her the official lookout.

Every morning Trapper looked like he was silently counting as he helped each one into the wagon. Four was always the last one in, with her pocket full of rocks.

When he lifted her in, Four would always pat his cheek and say, "Thanks, Tapper."

Trapper would secure the back of the wagon, then walk around and help Emery up. She thought of telling him she could climb into a wagon without any assistance, but she liked the gentle way he lifted her. She loved it when his smile reached his blue eyes.

As the days passed, he rode Midnight, circling the wagon and riding ahead from time to time. He'd always come back to her side of the wagon and check on the "little ladies."

When the wind changed at the start of the second week, the nights grew colder. She worried about Trapper sleeping outside on the ground, but he insisted the cold didn't bother him.

Emery liked to stay out by the fire long after the girls were asleep. Trapper talked about the weather and the plans for the next day. Thanks to him hunting and fishing, they had plenty of supplies. A wagon they'd past a few days back had told them of a trading post two days ahead. Emery agreed they'd stop there.

"I'd better turn in." She stood still, wrapped in her blanket.

As he always did, he walked her to the back of the wagon. When his hands went around her waist to lift her up, he whispered, "You know, that first night when I helped you up in the wagon, you kissed me."

"I remember." She could feel her cheeks warming. She'd been so grateful he'd agreed to take her.

"I was wondering if you'd thought about doing that again. It was a great way to end the day."

She looked down, surprised he'd asked. "I thought it was a nice ending to the day also," she answered. "If you have no objection, I'd like to do it again."

He was smiling when she looked up. "I wouldn't mind at all. I'd be much obliged."

She took his hand as she moved up one step to his height and leaned over and kissed his cheek once more. His face was hairy from the beard forming.

"Thank you, ma'am."

"You are welcome, Trapper. You're a good man."

He smiled. "No one's ever said that to me."

"Maybe no one took the time to know you." He'd never mentioned any family or friends. Maybe he was a man who wanted to live alone. Yet her light kiss seemed to mean a great deal to him.

When she moved inside, she thought how nice it was to know a man well enough to kiss him on the cheek.

Rain started before dawn the next morning. Trapper tied Midnight to the back and took the reins. He told Emery and the girls to stay inside. By noon the ruts that had replaced the road looked like tiny rivers, and the wagon rocked several times, almost tipping them over.

Emery covered her hair and leaned out when Trapper called.

"There is a bend up ahead." He pointed, as if she could see it. "It's got a rock formation behind a stand of trees. In a flash of lightning I saw a few wagons camped there. I think we need to pull over and wait this storm out."

She nodded, hating how he was exposed to the cold and the rain.

"Tell the girls to hold tight, and make sure all is tied down. Once we're off the trail, it's going to get rocky."

Emery pulled back in and began getting ready. She criss-crossed rope between the bows holding up the cover. Then the girls could hold onto the ropes. Anything tumbling would hopefully be caught in the web.

Trapper must have pulled off the trail and into open land. The wagon leaned first one way, then another, but they all held tightly. The girls were wrapped in their blankets to cushion them against any bumps.

"One!" Trapper yelled over the storm.

The oldest girl jumped up and climbed out to the bench.

Trapper handed her the reins. "I need to guide the lead horses. Hold tight to the reins and don't let them bolt." The last thing he yelled before jumping down was, "If the wagon falls over, jump and roll in the mud."

Emery couldn't just wait for the accident to happen. She had to help. In as calm a voice as she could muster, she said, "Now, girls, bundle up and hold on. I'm stepping out to help Trapper."

Their eyes watched her as she stripped off her jacket and skirt. Next came her petticoats and shoes. Without hesitation, she climbed out of the back of the wagon and headed toward the team of horses.

The wind almost knocked her down. She balanced against the wagon and moved forward. By the time she got to the lead horses, Trapper was already there, trying to control the huge animals.

She grabbed the bridle of one lead horse. Trapper had the other.

For a moment he didn't see her through the curtain of rain. "What are you doing here?" he yelled. "Get back in the wagon, Emery!"

"No!" she shouted. When she pulled the horse back in line,

they began to make progress. She felt like they were walking into an ocean. The rain was so hard she could barely breathe.

One step at a time they moved toward a thick stand of trees. It took what seemed like an hour to go the few hundred yards, but when they stepped behind the shelter of the rock outcrop, the wind slowed suddenly to a breeze as the rain dribbled.

Thirty feet more and they were in the shelter of the trees. Trapper pointed to a break in the tree line just big enough to pull in the horses and the wagon.

The wind and the noise of the pounding rain died, but the gloomy day remained. Now they were moving through a cloud sitting on the ground.

Emery held the reins, talking low to the exhausted team as Trapper began to unhitch the wagon. Four little heads peeked out of the wagon behind Number One, who still stood her post. She might be just thirteen, but she'd done her job better than most men could.

Trapper yelled for them to get back inside; then he helped One down from the bench. "You did great, Number One. I'm very proud of you."

She smiled. "I told you I could drive." She went to work, helping to settle the horses, and moved them twenty feet away to an opening beneath the overhang. It looked calm there in the shadows, and the grass was still green.

Emery started toward the wagon, carefully picking her steps in stocking feet. As she watched her path, she suddenly realized her bloomers were plastered to her legs.

She rounded the front of the wagon to the step up to the bench and noticed the thin material of her camisole was wet and lying like a second skin over her breasts. The pink of her nipples was showing proudly through the silk.

Before she could take the step into the wagon, she looked up and saw Trapper standing a few feet away. He seemed frozen as he stared.

There was nowhere she could run. If she stepped up, he'd see more of her, and if she turned to run to the back of the wagon, he'd see her backside.

She straightened and lifted her chin. "Turn around, Mr. Trapper."

For a moment he didn't move. She didn't think he was breathing. He was simply standing there. His eyes were wide open and looking at her.

"Turn around," she demanded.

"Why?" he whispered. "You're so beautiful."

The man had gone mad. You'd think she was the first woman he'd ever seen in her undergarments.

She glared at him, and he finally turned away, still smiling.

Emery climbed up as fast as she could and disappeared inside. Once in the wagon, she dried off with one of the blankets and removed her damp underwear. Then she dressed in her blouse, jacket and skirt, feeling strange with nothing between her skin and her clothes.

None of the girls seemed to notice. Two and Three had curled up sleeping after their frightening ride, and Four and Five were leaning out the back opening, trying to catch raindrops on their tongues.

Emery combed out her long hair and braided it, then carefully twisted it into a bun at the base of her neck. Finally, she felt respectable again. It was raining and gloomy when Trapper had seen her. Maybe he hadn't noticed how her camisole clung to her.

Maybe if she forgot that one moment he'd forget it too. She'd never mention it, and if he did, she'd say the shadows were playing tricks with what he thought he saw.

Voices sounded outside. Emery made out Number One's light laugh and Trapper's greeting. She slipped into her shoes and moved to the back of the wagon to stand behind Four and Five. She might be in shadows, but she could see the outline of a tall, very thin boy, maybe a year or two older than One. The middle-aged couple behind the boy was smiling and appeared to be tickled to find someone else near.

"Come on down, ladies, and meet our neighbors in the storm." Trapper raised his arms and tiny Five jumped into his hug. Four followed. Both the girls stood close to him, and he put his hands on their shoulders.

Mrs. Miller shook both their hands, but Em noticed they still clung to Trapper's legs.

"Like us, it looks like the Millers are trapped here until the storm's over. Number One, meet their son, Timothy. He noticed our horses and came to see if he could help." Trapper looked down at the little darlings hiding behind his legs, but his words were directed to the Millers. "We're playing a game right now. I've numbered the girls off by age. These two are the youngest, Four and Five. We're all explorers looking for Dallas."

The couple, standing a few feet away, laughed. They explained that they also had children, so they understood games.

Trapper looked up at Emery as she neared the edge. He lifted his arms. When she hesitated, he circled her waist and swung her down. He was polite making the introductions, but the light in his blue eyes told her he was thinking of how she'd looked before.

She thought of yelling at him again, but she doubted he'd noticed the first lecture she'd tried to give him. His eyes had been so focused his ears hadn't seemed to be working. Plus, if she showed her anger, strangers would notice, maybe even ask questions or try to smooth over the disagreement.

This was between her and Trapper. What he saw. What she'd shown.

She slipped her hand around his arm and tried to act like a lady and not a crazy woman running around in her underwear.

She didn't risk saying a word, but Trapper kept the conversation going as he patted her fingers on his arm.

The Millers were farmers driving two wagons west to land they'd bought sight unseen near Dallas. They had two boys in their teens and two girls about the ages of Four and Five. Four was shy, but Five seemed excited to meet someone her age. Beneath the overhang, the Millers had built a fire and invited Trapper and his girls to a potato soup supper.

The girls grabbed their blankets and rushed to find a place near the campfire. Emery walked a few feet, then remembered she could add biscuits to the meal. As she hurried back to the wagon, she heard Trapper say, "Go along and get them out of the rain. We'll be right behind you."

He caught up with her just before she reached the wagon. Without a word, he lifted her into the back.

When she had the basket of biscuits in hand, she stood at the opening. "I can get down myself."

"I know you can, but I like lifting you down, Emery."

His hands gently circled her waist once more and slowly lowered her to the ground. "You're so light, one might think you were a kid, but I know different."

His words reached her like a thought he hadn't realized he'd said out loud.

"What happened in the storm never happened, Trapper. Whatever you think you saw was simply shadows."

He was so close she could feel the warmth of him. "I can't unsee what I saw, Emery, even if I wanted to. Which I don't."

"Stop acting like you've never seen a woman in her underwear."

"It's no act. I never have. Not like that, with so little covering your skin you might have been bare. I saw the tips of your . . ."

"Forget that. If you were a gentleman, you'd forget."

"I'm not sure if I died I could forget. The sight of you will probably follow me into heaven. I mean no disrespect, but you're a hundred times prettier than a painting I saw in a saloon in New Orleans."

Emery fought down a laugh. "The way you talk. You'd think you've never seen a nude woman in your life."

"I'm telling the truth. I haven't," he whispered. "Not a live woman. Only paintings."

She turned and faced him then. "Never?"

"Never."

She laughed. "Well, I've never seen a nude man, but I doubt I'd just stand there and stare if I saw you."

"If you want, I'll strip, and that will make us even."

"No. I'm fine. Keep your clothes on. We have a dinner to go to right now. I'll ask later if I need a viewing." They both laughed loving this new teasing. Laughter made her less shy and somehow what had happened made her more comfortable when they could joke.

He offered his hand. "Shall we go, Mrs. Adams?"

"Yes, Mr. Hawkins."

As they walked, he asked, "Why did you take off your clothes in the cold rain?"

"This black dress is the only one I have. I didn't want to get it muddy."

He didn't ask another question.

She finally added, "I didn't realize how I'd look once the silk got wet."

He held a tree branch out of her way. The night was dark, making all the world only shadows. "May I just say that you are beautiful with or without your clothes?"

"No. Forget what you saw."

"Not a chance."

Chapter 6

By the time Trapper and Emery got to the Millers' campfire, the half-frozen kids had thawed out and were laughing and talking as if they'd known one another for years.

There was enough supper for everyone and the biscuits were all gone by the time the basket made the second circle around the fire.

Trapper sat next to Emery on a bench. The night was still stormy, with the roll of thunder far away and an occasional flash of lightning brightening the sky.

For some reason tonight he wanted to protect her. Not just because he'd seen her body, but because the lady only had one dress. She'd taken off her black dress so she could help him. She must have been freezing out there.

What woman doesn't pack a change of clothes?

A very poor one, he decided, or one running with no time to pack. If that was the case, what was she running from?

She was a beautiful mystery. He'd never forget how she looked standing in the rain. She was a rare work of art now hidden away in mourning black.

He braced his arm behind her so she could lean back. Now and then their legs brushed. Nothing anyone would notice, but something both were very much aware of doing. For the first time, he'd found a woman who was as alone as he was.

During the war there was no time to court and when it was over no woman would have looked at him twice.

While trying to keep up with the conversation, Trapper attempted to understand what had happened between them in the storm. First, he'd seen her naked, or almost. He told himself that she shouldn't be too upset. She was the one who took off her clothes.

When he was honest and told her she was beautiful, she got mad. Then she told him she'd never seen a naked man. How was that possible? She was a widow. Surely she'd noticed her husband walking by now and then.

Maybe he was shy and they only did it in the dark. But then the husband would have missed seeing her body so nicely rounded in all the right places.

To top off Trapper's confusion, she seemed to think this whole thing was his fault. All he'd done was stand in the rain and look.

She'd told him to forget about what he saw, but that would take a shotgun blast to the head.

He decided he'd try forgetting one part of her at a time. Those round breasts, just right for his hands to hold. Her hips, so nicely curved. Her waist so tiny. He'd lifted her and never guessed how small it was. And, her legs with the thin material hiding nothing.

This wasn't working, he decided. Maybe he should start with her toes. They were muddy. They'd be easy to forget. In fact, he didn't even remember them now. Maybe this was working.

No. He hadn't even looked down to her toes. There were too many other body parts.

Trapper tried to act normal, but that was impossible. Every time he looked in her direction, he pictured her nude. He thought of how the silk had bunched up between her breasts and how it indented at her belly button.

Maybe if she'd take off her clothes again, he'd think about her with clothes on, but he doubted she'd go along with the idea.

As it got darker, Number Five crawled up in his lap. She patted his chest and said, "Night, Tapper," then went to sleep.

Trapper saw Number One and the oldest Miller boy walk over near the trees and stand so close to each other they were almost touching. He told himself he'd go stand between them if they got any closer.

How was it he felt so old one minute and so young the next? When he'd been the Miller boy's age, he'd been riding through enemy territory with a midnight sky as his only companion. He hadn't even tried to keep up with what day it was. He figured he had too few days left to worry about it.

As they walked back to their wagon, Trapper wished he could have some time alone with Emery, but that wasn't happening. She climbed up in the wagon and helped the girls settle down to sleep. It had been a long day and they were all tired.

Trapper found enough dry wood to build a fire. With the low-hanging fog, no one would notice the smoke so he felt safe tonight, but he couldn't sleep. The vision of Emery standing in the rain was now carved on the back wall of his brain.

At dawn he was grumpy, but the girls didn't notice. The sun was out and the storm seemed forgotten. Emery wanted to spend the morning washing clothes in the creek and cooking up a few meals. "The girls need a bath," she said. "We can't go into town looking this way."

Trapper thought they looked fine. All the girls except Emery looked like they'd been rolling in the mud, but that wasn't unusual to see in little farming towns. He decided to saddle Midnight and ride ahead to make sure there were no problems around the bend. By noon he backtracked to make sure they were not being followed.

All was clear.

When he returned, Emery had fish cooking along with a pot of beans. The Millers came to supper and added cobbler to the meal. They talked of living near Dallas.

Trapper saw the widow yawning a few times and wondered if she'd had as much trouble sleeping as he had. She was in the wagon by the time he waved goodbye to the Millers, so he had no chance of a good-night kiss on the cheek.

At dawn the next morning, the girls helped him pull the wagon out of the trees and they were once again headed west. The Millers said they'd wait another day, but Trapper feared he'd lost too much time already. His goal was to get the girls home by Christmas, but he feared if more bad weather hit, he might not make it.

Once they were rolling, the girls were singing in the wagon and Emery was sitting beside him, so he thought he'd try to talk to her. "The girls look good with their hair in braids."

She smiled. "All but Eliza."

"Eliza. Who is Eliza?" Trapper asked.

The little widow smiled. "Trapper, you do know they have names."

"Of course, but I had it worked out with numbers. Once I hear or see something it sticks in my head."

"I'm aware."

When he glanced at her Trapper wasn't surprised to see her blushing.

He had a feeling one thing was on both their minds.

She tried to get back to their conversation. "Eliza is Number Three. The one who always wears a cap." She leaned close and whispered, "You want to know why?"

"Sure." He breathed in the scent of Emery. She smelled so good and he still smelled of trail dust and mud.

"She cut off her hair because she didn't want to go home. I tried to trim it, but I'm afraid she'll look more like a boy than a girl for a while if she takes off the hat."

"Why didn't she want to go home?"

"She says no one sees her there."

Trapper had no idea what Emery meant. Not being seen had kept him alive during the war. He felt like he'd gone half his life *trying* to be invisible.

When they stopped to make their circle, Trapper pulled farther off the trail than usual. Traffic was picking up. He'd seen two wagons coming from the trading post and a man on horseback rode past about an hour ago.

As the girls wore off a bit of energy and the horses rested, he rode to where he could see the road. Number Two wanted to follow along. She lifted her hand, so he pulled her up behind him.

She had done it before, but he'd barely noticed. One of the girls was usually walking close to him or sitting with him when he watched the road or collected wood. It occurred to him that maybe they were watching him or acting as his bodyguard. Who knows, maybe they were his tiny little angels.

When he knelt behind tall grass, Number Two did the same thing.

He hadn't waited long when four men, riding fast, came down the road. They weren't farmers. They didn't carry supplies on their saddles. Trapper touched his lips silently, telling Two not to make a sound.

Trapper had spent years learning to read people. These men were looking for trouble. Maybe running from someone, or riding toward something they wanted bad enough to exhaust their horses to get.

Who knows, maybe the men were even looking for him. Or worse, the girls. That knowledge felt like ice sliding down his back.

When the riders were out of sight, he swung Number Two onto Midnight and put his hat on her head. The big hat shadowed her face. "I'll stay here and watch to make sure they don't come back." He put his hand over hers. "You tell Mrs. Adams where I am, then tie Midnight's reins loosely to the saddle. She'll come back to me."

Two looked frightened.

"Don't worry, I won't let anything happen to you, baby."

"Two," she said straightening. "We like our code names and none of us are babies, not even Five." Then she was off smiling. She was on a mission.

Ten minutes later Number One showed up atop Midnight. She was carrying two rifles.

"Mrs. Adams said you might need these and me."

He took the weapons. "Can you shoot?"

One made a face. "I'm the colonel's daughter. I can shoot."

Trapper had no doubt.

"So can Two and Three. The little two will learn in another year."

They sat down behind a fallen log and watched the road. After ten minutes of silence One said, "Mrs. Adams wanted me to tell you that we're all going back to the wagon if you want to wash in the stream when we get back."

Trapper scratched his dirty hair. "You think I need to?"

"Yes. You do. We took a vote and it was unanimous."

They waited until sunset and then they rode back to camp. Wherever the four men who'd passed were, they wouldn't be riding back tonight. Maybe they were headed toward Jefferson. On horseback they'd make double the time he was making with a wagon. The road was more of a winding trail now, too uneven to chance at night.

His little nest of ladies was safe tonight.

When he got back, supper was almost ready.

Trapper handed One the rifles and told her and Two to keep watch while he walked down a slope to where the horses were grazing. The sun was setting, with just enough light to see the towel and soap a foot from the stream. His saddlebags were there also.

If he was going into town, even though it was probably little more than a trading post and a few huts, he'd clean up. Trapper stripped and dove in. The water was cold, so he didn't waste any time. In ten minutes he was out of the water, dry, and putting on a clean set of clothes.

When he sat down by the fire for supper, each one of the girls walked past him and patted him on the shoulder. Number Four even kissed his cheek.

As they ate, he explained that tonight would be the first night he'd have a watch. After midnight he'd wake One and Two to stand guard while he slept a few hours. Emery said she'd take another two hours. Before dawn he'd take back over.

He felt they were safe tonight. They were too far from the trail for anyone to see their small fire. If a raid came, it would be after dawn.

To his surprise the girls asked questions. For them this might still seem like a game, but they wanted to know the rules.

If danger was coming their way, they needed to know what to do. Where to shoot to stop a man, but not kill him. How to hit a man twice their size and make him drop. How to read an attacker's movements. All that he'd learned in the army about staying alive poured out. They would have to be his troops if trouble came.

"If you can't convince them you're meaner and bigger, all you have to do is act crazy. Anyone with sense is afraid of crazy. Remember, anything can be a weapon."

Number Five crawled up in his lap and went to sleep, but the others listened and asked questions. They were little girls, too young to have to know all he said. But someday maybe they'd remember how to fight, and what he was teaching them might save their lives.

Chapter 7

The moon was only a sliver in the midnight sky when One and Two took over the watch. Trapper planned to stay awake, but he dozed, knowing they'd wake him if so much as a twig snapped.

Two hours later Emery took over the watch.

Trapper tried to go back to sleep, but he couldn't with her so near. They'd been little more than polite strangers for two days. He couldn't make himself wish he hadn't seen her almost bare, but he did wish they could go back to being close. He liked looking forward to her light kiss on his cheek, and the way she leaned close to whisper something. He liked watching her and seeing her smile when she caught him doing just that.

After a while he sat up and looked at her across a dying fire. "You going to talk to me ever again?"

"I talked to you today." She didn't look at him.

"Pass the bread. Tell Number Five to wash her hands. Do you want the last of the coffee?"

When she didn't comment, he added, "All that isn't talking, Emery."

She didn't argue. She wasn't even looking at him.

He tried again in a low voice. "I can't figure out what I did wrong. I didn't cause the rain or the storm. I didn't take off your clothes or tell you to come out to help. I couldn't act like I didn't see something so beautiful."

She was silent for a while, then she answered. "You are right. It wasn't your fault. I didn't think. It's all my fault."

"So you're not mad at me?"

"I'm not mad at you. I'm sorry, but you have to understand, it's hard to talk to someone who has seen me like that. I'm embarrassed."

"You have nothing to be mad or embarrassed about. You were just trying to help." He stood and moved to her side of the fire. He sat a foot away from her. "So we're friends again?"

She nodded.

"And you'll kiss me on the cheek when we say good night."

Emery leaned over and kissed his cheek. "I was never mad at you. I was mad at myself."

Trapper smiled. "Next time you're upset with yourself, would you mind telling me so I can get out of the way while you're beating yourself up?"

She laughed.

"And now that we're talking again, I need to remind you you're two kisses behind."

She leaned near and kissed his cheek, lingering a moment longer this time.

"That's one," he whispered.

He met her halfway when she leaned near again, and this time his lips met hers.

He knew she felt the spark between them as much as he did. Trapper raised his hand and lightly brushed the back of her hair as he held her in place. Her kiss was soft and he didn't want it to end.

Slowly, he learned the feel of her lips. When he ran his tongue over her bottom lip to taste, she shivered.

He put his arm around her and pulled her gently into his lap; he wanted her closer. When he opened her mouth slightly to deepen the kiss, he feared she'd pull away, but she didn't. She put her hands on his shoulders and drifted into the pleasure with him.

His hand rested at her waist as she moved her fingers into his hair. "I like touching you," she whispered against his ear.

He wasn't sure he could form words. He just held her and kissed his way across her face.

A thump came from the wagon, and Number Five climbed out. "I have to go take care of private things," the four-year-old mumbled as she tried to climb down.

Emery was gone from his arms in a moment and caught the little girl in flight.

"I'll take her to the other side of the wagon."

Trapper felt the loss of Emery in his arms. "I'm getting a chamber pot at the trading post."

He heard Emery's laughter from somewhere in the darkness.

When Number Five came back, she walked past the step up to the wagon and went straight to Trapper. Without a word, she curled up in his lap and went to sleep.

Emery stood in front of him. "It appears I've lost my spot."

"Any time I'm open, you're welcome to come on in. I loved holding you. For a few minutes I had heaven in my arms."

She winked. "I felt like that too."

Before she could say more, Number Four poked her head out of the wagon.

Emery lifted down the chubby angel, and without a word they went behind the wagon.

When she returned, Emery climbed up and tucked Four in,

then reached out to take a sleeping Five. "Tomorrow," she whispered.

"Tomorrow," he answered, thinking a kind of happiness he'd never known had just slammed into his heart.

Trapper stayed wide awake. He knew trouble was coming. He could feel it in his bones. It was one of the reasons he'd stayed awake during the war. Only this time he wouldn't be able to run. He had five little girls to worry about, and one little widow. They couldn't disappear up a tree or roll in mud to become part of the land.

This time he might have to stand and fight.

And he would. He'd do whatever he had to do to keep them safe, even if it meant his life.

Chapter 8

They reached the trading post at about noon. The settlement was bigger than Emery had thought it would be. The stage line had opened a route a few months ago, but it wasn't dependable.

Em shuddered at the thought that if Trapper hadn't taken her with him, her father would have found her. He'd beat her, but not so hard that she couldn't go back to work.

She had enough money in the Bible to buy a ticket on the paddleboat, but it would have been hours before it was loaded. Years ago he'd beat her oldest sister for talking to a boy. Her sister had run away as soon as she recovered with that same boy. They were already married by the time her father found them.

Emery forced a smile. No thinking of the past. From now on she'd only look forward. This was a new world, wild and beautiful, she thought as she looked around. Even if Trapper moved on after they reached Dallas, he'd taught her there were men worth knowing.

Across from the trading post, someone had built a small bar furnished with barrels and boards stacked atop. There were a few tables for the stage customers to grab a meal under the overhang of the roof. Em could almost see the beginnings of a town that looked like a good wind would blow it away.

Trapper tied the team in front of the store and began helping each girl down. Number Five had lost a shoe again, but she didn't want to wait. She promised she'd just hop around the store.

Emery was as excited as the girls. She wanted to buy them all ribbons for their hair. She needed a proper gown to sleep in, and if the material wasn't too expensive, enough cloth for a proper dress. She pulled out three dollars from the Bible hidden away in her leather bag.

If the weather held, Trapper had told her, they had eight, maybe nine days of travel left. When he'd asked her if she needed any more supplies, Emery had given him a list of baking goods.

The little girls had pulled out little change purses. They weren't any bigger than her fist, but each had flowers embroidered on them. "We have money left over from our monthly allowances," Number One announced. "Is it all right if we buy candy, Mrs. Adams?"

Em loved that they asked her. "If you only buy what will fit in your bag."

When they walked in, all the girls stopped to stare. The rough, wooden building of logs with bark left on was filled with wonders. Hats made out of animal hides, bolts of material stacked high, rugs, guns, and knives beside pots and pans. Books, candy, and wood carvings of birds. Anything you could think of to buy was on display.

As near as Emery could tell, no one was in the store except an old man sleeping at his desk with a half-empty whiskey bottle beside him.

"Morning." Trapper woke the old guy. "Mind if me and my family look around."

"Nope. You're the first folks I've seen today." His words were straight, but his eyes didn't seem to be focusing on anything but his nose. "Wake me up when you're ready to check out." His head hit the desk so hard it rattled the whiskey bottle.

Trapper wandered off with his list in hand, and Emery moved to the material. She was deep in thought, trying to picture a dress made from each bolt, when Number Three and Four moved close to her.

"Mrs. Adams," Number Three whispered. Her hat hid her eyes from view. "May I buy a pair of Levi's and a flannel shirt? I got the money."

"Why, Eliza?" Emery asked. "Wouldn't you rather buy something pretty?"

She shook her head. "It'd make it easier to ride. I like riding just like Two does but it's not easy in a dress. When we met the Millers, the mom thought I was a boy in a dress when my hat got knocked off. I can't do anything about my hair, but I thought if I put on pants and a shirt, I wouldn't have to wear the hat all the time. I don't care if folks think I'm a boy."

Four pushed closer. "If she does, I want to get them too."

Emery thought of the terrible sack of a dress her mother had made her wear so no one would see her as a woman. In truth, Levi's and a shirt made much more sense on this journey.

"I don't mind at all."

Thirty minutes later Emery met Trapper at the counter with her material, ribbons, and a simple white nightgown. She feared she was spending money she'd need to get by in Dallas.

Trapper had collected all the supplies and a chamber pot.

He'd also bought Number One a pair of leather gloves for when she drove the team and Emery a sensible pair of boots. Ladylike, but practical.

He wanted to make sure Number Five now had a new bonnet; she'd lost hers on the second day out. Number Four had a leather bag to keep her rocks in.

Two would have her own fishing pole and Three would have a book to read because she'd told them she loved books.

"You're a pushover." Emery laughed, brushing his arm.

"I've never had anyone to buy anything for. It was fun."

When Trapper reached to shake the old man awake, Emery stopped him with a touch. She glanced around and saw there was no one around, then stood on her toes and kissed him on the mouth.

Trapper's blue eyes darkened when she pulled back.

"Why'd you do that?"

"I didn't want to wait all day to kiss you." She stared in his eyes. They both knew there was no time for more. No place they could be alone. But she saw what she'd hoped to see in his face. He felt the same way she did.

"One day, Emery."

"One day, Trapper."

The unspoken promise passed between them.

The old man lifted his head and looked at them as if he'd never seen them before. Trapper moved a respectable distance away from her.

"Where are the kids?" He looked around.

"They are changing. I told Two she could wear pants if she wanted to."

About that time she heard the tap of boots moving their way. As they moved out from behind the bolts of material, Emery smiled as five little princesses dressed in Levi's and flannel shirts stood before her. Each had on boots almost to their knees and wide hats like Trapper wore. Their shirts were dusty red and sagebrush green and their smiles were pure sunshine.

Except for a few braids hanging down, she could have sworn she was looking at boys. Number One swung a rain slicker over her shoulder and Two, Three, and Four did the same. Five tried but her jacket flew behind her.

Trapper cleared his throat. "Whose idea was this?"

Emery looked at the girls "It was Eliza, I mean Three, and

mine. If someone is looking for a wagon filled with little girls, they won't find them.

"I needed a vest too," Number One commented.

Four giggled and added, "She's starting to bud."

Trapper looked like he had no idea what they were talking about.

Number One moved forward as she changed the subject. "I saw a corral full of horses when we came in. If we can buy a few, Two, Three, and I can take turns riding beside the wagon. We'd have a wider view of the surroundings."

All looked at Trapper. If he didn't like the idea, they'd all be heading back to change clothes.

"It is a brilliant idea," he said, smiling, "but I don't know if I can afford all this."

One ended his worries. "We've got enough to pay for the clothes and the horses."

"They'll cost you ten dollars a head," the drunk behind the counter finally joined in.

One turned directly to him. "That's outrageous, but I'll pay your price providing I pick the horses."

The drunk raised an eyebrow but finally nodded. "You do that, little girl."

As they headed out, Emery heard Trapper ask One how come they had so much money in those tiny purses."

She said simply, "The colonel doesn't want his daughters to ever go without what they need."

Trapper looked over at Four and Five, carrying two corn-husk dolls each. "I see some of the needs are questionable."

"No, sir." One smiled. "They needed them."

Trapper scratched his head. "You know, One, someday you are going to run the world."

"No, sir. I'm going to run the Rolling C Ranch."

Trapper looked at Emery and whispered, "I have no doubt she will."

Chapter 9

Trapper walked out of the trading post fully aware that the girls were imitating every move he made. They took long steps. Stuck their thumbs in their waistbands. Lifted their hats forward to shade their eyes.

He leaned close to Emery. "I have my army." He grinned. "They may be small, but I wouldn't trade them for gunslingers."

When they got to the wagon, each one insisted on swinging their now-free legs into the wagon. Five tried twice and almost made it the second time before she fell back into Trapper's waiting arms.

He tossed her inside, then touched two fingers to his hat in a salute. Number Five smiled and did the same. "Thanks, Tapper."

When Number Three climbed in, her short, auburn hair was now free of the ugly wool cap. "I started something, didn't I?"

"Yeah," he answered.

"What do you think the colonel will say about this? Your father's bound to notice."

"I doubt it. He doesn't spend much time with us. Now and

then he looks like he's counting us, as if to make sure we're all there or maybe he forgets how many daughters he has."

"He remembers the number and each of you. He's probably just making sure you're all there." Trapper had no doubt he'd counted to five a thousand times already.

He moved the wagon near the corral, and everyone seemed to have an opinion about which horses they should buy. Most looked worthless. Five wanted only white ones and Four wanted all the ones that looked like they were wearing socks.

One, Two, and Three climbed over the fence, laughing at how easy it was to do in Levi's. They walked among the horses and chose three.

Trapper joined them and checked each horse's teeth, legs, and eyes. He ran his hand from mane to tail and back again.

Each girl did the same.

"Pick your own mount, ladies. You'll be the one taking care of them."

Once they'd picked, Trapper took the time to show each girl how to saddle her horse. None of the mares were as big or would be as fast as his Midnight, but Trapper figured they'd do.

While the girls rode their horses around the corral, Trapper noticed the old drunk from the trading post was finally out in the sun.

"You picked my three best horses. Damn it."

"I didn't, they did," Trapper answered.

"I didn't sell you the saddles. You just going to take them? They are worth as much as the horses."

"I'll give you a twenty for the three."

"Twenty-five."

"Twenty. The girls can ride bareback to the next trading post if you don't take the price."

"Damn. You're as tough to trade with as your daughter, mister."

Trapper didn't correct the old goat.

A few minutes later he told One to drive the wagon, and he rode ahead with Two and Three traveling beside him.

They were not as skilled as Number One at riding, but both could handle their mounts. As the miles passed, he told them how to watch for trouble. How to move leaving fewest footprints on the land. He said they had to feel trouble in their gut before their brains.

As the day aged, he traded places with One and let her ride with her sisters. The only rule was to stay in sight of the wagon, and the three ladies pushed that limit to the edge.

Before sundown they camped.

Emery and the two little ones made biscuits that looked like rabbits as Trapper made sure the older three took proper care of their horses. When he came back to camp, he whispered to Emery that he'd seen Number Three smile twice that day.

The old wool hat was retired to become the cornhusk dolls' bed.

After supper all the little ladies turned in. Trapper said he'd wake up One at midnight so he could sleep for a few hours.

She nodded. He swore she'd matured these last two weeks. No bedtime stories or songs tonight; the girls were all tired.

Trapper kept the fire low even though the wind was kicking up from the north. He figured if the four riders were looking for them, they would have already been traveling back. Once they passed the trading post, it wouldn't take long for them to catch up.

Maybe not tonight, but Trapper guessed he'd be seeing them sometime tomorrow. Of course, it was just as likely that the men were simply riding fast toward Jefferson, but Trapper felt they were coming. Gut, not brains.

The next morning he was on edge. The wind was strong, with a bit of snow blowing like sand. All the girls stayed in the back of the wagon except Number One. She and Emery took turns riding shotgun.

By midafternoon the snow increased but still blew sideways from the north. The heavy clouds seemed to boil above them, promising a storm. Trapper ordered everyone inside the wagon as he drove, fighting to see the trail on a ground turning white.

Finally, before dark, he found a ravine about a quarter mile from the trail. It wasn't much deeper than the wagon was tall, but it would break most of the wind.

Though not perfect, he took the stop knowing that the horses needed rest. His three riders jumped out of the wagon and helped him with the horses. They walked them to the deepest part of the wide ditch. It was too rocky for the wagon, but here the animals were out of the wind, and they found a spot to form a corral.

When they got back, all the girls helped to push the wagon into a pocket in the ravine, taller and longer than the wagon. Trapper chopped down a few branches and small trees to block the one side of wagon that was exposed. The barrier might not keep out all the wind, but it would help.

Emery had a supper of apples and biscuits with leftover bacon sitting out on a tiny table made of bags. They all knew there would be no campfire tonight. They'd eat in the wagon.

Halfway through the meal, Number Five stood up and said that Tapper was staying inside with them tonight. It was too cold to sleep out, even if he did have a P-gun and didn't need the chamber pot."

"What's a P-gun?" he asked.

Emery whispered, "I believe it's spelled p-e-e gun."

He was the only one who blushed. The others all laughed.

"I never knew little girls thought of such things."

"We've seen them on babies," Three announced. "You take off their clothes and the pee gun shoots up like a fountain."

Two added, "Don't boys think things about girls?"

"We are not having this conversation." If he got any redder, he'd be stepping out in the blowing snow. He sat on the bench by the back opening that was now draped with the girls' dresses. Looking down at all of them settling in, he felt like an eagle watching over his nest of chicks.

Emery moved over to sit beside him. He wrapped his blanket and his arm around her. She spread her blanket over their knees.

He pulled her close and kissed her forehead, then looked at the sleeping girls. "I'm going to miss them," he whispered.

"Me too," she answered.

As the last light faded and the inside of the wagon was black as a mine, she touched his chin and turned his face toward her. This time she kissed him slowly and tenderly for a long while.

He didn't feel the cold or worry about the darkness. He was floating in heaven. He encircled her waist and pulled Em on his knee so he could feel her heart beating against his. As they kissed, he untied the shawl and pushed it back so he could feel the soft cotton of her nightgown.

She shifted so his blanket covered them from the shoulders down.

He spread his hand over her ribs and felt her breath quicken. When the kiss deepened, he knew she loved his touch as much as he loved the feel of what he'd once seen on a rainy night.

His hand moved up until his fingers passed over her breast and he caught a tiny cry of joy before it could escape.

He moved close to her ear and whispered, "You all right with this?"

She nodded, then turned to whisper back, "I'm loving it. I've never felt anything like this."

He wanted to tell her how soft she was, how perfect, but words would be dangerous. If one of the girls woke, what they were doing would be a lot harder to explain than the pee gun.

He moved to the buttons of her gown and slowly worked one at a time. Then he slid his hand beneath the cotton and felt her skin on skin. His hand was rough on the softest thing he'd ever felt. Her nipple peeked and he laughed in surprise.

They'd had no time to say the words of how they felt about each other. No mention of love or forever but he hoped she felt it in his touch.

Maybe neither believed in forever. But at this one moment in time, he wished he did. He had nothing to give her. She'd lost one man. What if she wasn't willing to lose another?

What if this one touch was all they'd ever have? It wasn't enough. He had a feeling that a lifetime wouldn't be enough.

He kissed her one more time and brushed her breast once more as he tried to memorize the feel. Holding her so close he felt like they were one person with two hearts.

Then, he relaxed. She rested her head on his chest and slowed her breathing.

He held her against him all night. It might be the only night they had. Tomorrow he might have to fight. He swore he'd die before he'd let anyone take Emery or the girls from him.

Chapter 10

The silence woke him at first light. The raging wind that had whistled down the ravine had finally settled. The storm was over.

He stood and gently lowered Emery to the bench. Covering her with his blanket, he kissed her head tenderly. He'd danced with a few women when drunk, and talked to a few when necessary, but holding Emery in his arms was a paradise he'd never expected.

Trapper had no way to put it into words.

Moments like this in his life were tiny stars in a million miles of darkness. They made all the hard times bearable. One night like this would carry him through seasons of loneliness. Strange, he thought, how he hadn't known how hollow he was until Emery filled his heart.

As he buttoned his coat, he stared at the girls sleeping. Texas princesses born on this land. Number Five, Sophia May, she'd reminded him yesterday of her real name, had wiggled out of her blanket, but One, Catherine Claire, was holding her close and sharing her blanket with her little sister.

Number Four, Helen Wren, had hidden so many rocks beneath the back of the front seat he wouldn't have been surprised if they weighed more than him. He couldn't bring himself to tell her she had to toss out even one.

Four might be the next to the youngest, but she could read him. When he had to stop for the third time in one morning for the girls to "take care of private things," or Trapper was forced into one of their games, Four always came near and patted him on the cheek, like that one thing would calm him.

Strange thing. It usually did.

When he studied Two and Three, he couldn't believe he'd thought they looked just alike when he met them. They were as different as night and day. Number Two, Anna, was shy and organized, with a love of horses he'd rarely seen. Number Three, with her short hair and shorter temper, was emotional, unpredictable, and could talk him into anything.

As Trapper climbed out of the wagon and crunched his way down the ravine to the horses on a thin layer of frozen snow, he thought about what kind of men his girls would marry. He wished he could stay around to run off most suitors. If he were the colonel, he'd only let one in a hundred through the front door.

Trapper frowned. The colonel might want to think about nailing Number Three's windows closed. Short hair or not, she'd be a beauty and probably would grow up to be wild as a jackrabbit.

He thought he heard the horses moving restlessly farther down the ravine and was glad he'd corralled them so far away from the wagon. They might have kept the girls awake during the storm. Then Two would think she'd have to go check on them, and of course he'd have to go with her.

He'd better go check on them early, before he had two or three of the girls following him.

He'd like them to sleep a bit longer, for this morning there was no campfire to warm up around.

As he walked toward the makeshift corral, he realized something was wrong. Maybe some animal was trying to get to them. He'd heard that in cold winters mountain lions would come down this far looking for food.

He heard something strange on the wind. The tiny giggle of a spur. The sound of leather rattling and the shuffling of human feet.

Trouble! That gut feeling he always got. Every nerve in Trapper's body went on full alert.

He raised his rifle to the ready and moved into a heavy fog that had settled low to the ground.

Just as he turned a bend, something slammed into the back of his head, knocking Trapper to the ground. Someone or something hit the dirt a few feet to his left. Trapper turned left, but the fog blocked a clean shot.

Trapper took one step left as two more men, dressed in western clothes, dropped from above on his right. One man's knee hit hard into Trapper's middle, while another's fist got in two hard blows before Trapper could get in just one.

He was a trained fighter, but so were they. After delivering several blows, two of the men caught his arms, and the third man, with the stance of a boxer, delivered a fist to his chin that knocked back his head.

Trapper's world went black and he could no longer respond, but the boxer continued hitting as his partners kept Trapper from collapsing.

He hurt in so many places he could barely feel the new blows coming. He was seventeen again, thinking his midnight rides through the lines were exciting. Bullets flew past his ears, but he rode on believing he was somehow saving lives.

Suddenly, in his mind, he couldn't draw in enough air to

breathe and his horse slowed. Now he was running. Not riding for a cause he didn't understand. Not trying to save lives. Just running.

In his nightmare he was reaching out, trying to touch someone. Running to Emery. He called her name, but the sound never met his ears and night closed in around him. The ground finally rose up to slam against him and all was silent.

When Trapper finally fought his way awake, the sun was high. The first thing he heard was snow dripping as it melted. All was silent around him.

Both his eyes were swollen, but he could see out of the left one. The three men who'd attacked him were huddled around a tiny fire drinking coffee. The boxer who'd delivered more blows than Trapper could count was beefy and bear-shaped. The other two looked more like gunfighters, with their gun belts worn low and strapped to their legs.

Trapper didn't have to ask what they wanted; he knew. He'd been watching for them to arrive, waiting for them since he left Jefferson.

Last night he'd talked to Emery and the oldest three girls. They'd agreed that Trapper would step out early and scout around until he was sure they were safe to travel. Then he'd come back and they'd head out. From this time on they'd be traveling off the trail. Only now it was too late. The bad guys had found them.

The plan was still sound. The wagon was hidden. If Emery could keep the girls in the wagon, they'd be safe for a while. Only, Four might slip out looking for rocks or Two might decide to test her skills in tracking him. One of them could refuse to use the chamber pot and want to make their circle in the open. Number One might decide it was time for her to take over the world.

Trapper knew one fact: With Colonel Chapman's daughters, he needed to expect the unexpected.

His head was starting to hurt more from worrying than he did from his black eyes or split lip, or bruises and cuts.

A short little man who looked like the reincarnation of Napoleon appeared and strutted over to Trapper. The new-comer rocked back on his heels as if he was teasing. "You must be Trapper Hawkins. I must say, you are far more trouble to track than that fat teamster. We lost your trail the third day out. Since then we've been riding back and forth, trying to guess where you were. It was pure luck we found your horses last night."

Trapper didn't speak or move. It wasn't hard for him to look half dead; he pretty much was.

The little man turned and yelled at his men, "I told you to capture him, not beat him senseless. If he dies, one or two of you will be buried in the same grave."

The beefy guy grumbled and finally said, "I don't see that it makes any difference. You told us we was gonna kill him anyway."

"And that little widow with him," another added. "But I'd like to spend some time with her first."

All three started arguing over Emery.

Trapper sat calmly on the ground with his hands tied behind him and blood dripping from several cuts on his face. His one thought was which one of these outlaws he'd kill first.

The little Napoleon pushed them aside and stood in front of Trapper.

"Sorry about my men. They can't seem to follow orders," he said, as if there was nothing unusual about Trapper being tied up.

Trapper stilled. "Those are my horses. Take them and be gone and I won't shoot you."

The thin cowboy hiccupped a laugh and asked, "How you gonna shoot us? Your hands are tied and you don't have a gun."

He tapped the barrel of his rifle against the back of Trapper's head.

The leader shrugged, as if not interested in anything the thin cowboy said. "I didn't spend two weeks tracking you just to take the horses. You insult me by even thinking I'm a horse thief. That's not what I came for."

Trapper saw no gun on the man. He might give the orders, but he wasn't a fighter.

"I heard you fought for the South, Trapper. Thought I'd make you an offer. One chance, you might say, from one soldier to another."

"You're here for the girls." Trapper made a statement. He wasn't asking a question.

"Yes, we are. We're not going to hurt them. They're worth too much alive. We just plan to keep them until their papa gives us enough money. Then we'll give them back, take the money, and head for California."

"I'm not turning them over." Trapper steadied himself. He sensed another man was standing back in the fog even though he could not see him. Once the shooting started, Trapper had to get two, maybe three, before they killed him. The man hidden in the fog was a wild card in this deadly game they played.

The three who'd beat him up were not ready for a gunfight. They'd done their job of beating him. The man in the fog might be the assigned killer.

Trapper put his palms together and twisted hard on the wet rope. It gave just enough to slip one hand out.

The short man was too busy making his point to notice. "Now think about it, Reb. You can get on your black devil of a horse and ride away, or you can die right here. Either way is fine with me." He smiled. "Either way we take the girls."

Trapper figured if he could bide his time a little longer, the sun would burn away some of the fog and his chances would be better. "What's in this for me? I'd already be dead if you didn't want something else from me. So, tell me what you want."

The outlaw leader laughed. "You're right. The old man at the trading post told us you were well-armed and you bought more. I only see one rifle on you, which means the others are in the wagon."

"They are." Trapper saw no reason to deny what they already knew.

The short man shrugged. "I'll give you a hundred dollars, your horse, and your life if you'll go tell the girls to come out unarmed. That includes that little woman you've got traveling with you."

Trapper shook his head and caught a glimpse of his rifle leaning against the ravine wall. If he rolled, he could grab it and get two, maybe three shots off before the men around him could raise their guns. But, the shadow in the fog standing twenty feet back might be ready. If so, Trapper would only get one man before he was shot.

The odds weren't with him this time, but he had no choice. He had to fight.

Chapter 11

Emery opened her eyes. Trapper wasn't holding her. Looking around, she realized he was gone. All was quiet. He was simply scouting around, checking on the horses, nothing more.

Maybe he'd gone to gather firewood for a meal before they started out.

She closed her eyes for a moment and remembered how he'd touched her. Very few words were spoken. He'd told her how he felt about her with his light strokes.

There was no time for words now, or maybe ever. He was a drifter who might not want to settle. But, last night, she'd felt cherished and his touch would stay with her no matter what happened next.

As quickly as she could, she changed into her clothes. They all needed to be dressed by the time he got back. One by one she woke the girls. Before they were finished dressing, she heard a horse stomping, as if the devil was chasing him.

No breakfast. They'd be moving out soon, she guessed.

One and Two shoved on their boots. "That's Midnight," One whispered.

They were gone before Emery could stop them.

She ordered the three other girls to stay put and ran to the opening where One and Two had disappeared.

Branches caught her skirts for a minute, and she wished she'd been smart enough to buy Levi's like the others had.

Both girls were trying to calm Midnight.

"His right front leg is cut," Two said as she cried. "He won't let us close."

Emery didn't know much about horses, but she'd watched Trapper. He always talked to the horse before he touched the animal.

"Easy, Midnight. Easy. I'm not going to hurt you. Easy."

Midnight watched her, his eyes still fired with panic.

Emery kept talking. "I wish you could tell us where Trapper is. Did he go looking for you? Trapper will be worried about you."

The horse seemed to calm a bit as her soothing voice continued. "We want to help you, Midnight."

Finally, he stilled.

Number One touched the rope around his neck. "I've never seen Trapper put a lead rope on Midnight."

"Someone else must have." Emery felt fear cut off her breathing. "We need to hide, girls. Get back in the wagon. If someone besides Trapper is out there, we don't want them to see us."

Catherine Chapman straightened to her full height. "No, Mrs. Adams. We have to split up. Eliza and you stay in the wagon with Helen and Sophia. If anyone you don't know comes near the wagon, start firing. Even if you don't hit anyone, they'll stay back."

Emery nodded. The girl was right.

"Anna and I will go look for Trapper. If he's hurt, we'll get him back here."

Emery agreed with the plan except for one detail. "Eliza will go with you. I'll make sure no one comes near the little girls. You may need her."

Eliza climbed out of the wagon, her arms full of rifles.

A tear ran down Emery's cheek. Three little girls, thirteen, eleven, and ten. Barely half grown, but they were now warriors.

And, they were all better shots than she was.

One took the lead and all three disappeared in the fog.

Emery asked the little ones to bring her bag and sewing box. Four and Five brought them, then stood close beside her, as if it was their time to be on guard.

While she ripped her ugly wool dress and bandaged Midnight's leg, they both asked questions.

Emery kept her voice low and calm. "One, Two, and Three have gone to get Trapper. We will stay here and on guard. If trouble comes, I want you both to get low in the wagon and stay silent. No matter what, don't say a word. Just hide."

Five straightened. "My father says Chapmans are fighters, not hiders."

When she finished tying the bandage, she pulled the rope off Midnight and whispered, "Go find Trapper."

As if the horse understood, he turned into the fog and vanished.

Chapter 12

Trapper sat with his hands still behind him, waiting for just the right moment. The shadowy figure in the fog was moving. Disappearing, almost becoming solid again.

The little man ordered the beefy boxer and one of the cowboys to saddle up. Trapper was pleased to see that the thin cowboy had a broken nose. The other cowboy close to Trapper was still cussing under his breath, like it was a twitch he couldn't stop. He circled around him and pointed his rifle at Trapper's face.

"Last chance. You go in and bring the girls out to us and we'll let you ride away." Little Napoleon moved in close, his tone low.

"They're nothing to you. Five little rich girls who won't ever amount to anything. Even if you got them back to their father, he probably wouldn't take the time to thank you." Napoleon shrugged. "And that little widow is nothing to no one or she wouldn't be traveling alone. If she vanishes, no one would miss her."

The little man put his hands in his pockets and rocked on his heels. "You're a good fighter, Trapper. If one of my men hadn't slammed you in the head, you would have taken all three of them down, even Big Hank. I wouldn't mind having a man like you in my gang."

"I'm finished fighting," Trapper lied. He kept his voice low and noticed the stranger in the fog moving closer.

With Big Hank and one of the cowboys gone to get their horses, there was a chance Trapper could shoot two of the three before they got off a shot.

But he didn't dare act until the rifle moved more than an inch from his head. The cussing outlaw kept tapping the barrel against his chin, as if teasing him.

Trapper growled as he looked away from the dumbest one of the group. In the blink of a moment, he saw blond hair move just above the top of the ravine. One.

Trapper forced his almost-closed eyes open and studied the edge of the small rise. Two's long, auburn hair flashed and disappeared. Two. Then he saw Three, ten feet away from her sister.

Trapper turned back to the head outlaw. "What if I did join up with you?"

Little Napoleon looked excited at the possibility.

To Trapper's surprise, the short man glanced at the man in the fog. The day was warming, and the stranger wouldn't be hidden for long.

"If I rode with you, would I get a cut of the ransom money?"

The short man hesitated, and Trapper knew that the true leader was in the fog, not standing before him. "Who's the shadow in the fog?" Trapper demanded.

"You never mind him."

"Oh, come on, Shorty, who is he? He's standing right behind you."

"Don't call me Shorty."

"Why not? I'm calling this one Drippy. Tell him to stop

bleeding on me." Trapper pointed with his head to the man with the rifle pointed between Trapper's eyes.

Trapper raised his voice. "If I joined, I'd have three rules. One: Get rid of the shadow, Two: Drippy is yours, and Three: Take Shorty down. *Now!*"

Three guns blasted as one, ringing through the ravine like a cannonball.

Trapper rolled to his rifle and stood. Shorty was screaming that his kneecap was shot off. Drippy had been shot in his gun arm and was struggling to lift his weapon with his left hand.

Trapper kicked away Drippy's gun as the girls slid down the ravine, their rifles ready to fire by the time they hit the dirt.

When he saw Number One standing over the shadowed stranger, he limped toward her.

"You all right, One?"

She shook her head. "No. I know him. I think I killed him."

Trapper put his arm around her trembling shoulders. "Who is he?"

"He's the foreman at our ranch. I've known him all my life and he was trying to kidnap us."

Trapper knelt and pushed the blood away from the foreman's forehead. "He's not dead. You just grazed him. He'll live long enough to hang.

"Two," Trapper yelled. "Grab the rope off their saddles. We'll tie them up and doctor them later. I got to get to the wagon.

"One, come with me. Two and Three, keep an eye on these three. I'll be back as soon as I know the others are safe."

As soon as they were tied, Trapper grabbed one of the outlaws' horses.

Just before they rode out, he heard Three telling the prisoners that if they moved or cussed, she'd shoot their toes off one at a time.

Trapper smiled as he rode toward the wagon. He hadn't

heard any shots coming from the wagon's direction. That might be a good sign.

The first thing he saw was Midnight, standing near where they'd hidden the wagon.

Big Hank was pulling off branches and dodging rocks.

"Stop that, lady!" Hank screamed in pain as one the size of a sharp egg hit his eye.

More rocks rained down. Some bounced off his big frame, but now and then one hit him and left a cut.

Trapper raised his rifle. "Step back, Hank, and raise your hands."

The beefy man did as he was told while rocks continued to pound on him.

Trapper handed his rifle to Number One. "Shoot him if he moves."

"Yes, sir," she answered.

"Emery, are you and the girls all right?"

"We are," Number Five answered. "Can we keep throwing rocks, Tapper?"

"Sure." He climbed into the wagon and hugged both girls, then let them go back to throwing rocks.

Trapper moved to Emery. He pulled her close, and they just held on tight to each other. Neither said a word. When he pulled away enough to kiss her, Trapper heard the girls giggling.

"There's one more man," Trapper whispered, not wanting to frighten the girls.

"We know," Emery said in a normal voice. She pointed to the back of the wagon. "He must have crawled under the wagon. When he started coming into the wagon, I was busy with that giant out there.

"The girls hit him with the chamber pot. It was full. I'm afraid the man doesn't smell so good."

Chapter 13

The next few days were hard. Trapper hurt all over. Hank had broken two of his ribs, but Trapper was able to drive the wagon by the second day. Five and Four stayed on either side of him on the front bench, wiping blood from his cuts and constantly talking about how bad he looked. The three older girls and Emery rode, surrounding the wagon as if guards.

They passed through the edge of Dallas but didn't stop. Number One was setting the pace and directing them over open country to her home.

Emery had insisted on doctoring the outlaws. Then Trapper tied them in the wagon and put the luggage on their horses.

When Number One said they were on Chapman land, Trapper thought they were home. He had no idea it would take two more days.

As the ragged, exhausted group neared the huge ranch house, armed riders rode out to meet them.

"What is the meaning of this? Are you drifters unaware you're on Colonel Chapman's land?" the leader of the not-so-friendly greeters demanded.

Before Trapper could answer, One moved her horse forward. The young girl not fully grown sat tall in the saddle. "Are you men aware I am Catherine Claire Chapman?"

All the men looked at her in shock.

"We were ambushed on the trail and almost killed. We have the outlaws tied in the back of the wagon. I want you to make sure they are locked up until my father decides what to do with them."

Catherine rode over to the wagon and lifted little Sophia May from the bench, then looked at the man closest to her. "Give Mr. Trapper Hawkins your horse and drive the prisoners in. We'll race to the house just like all Chapmans do."

All the men followed orders. One older rider, with a mustache that went from ear to ear, offered his arms to Number Four. "Come along, Miss Helen Wren, I'll ride you in."

"All right, Sam," Number Four said politely, "but while I'm here I plan to learn to ride all by myself. Will you teach me?"

"Of course. Just like I did your three big sisters."

Trapper slowly climbed onto the mount he was offered, then asked the cowboy to lift up the widow to ride with him. "My horse is almost lame, can someone see to him?"

Again the older man answered, "We'll see to it. Mr. Hawkins, right?"

Trapper nodded. "So you knew we were coming?"

"We did, sir. The nurse wired us. She said you'd make it by Christmas."

"Did we?" Trapper had lost track of the days.

"You did, sir."

Emery looked frightened when one of the men lifted her up in front of Trapper, but she obviously wanted to hold on to Trapper. All the little ladies seemed to think he might pass out at any minute.

Number One raised her hand and pointed toward home. "We ride to home."

They all took off, laughing and yelling. The cowboys at the wagon raised their rifles and fired in salute. The Chapman princesses were home.

By the time they reached the steps, everyone on the ranch was watching.

Trapper had no problem recognizing the colonel. White beard, white hair, and standing strong and tall. For a moment he frowned, as if he didn't know who was invading his ranch.

Number One lowered the four-year-old to the ground and she ran toward her father. She was halfway up the steps before anyone recognized the youngest daughter.

The colonel hugged her so hard, Trapper thought he might crush her. Within a minute all his daughters were around him, talking and hugging and laughing. He took each girl's face in his big hands and stared at them, then smiled. No matter how bad they looked or how they were dressed, his girls were back.

Trapper stood watching. He'd done it. He'd got them home by Christmas.

As the chaos began to settle, Trapper wasn't surprised to see the colonel's eyes focused on him.

"Mr. Trapper. I'd like to have a word with you. Now!"

Trapper remembered what the teamster had said about the colonel threatening to kill him if the girls arrived with one scratch. The girls were all sunburned and bruised, with scrapes and blisters.

He tried to stand up straight as he moved forward, but Number Three cut him off when she ran in front of him, almost tripping him.

"Now, Papa," she began, with her fists on her hips.

The colonel pointed his finger. "What happened to your hair, Elizabeth?"

"Never mind that. Right now Trapper needs a doctor and some rest. He is hurt and hasn't slept in days because, even injured, he's always watching over us." She crossed her arms.

"And I go by Eliza or Three. You'll not lecture Trapper. I will not stand for it."

Anger reddened the colonel's face. "You telling me what to do, daughter?"

All five girls stood before him with their arms crossed and their boots set wide apart as if ready for a fight.

Anger looked like it might explode out of the colonel. Obviously, no one ever told him what to do. No man. No woman, and certainly no daughters.

The girls didn't back down.

To everyone's surprise, the littlest one stepped closer to her papa. "We're not taking a bath until you take care of our Tapper. He's still dripping."

"Who is Tapper?" The colonel lowered to her level and his tone softened slightly.

All the girls started explaining that Five never got the name right. And Trapper had told her she could call him by any name she liked.

"Who is Five?" The colonel tried to yell above them.

Then they all began with how they met on the dock.

Finally, the colonel yelled, "Stop." When all was silent, he said in a normal voice he rarely used, "Sam, go get the doctor."

"Yes, sir." Sam smiled, obviously happy to be leaving.

"Martha." The colonel yelled again.

A woman with an apron on, stepped from the crowd watching. "Yes, Colonel."

"Tell the kitchen to cook up a meal and keep buckets of hot water headed upstairs." He stared at his girls. "My daughters will be taking baths and dressing properly for dinner in one hour. I'll be busy taking care of our guests."

The girls all smiled and walked past their father. Each kissed him, and as they started up the stairs, Chapman grinned as if he just hadn't lost the first argument in his life.

When he turned back, he seemed to notice Emery for the

first time. "Madam, I assume you are the girls' traveling companion."

"Yes. I met them in Jefferson."

"I'd be honored if you'd stay with us through Christmas. Martha will send a bath to your room, and I'm sure we'll find clothes that will fit you. I see you are a widow."

"Yes."

Trapper's hand was resting on the small of her back, and he could feel her shaking.

"Thank you for seeing my daughters here safely. I hope we have time to talk over dinner. It isn't often we have such a lovely lady among us."

Martha took Emery away. Trapper couldn't help but notice she hadn't even said goodbye to him. But then, the little widow hadn't said anything to anyone but the colonel, and that was "*yes.*"

Sam moved up behind Trapper. "I'll see you to your room, sir. The doc will be here as soon as he sobers a bit. He always comes for Christmas, but he prefers to stay in the bunkhouse.

"We have two guest rooms through here." Sam started down the same long hallway where Emery had disappeared.

Trapper followed, suddenly feeling the lack of sleep catching up with him.

"The old man was sure polite to the widow," Trapper said to Sam.

Sam nodded. "He's always nice to his wives and future wives."

Trapper decided he'd better stay awake a bit longer.

Chapter 14

Emery loved soaking in the big tub. They'd made the trip in less than three weeks, but it seemed like a lifetime. Someday she'd write down all that had happened and save it for her grandchildren to read. And there would be grandchildren, because after knowing the girls, she wanted a dozen kids, all girls.

Martha brought her a warm dress made of the softest fabric she'd ever felt. Without a word, the housekeeper took all her dirty clothes to be washed.

Emery's hair was clean and still wet. She combed it out and let it fall in curls down her back. When she stepped into the dining room an hour later, all the men stood.

Her gaze was drawn to Trapper. His wounds were all doctored and bandaged. His clothes looked new. His smile was the same as it always was when he looked at her.

Before she could take a seat at the table, the girls stepped in. They looked every bit the little ladies they were. Emery and Trapper remained silent as the girls entertained their father with stories of the trail.

She noticed none mentioned the trouble they'd faced in the snowy ravine. Maybe they didn't think it was proper conversation over dinner.

The girls invited Emery to join them for dessert in the kitchen so the men could talk. This apparently was a ritual in the house. Martha and the kitchen help had raised the girls and they wanted their time to talk.

Emery excused herself after two pieces of pie and retired to her beautiful room. She slipped into a nightgown far fancier than the one she'd bought at the trading post and brushed her hair until it shined.

Then, she stepped into the hallway and tried the door across from hers. Martha had mentioned it was Trapper's room. She wanted to check on him. He'd looked tired at dinner.

The room was dark except for the low light from the fireplace. She tiptoed to the bed and saw he was sound asleep. The man she thought was the bravest she'd ever known finally let down his guard and slept.

Without giving it much thought, she crawled into bed with him, rested her head on the one spot on his chest that wasn't covered in bandages, and closed her eyes.

They'd never talked of the future. He'd never mentioned marriage. Neither had ever said they loved the other. But there was nowhere in the world she wanted to be but by his side.

Deep in the night, he moved and found her next to him. Without saying a word, he pulled her close and kissed her.

When he finally pulled free, he whispered, "Am I dreaming?"

"No, I'm here."

He sounded half asleep when he asked, "Will you have kids with me?"

"No," she answered. "We're not married."

"Then will you marry me?"

"No. You don't know me."

"Sure, I do." He moved his hand over the soft cotton of her gown. "I know the way you kiss and the way you feel and how gentle and shy you are."

She had to tell him the truth. The whole truth. "I'm not a widow."

His body tensed, and she knew he was totally awake now. "Are you saying that your husband is alive? Did he leave you? Did you leave him?"

"No, he never was. I found the dress and the ring."

Trapper scrubbed his face. "You are not married. You were not in mourning?"

"Right."

"Can we go back to sleep, Emery? I don't want to think about this until morning."

"Why?"

"Because I've been keeping my distance from you for this whole trip because I thought you were a widow wearing mourning black. I couldn't tell you how I felt."

She laughed. "Start talking, cowboy. If we're going to make babies, I need to hear the words."

He pulled her close and told her what he'd wanted to tell her. If she'd give him a chance he'd love her every day and every night for the rest of his life.

The next morning everyone was up early for a Christmas breakfast.

Everyone had gifts under the tree and the girls' laughter filled the great room.

After breakfast the colonel finally got the chance to talk with Trapper. He made Trapper tell him everything that had happened.

Trapper swore the man's chest swelled with pride when Trapper described how the girls saved him.

When Trapper left the room, all five girls were standing outside the study.

He watched them walk into their father's study with determination in their eyes. Five closed the door.

He went in search of Emery. Whatever the girls were saying to the colonel, it had nothing to do with him.

Chapter 15

Trapper found Emery sewing with the women, and she seemed in no hurry to leave, so he wandered onto the porch and relaxed.

He had a great deal to think about but within five minutes he was asleep.

The colonel's booming voice woke him up.

"Mr. Hawkins, I believe we have business to finish. I owe you five hundred dollars, sir."

Trapper straightened in his chair. He hadn't given the money much thought. Getting the girls safely to the ranch had been his goal from the minute he'd seen them.

The colonel offered him a whiskey in his study, then sat across from him. "On another matter, I've just finished talking to my daughters, and they've informed me that you need to marry the widow right away."

"Why?" Trapper hoped the girls hadn't mentioned the pee gun again. A father might not think the conversation proper.

"They told me you like to hug her."

"I do." Trapper could not lie.

The colonel raised an eyebrow. "Does she return your affection?"

"She does," he answered remembering that she'd crawled in his bed last night. "But, she's a proper lady." Trapper felt he had to add.

"Then you've no objections to the idea of marriage?"

"None," Trapper looked down. "I don't have anything to offer her. It wouldn't be fair to her."

"You'll be a rich man with five hundred dollars in your pocket and I'm offering you a job. I'm in need of a smart man to be in charge of security. Nothing like this is ever going to happen again to my daughters. They said you risked your life to save them."

"Your daughters can take care of themselves."

"They will be able to do just that with your help, so what about taking the job?"

Trapper studied the man. "Did your daughters talk you into hiring me?"

"Of course not. No woman could ever run my life." He smiled. "I did love my wives. All three of them. I acted like I wanted boys, but truth be told, I wouldn't take ten sons for any one of the girls."

Trapper kept grinning. "They put some pressure on you?"

"Of course. Anna tried reasoning with me. Catherine told me she wanted you for her foreman when she takes over running this place. But it was Sophia who settled the debate. She said she wouldn't wear shoes ever, ever again if I didn't try my best to keep her Tapper around. From what I see, she's already halfway barefoot as it is."

Trapper leaned closer. "I'll make you a deal, Colonel. If Emery says yes to marrying me, I'll take you up on the job."

"Good. I'll have the former foreman's cabin cleaned out. It's about the right size for newlyweds."

"What's happened to the outlaws I brought in?"

The colonel shrugged. "I had a man ride into Dallas to get a Texas Ranger. He'll take them in as soon as their wounds heal, and I'll send a dozen men to ride along to make sure they make it to a trial."

"You mind if I'm one of the men going along?"

"It'll be your first assignment."

The colonel stood, happy with the deal, but Trapper feared the hardest part was yet to come. He had to ask the little widow to marry him first. Since she was already thinking she'd like to have kids with him, he thought he knew what the answer would be.

It was evening before he caught her alone in a big room the housekeeper called the great room. The fireplace was tall enough for a man to stand in, and tonight candles lined the windows. Garland climbed the staircase. The center table was covered with sweets for the neighbors and the employees and their families. It didn't take long for Trapper to realize the ranch was a small town.

When Emery entered, dressed in a dark-green dress with white lace, she took his breath away. He took her hand and pulled her into the empty study.

"You're beautiful." He kissed her hand. "Almost as beautiful as you were that night in the rain."

"Thank you."

She seemed so shy now, as if they hadn't spent three weeks together. As if he hadn't touched her. As if she hadn't slept in his arms.

"I don't know the words, Emery."

"What words?" Her shy whisper brushed his heart.

"The ones to tell you how much you mean to me. I feel like I've been walking around holding my breath all my life and suddenly I'm can breathe. I've been half dead for years and you make me want to live forever."

When she didn't answer, he looked away. "I don't have anything to offer. I own a horse and a wagon." He took a long breath and let it all out. "I do have enough money to buy a little place or the colonel offered me a job. But without you I don't think I could settle down."

All at once he couldn't find the words. He'd lived from day to day, never dreaming for so long he was afraid to wish for more.

She smiled. "What do you really want?"

"I want you to be with me forever. I want to have a bunch of kids. I want to sleep next to you until I die."

"You have me," she said so low he wasn't sure he heard her. "You've had me since the day we left Jefferson and you couldn't be stern with Four. You had me when you let Three be her own person and you let One become a leader. You watched over us all.

"I know who you are, Trapper Hawkins. I saw the truth the first time I saw your blue eyes. You're a good man. You have everything I want even without the money or the land or even the job. I want you."

"Any chance you'd marry me?"

She smiled. "You can bet on it."

As he kissed her, Trapper swore he heard five little girls laughing just outside the window.

"Look, One," a four-year-old whispered, "Tapper got what he wanted for Christmas."

Read on for a preview of Jodi Thomas's next book . . .

PICNIC IN SOMEDAY VALLEY

A Honey Creek Novel

Available Spring 2021 wherever books are sold

Chapter 1

Marcie

Marcie Latimer sat on a tall, wobbly stool in the corner of Bandit's Bar. Her right leg, wrapped in a black leather boot, was anchored on the stage. Her left heel was hooked on the first rung of the stool so her knee could brace her guitar. With her prairie skirt and low-cut, lacy blouse, she was the picture of a country singer. Long, midnight hair and sad, hazel eyes completed the look.

She played to an almost empty room, but it didn't matter. She sang every word as if it had to pass through her soul first. All her heartbreak drifted over the smoky room, whispering of a sorrow so deep it would never heal.

When she finished her last song, her fingers still strummed out the beat slowly, as if dying.

One couple, over by the pool table, clapped. The bartender,

Wayne, brought Marcie a wineglass of ice water and said the same thing he did every night. "Great show, kid."

She wasn't a kid. She was almost thirty, feeling like she was running toward fifty. Six months ago her future was looking up. She had a rich boyfriend. A maybe future with Boone Buchanan, a lawyer, who promised to take her out of this dirt-road town. He'd said they'd travel the world and go to fancy parties at the capital.

Then, the boyfriend tried to burn down the city hall in a town thirty miles away and toast the mayor of Honey Creek, who he claimed was his ex-girlfriend. But that turned out to be a lie too. It seemed her smart, good-looking, someday husband was playing Russian roulette, and the gun went off not only on his life but hers as well.

He'd written her twice from prison. She hadn't answered.

She'd tossed away the letters without opening them. Because of him, she couldn't find any job but this one, and no man would get near enough to ask her out. She was poison, a small-town curiosity.

Marcie hadn't known anything about his plot to make the front page of every paper in the state, but most folks still looked at her as if she should have been locked away with Boone Buchanan. She was living with the guy; she must have known what he was planning.

She shook off hopelessness like dust and walked across the empty dance floor. Her set was over; time to go home.

A cowboy sat near the door in the shadows. He wore his hat low. She couldn't see his eyes, but she knew who he was. Long, lean legs, wide shoulders, and hands rough and scarred from working hard. At six-feet-four, he was one of the few people in town she had to look up to.

"Evening, Brand."

"Evening, Marcie," he said, so low it seemed more a thought than a greeting.

She usually didn't talk to him, but tonight she thought she'd be civil. "Did you come to see me play?"

"Nope. I'm here for the beer."

She laughed. One beer wasn't worth the twenty-mile drive to Someday Valley. He'd had to pass two other bars to get to this run-down place.

"You ever think of buying a six-pack and staying home for a month?"

"Nope."

Marcie couldn't decide if she disliked Brandon Rodgers or just found him dead boring. If they spoke, they had pretty much the same conversation every week. He was a Clydesdale of a man, bigger than most, but easy moving. She had no doubt he talked to his horses far more than he ever did people.

It wasn't like she didn't know him. He was about three years older than her, owned a place north of here. Ran a few cattle and bred some kind of horses, she'd heard. Folks always commented that the Rodgers clan kept to themselves, but lately he was the only Rodgers around. His mother died and his sister married and moved off. He'd never dated anyone that she knew about. In his twenties he had gone off to the Marines for six years.

"You want to sit down?" He dipped his worn Stetson toward the chair to his left.

She almost jumped in surprise. He'd never asked her to join him. But Marcie didn't want to make a scene. He never talked to anyone and no one talked to her, so they could sit at the same table in silence together.

In a strange way they were made for each other, she decided. "Sure."

"You want a drink?" His words were so low they seemed faded by the time they reached her.

"No." Marcie folded her arms and stared at him. They'd run out of conversation, and with his hat on, she couldn't see anything but the bottom half of his face. Strong jaw. A one-inch scar on the left of his chin was almost camouflaged by his week-old beard. He wasn't handsome or homely.

She decided to wait him out. She guessed he wasn't a man to enjoy chatter.

"I'm not trying to pick you up, Marcie," he finally said with the same emotion he'd use to read a fortune cookie.

"I know. 'You want to sit down' is the worst pickup line ever." She raised her voice slightly, as a half dozen good ol' boys who smelled like they'd been fishing stumbled in. They all lived around Someday Valley, most with their folks, and even though they were near her age, not one had a full-time job.

Joey Hattly, the shortest of the pack, bumped into Marcie's chair. He must have heard her, because he grinned.

"I got a line that never fails." The stinky guy pushed out his chest as if performing to a crowd.

Marcie smelled cheap liquor on his breath and fish bait on his clothes. She moved an inch closer to Brand. She wasn't afraid of Joey, but she didn't want her sins listed again. Some of the bar regulars liked to remind her that she was a jailbird's girl-friend.

Luckily, Joey was more interested in talking about himself tonight. "I can pick up any gal with just a few words. I walk up to a table of pretty gals and say, 'Evening ladies. This is your lucky night. I'm single and here to dance. I've got a college ed-ucation and I know my ABDs.' "

He held up a finger to silence everyone before adding, "Wanta C what I can do?"

The fishing buddies laughed. One slapped Joey on the back. "Don't waste your lines on Marcie; she's not interested. She's sworn off all men since she slept with the bottom of the barrel."

She didn't much like Brand, but right now he was the safest bet in the room. A pack of drunks was never good, and they all appeared to have more than a few bottles of courage in them.

Another fisherman mumbled, "Yeah, she was shacking up with a killer. They say a man who thinks about burning folks alive is sick in the head. If you ask me, she knew what he was planning. She don't deserve to just walk away free when that fire Boone set almost killed four people. Least we should do is give her a spanking."

The oldest of the group added, as he scratched his bald head, "Maybe we should strip her and paint an A on her chest, like they did in that old book Mrs. Warren made us read."

"They stripped a woman in *The Scarlet Letter*?" Joey's squeaky voice chimed in. "Maybe I should have read that."

His buddy added, "There were no pictures, Joey."

The sound of the bartender racking a shotgun silenced the room. "Closing time. One more drink and I'm turning off the lights."

The gang turned their attention to the bar. Marcie had never seen the bartender fire the shotgun, but Wayne had slapped a few drunks senseless with the stock.

The bald guy gave her a wicked look before he joined his buddies.

Brand slid his half-empty beer across the table and stood. "Get your guitar. I'm taking you home."

Marcie managed to force a smile, proving she wasn't afraid. "Brandon, that won't be necessary. I live across the street in the trailer park. I can walk home."

"It's not a suggestion, it's a favor, and I told you, I'm not picking you up. That trailer park isn't safe to walk through in daylight, much less after midnight."

She looked up, and for once she could see his coffee-brown eyes. He looked worried, almost as if he cared. "I'm not your problem." Marcie laced her fingers without making any move to follow his orders. "I'm no one's problem. I didn't think you even liked me, so why act like you care now?"

She'd slept with some truck driver a few months after Boone

went to jail. He had bragged that she'd told him all kinds of things about what Wild Boone did in bed, and then claimed she'd said the driver was better than crazy Boone. He must have known she wouldn't say anything. If she had, no one would believe her.

She looked up at Brand Rodgers. He seemed to have turned into a six-foot-four tree wearing a Stetson. Silent. Waiting beside the table.

"Oh, all right," she said, as if they'd been arguing. "I'll let you drive me home."

The Mistletoe Promise

SHARLA LOVELACE

To all the women back then who made eye contact and wore pants. You made this possible.

Chapter 1

1904 (present day)

Josephine

I would prefer to be dragged behind my horse. Through manure. And then run over by what was left of our meager cattle herd.

"Repeatedly," I added through my teeth as I told all this to the only woman who would understand. "This party is—" I shook my head, making the stupid curls I hated bounce around my shoulders. "The most mortifyingly horrendous thing I've ever stooped to do."

Lila, a slight, elderly woman with sharp eyes and a quick mind that had kept me in line since I was a baby, pinned back a rebellious lock of my hair that refused to be manipulated. I felt its pain.

"The *most* horrendous?" she asked, lifting a gray eyebrow as her gaze darted to mine. "I highly doubt that."

"Then you'd be wrong," I said.

"Josephine."

"Lila," I retorted.

"You will be fine," she said, walking away from me to carefully unwrap something from yellowed paper. I hadn't noticed it lying on my cedar chest when she came in.

"I will be the laughing stock of the community," I said. "Henry Bancroft's society-scoffing, failure of a rancher, failure of a *daughter*. Still scandalously unmarried—"

"Interesting that you listed that last," Lila muttered.

"—who *never* steps a foot on Mason Ranch property," I continued, closing my eyes. "Ever. Now shows up begging with her tail between her legs."

"Honestly, Josie," Lila said, looking up from her unwrapping, her brow furrowed in disapproval. "I realize you're more comfortable on a horse than in a dress, but have some couth."

I stood there in my underthings in front of the wood-framed, full-length mirror that once belonged to my mother. Where Lila used to dress *her* for galas probably much like the one across the bridge tonight, because my mother's family came from some of the original money that settled in Houston, Texas. Marrying my father and taking on the cattle-ranching lifestyle on the outskirts may have changed some things, but she would have loved this party. From what I understood anyway.

She died the night I was born.

"All my couth disappeared, Lila," I said, gazing into my own dark eyes.

"Nonsense," she said.

"When the storm wiped out Galveston and cut us off," I said. "When the herd got sick, when buyers stopped buying, and the Masons took part of our land, and then Daddy—" I shut my eyes tight against the burn.

"Listen to me, young lady," Lila said, coming back up behind me, something draped over her arm. Her pale-blue eyes glittered with something between love and a desire to put me over her knee. "Your daddy was the most honorable man I've ever known. And he raised you to be the same. He knows that you've been pulling out all the stops and doing everything in your power to keep the Lucky B going since he passed. You are not a failure. He *knows* that you're struggling. But he also expects you to hold up your head and be the lady of this house now. It's been three years since he—"

"I've never been a lady, Lila."

"Bullshit."

My mouth fell open, and not even a shocked laugh could fall out. In my twenty-three years of life, I'd never heard Lila say anything stronger than "cockleburs," and that was when I nearly burned down the kitchen attempting to fry sausage.

"Lila!"

"Oh, don't act like you have virgin ears, baby girl," she said, waving a hand. "You *are* a lady. You come from the finest lady I ever had the privilege to—call my friend," she said, her eyes tearing up before she blinked them away. "And I did everything I could to nurture her spirit in you. You may not live it actively, Josie, but you have stronger stock in you than you think. And your parents would expect you to call upon that now. You've done everything else."

"Everything else," I said bitterly. "Except find a husband to save me?"

"To save this ranch," she said, her jaw twitching with the same pain I felt. She averted her eyes to check my hair for the fiftieth time, as if it held all the answers. "I know how you feel about going to the Mason Ranch, but at least the party is no longer held on Christmas Eve, so there's that. And there will be benefactors there, Josie. Possibly even that Mr. LaDeen, who has some calling twice."

"Benefactors," I said, swiping under my eyes. "Such a nice,

benign word for available, rich men. And Mr. LaDeen is old enough to be my father. He never looks me in the eye either. He's . . ."

"Rich?"

"Creepy."

"Call him whatever you want, my girl," she said with a sigh. "But the cold, hard truth of the matter is that you need help. And fast. You like saying 'Masons' like there are hordes of them lying in wait, but you and I both know there's just one now. And you may not want to believe it, but Benjamin Mason didn't *take* the bridge and creek junction of Lucky B property. He bought it fair and square to help your father."

"He bought it to stick it to me," I snapped—a little too hard. I took a deep breath and tried to blink back the sudden burn.

"You need to let all that go," she said, walking up behind me and meeting my eyes in the mirror with a tired hardness. "Men make pretty vows when it serves their purposes, and a promise made under a silly plant is about as solid as oatmeal."

I refused to let my mind drift back to the worn-out memory.

"Didn't my father propose to my mother under the mistletoe?" I asked dryly. "I'm quite sure I've heard that story a time or twenty."

"Your father was a romantic git," she said. "And one of the few who always kept his word. Don't think for one moment that because you've carried around this anger the past five years that Benjamin Mason had any memory of it two weeks later."

"It wasn't about any stupid promise," I said. "It was all the lies preceding it." I shook my head, pushing away the old memories. It served no purpose going there now. "It was personal, Lila, him buying that particular section," I said. "I knew it, and so did he. If he'd really wanted to help us out, he could have just given Daddy the money free and clear."

"If you think *that* was ever a possibility, sweet girl," Lila said, scoffing, "then you didn't know your daddy at all." She held up what was on her arm. "Now—enough of this. Quit crying; you'll mess up your face. Time to put on the dress."

"I should go looking like I really do every day," I said, crossing my arms over my chest. "If I'm trolling for a husband, shouldn't they know what they're paying for?"

"Josie, if you go over there dressed in men's riding breeches and a top shirt, you'll get more attention than you ever want, and not the good kind." She hung the dress in front of me, layering a corset in front of it. "Put this on."

The dress was a deep burgundy velvet, and simpler than what Lila had pushed on me in the past. A simple cut with a scalloped neckline and a tailored waist. The full-length sleeves were sheer. It was actually beautiful.

"Where did this come from?" I asked. "I haven't seen it before."

"Just put it on."

"I'm not wearing the corset."

"Josie."

"It's torture," I said. "And they are going out of fashion anyway."

She closed her eyes. "So am I, but I'm still necessary, it seems."

"The dress?" I asked again.

Lila opened her eyes. "Was your mother's."

Staring at myself in my mother's gown was . . . eerie. Not that I had memories to pull from, but I'd seen photographs. Elizabeth Ashford Bancroft had been a stunning beauty, with wavy, chestnut hair and an easy smile. Her eyes were light in the images, a pale blue according to Lila and my father, whereas I had inherited his dark-chocolate ones. Outside of that, I could pass for her. With my dark tresses done up and curled instead of the quick, single braid I went with daily, and her incredible dress forming to my every *natural* curve—to *hell* with that damn corset—it was like seeing that handful of photographs come to life.

The tears brimming in Lila's old eyes said the same.

"I wish your father could see this," she said, blinking them free and swiping them away.

"I never saw this in her trunk," I said.

Lila waved a hand, tightening the laces in the back of the dress to make up for my audacity. "When we finally sorted her things, he asked me to keep this aside for you. He knew the Ashfords would go through the trunk and plunder her things, taking what they wanted, and *he* gave her this gown as a Christmas gift right after they married. He wanted it for you."

I ran my hands along the elegant fabric. A gift from my father. Twice.

"Why didn't he give it to me sooner?"

She shrugged. "Probably because he knew you'd never wear it."

This was true. Running a cattle ranch didn't call for fancy gowns and pretty coifs. I didn't make up my face or stay out of the Texas sun to insure the feminine, milky-white complexion that men loved. I spent my days either on my horse—full saddle, thank you—checking on the dwindled herd, working with the stable manager on supplies, riding the perimeter for issues, or at my father's desk poring over bills. Lately, that last one took up more time.

None of it worked well with skirts in the way. It never had. Even when we had more staff and I didn't have to do as much. Ranch life was too busy for frilliness.

It was too busy for *anything* else.

I was the son my father never had, and I desperately needed to help him with the ranch. I was also the daughter he adored and very much wanted to see accepted into nearby Houston society and married off—mostly to appease my grandparents. I couldn't pull off both and was actually okay with that.

It wasn't that I was averse to the idea of marriage and family, or even of men. I liked men. I accepted an occasional lunch date or a picnic out to my favorite pecan grove if the man could work it around my schedule and didn't mind taking a horse-back ride, but most didn't understand that. Or me. Rarely did anyone come calling a second time.

I'd even go so far as to say I'd loved a man once, but that was a hard lesson learned.

It was also the reason for the dull ache behind my temples tonight, and the clamminess of my palms as I rode silently in the covered buggy we kept in the stable for special occasions. The damp chill was right on par for mid-December in Texas. No snow yet, but cold enough to seep into the bones after sun-set and make me pull my coat tighter around me and adjust the blanket higher on my lap. It could have been thirty below, however, and my palms would still be sweaty as I headed to Benjamin Mason's home.

Lila was right about one thing: We needed help, quickly. This evening would make or break the Lucky B. With everything failing so abysmally, taxes had been in arrears for the last two years. We'd limped our way through calfing season. All that I knew, all that I kept trying fell flat. Now we had till year's end—literally less than two weeks away—to pay our debt in full.

I didn't have it.

And unless I successfully sold my soul to one of the wealth-ier men tonight, convincing them to take on a hobbled cattle ranch as a dowry and bail me out, the Lucky B would belong to the bank on New Year's Day.

My stomach roiled just thinking about it. My father would turn over in his grave.

Lila was right about something else as well. At least it wasn't Christmas Eve, my birthday. That would have been too much. Benjamin's uncle, Travis Mason, had always held this "commu-

nity get-together"—that was what he'd called it—on the holiday itself back in his day. When Benjamin inherited the ranch
and married, he'd carried on the tradition at first. Since his wife
died giving birth to his daughter shortly afterward, however,
he'd changed it to a few days prior. Probably in mourning over
the love of his life. As if he knew what love was.

I shifted in my seat. Malcolm, the last stable manager left
who I could afford to pay, insisted on driving for propriety's
sake, and sat silently as we jostled and listened to the carriage
horse's hooves. As with Lila, I let him have his way. Most of the
time. They were only looking out for the woman they still saw
as a girl. To be honest, I kind of felt like that girl again as we
crossed the bridge that once connected our separate properties.
Before Benjamin Mason made it his.

I'd made it a point not to come here except in passing, to in-
spect the fencing over the last five years, but once upon a time
that young woman who'd thought she was all grown up then,
met up with a certain ranch hand just on the other side on a
fairly regular basis. To the little stone formations that were hidden from the eye on the other side, that made their way down
to the water and a little cubby under the bridge. A beautiful,
private spot.

That young woman had been a fool.

Chapter 2

1899 (five years earlier)

Josie

I slid down from my saddle, running a loving hand over Daisy's neck. She turned to nuzzle my cheek, and I chuckled. Anyone could say whatever they wanted—and they usually did—but horses were the best kinds of friends. Loyal to a fault, silly when they wanted to be, fiery when they needed to be, and they were the absolute best keeper of secrets.

Daisy knew all of mine.

Being the only girl my age among a world of cattlemen didn't provide much in female companionship, so when the mysterious new ranch hand arrived at the Lucky B, she heard all my thoughts.

Ben—I never asked for a last name, and he never offered one—was different from the others. Quiet and to himself. A little dark and sulky, maybe, but oh so beautiful. Light hair that wasn't quite blond but not brown either, peeked out in wavy locks from beneath his wide-brimmed dark hat. Hazel, gold-flecked eyes gazed at me boldly when I'd gotten close enough to see them the first time, sending my insides into a flutter I'd never experienced before.

And at eighteen, I'd had plenty of opportunity lately.

My grandparents on my mother's side were active in Houston's social circle, and hell-bent on pulling me from "that ranch life" that they felt was beneath me. It was beneath *them*, really. I couldn't wrap my head around the endless galas and dinners and teas and formal etiquette they loved so much. I'd find myself on the other end of some boring so-and-so's son's diatribe about what he was going to college to do, or what business his father or uncle or grandfather was in to . . . and staring out a window at the land in the distance. Fantasizing about being back on my land. Sitting under the pecan groves and feeling the grass under my fingers. Riding Daisy until my hair shook loose from my perpetual braid.

My father insisted I go. I knew it was to keep the peace with his in-laws. Maybe even assuage some guilt that my mother left them behind and then died having me . . . I didn't know exactly what his reasons were. But he told me to keep my mind open, and that I could do both. I could love the ranch and still be cultured in polite society. I could marry a suitable businessman and still be connected to my own family's legacy. The ranch was doing well, rising in status every year in the cattle auction circles. The Lucky B was making a significant name for itself, and I would be considered quite the catch.

I felt *quite the catch*, all right, every time I met a new suitor. Like I had a sign around my neck listing my assets for bidding.

Ben, however . . .

Ben wasn't interested in my assets. Or not *those*.

Ben would smile when I'd accidentally on purpose ride by where he was working, or resting, or taking a break. While the other hands I knew were warned not to look at me that way or speak to me in any manner other than as the boss's daughter, he would meet my gaze and the darkness would leave his face, and that smile—that smile made my whole day. Every day.

And once we started talking, we never stopped.

He knew about my mother, my life, my inevitable shoveling off to some business heir one day. I learned that he was four years older and from Colorado. A rebel of sorts, come to Texas to work for the great Travis Mason, our nearest neighbor and a horse rancher, and my father's oldest friend. Mr. Mason soon traded Ben for one of our hands, sending him to work for us. Ben hinted at disagreements being the reason, but that wasn't my business. He was trying to stay out of trouble, he said.

I told Ben that I secretly dreaded Christmas because it made my father sad. I knew he tried not to be, to give me the excitement of Christmas and my birthday, but I always saw it in his eyes.

I learned that Ben had recently broken off a serious relationship back home—with a tempestuous girl who he realized he barely liked anymore, much less loved. Leaving his whole world behind, he'd come here to start over. He said that he didn't have to worry about marrying anyone now because no one would want to deal with his past, and he learned with our first timid kiss that I very much wanted him. Past or no.

My father would hate it. My grandparents would revolt. It was unacceptable and improper from every possible angle for Ben and me to meet in secret the way we did. The way I was today, waiting in our spot under the bridge that connected the Lucky B to the Mason property.

I didn't care. Once he'd kissed me, it was all I could think about. Those lips on mine. His hands, rough and callused, on my face, threading into my hair, which I'd pull down loose just for him. The way he'd groan against my mouth when I'd press close, and then break away, holding me at arm's length but looking at me with those eyes like—oh, God, I knew it was wrong and improper in a hundred different ways, but I couldn't get enough. I was falling for the wrong man and couldn't stop it if I tried.

I was shaking with anticipation when I heard the gait of hooves overhead, and pushed my palm against my stomach to stem the flop it did when he appeared, jogging down the rocks that ran alongside the little bridge, ducking to avoid hitting his head as he joined me on the rocky ledge. It was beautiful here, watching the water bubble by, tucked away in our own little world. Even more beautiful, as he set his hat on a protruding stick and sprawled out on his side next to me, his head propped on his hand.

Something was different, though. There was trouble in his eyes. Trouble he didn't want me to see as he smiled and reached for me.

"You aren't cold?" he asked, noting my riding jacket on the rock underneath me.

"It's a beautiful and rare dry day. It doesn't get better than this in Texas," I said with a smile. "Haven't you learned that yet, Colorado boy?"

"Come here," he said, tugging gently on my hand.

"What's wrong?" I asked.

He shook his head. "Nothing that the next five minutes won't cure," he said, pulling my head down to his.

I couldn't agree more. Kissing Ben made the whole world go away. All the incessant letters from my grandmother, the stress on my father's face, the nagging from Lila to be a lady, when all I really wanted to worry about was whether the herd had food and medical attention, and what calves were due to be birthed. What fence needed tending.

And lately . . . how I could keep my tumbling, crazy heart at bay.

"Ben," I said breathily against his mouth, almost lying next to him but holding myself up by sheer will. "Tell me."

He shook his head slowly, narrowing his eyes as if studying me. Or gauging what to say. His fingers played with a lock of my hair.

"It's not important."

"Important enough to make you frown," I said, running a finger between his eyebrows and relaxing the muscle there. I kissed it, and he closed his eyes. "Talk to me."

"The Christmas party is coming up," he said.

Thrown by that, I backed up an inch. "Mr. Mason's party?" I asked. "The one he has every year?"

"Yes."

I lifted an eyebrow, waiting. "How do you even know about that? And why would that bother you?"

Travis Mason had hosted a Christmas Eve party at his house every year for as long as I could remember. Adults only. He and my father would frequently plan it over cigars and whiskey. This year brought my first invitation, even though I'd technically qualified last year, turning eighteen that day. Although I generally avoided any event I wasn't forced to attend, this invitation was something I'd waited my whole life to garner. It was a thing. Probably a really boring thing, but the mystery made me want to see for myself.

"Have you ever been?" I asked when he didn't answer, something feeling off.

"No," he said, blinking away. "Of course not. I'm new here."

I brought his face back to mine. "Don't lie to me, Ben. We have enough secrets to keep up with."

That sentence looked to settle on him like a dark blanket as he met my gaze.

"I just have a little too much on my mind these days," he said, caressing my cheek. I knew he was diverting, but I didn't push. I wanted that smile back. "One being the thought of you paired off with some guy with manicured hands."

I laughed, and the smile I needed so badly lit up his face.

"There aren't too many of those around here," I said. "Not to worry. Maybe in the city, but around here it's mostly smelly cattlemen and ranchers." I balled my fists, not wanting him to see the state of my unladylike hands. "They put on suits and forget about the manure under their nails."

He took my left one in his hand, opening it and caressing my palm with his thumb. Tingles shot up my arm.

"I know you want to go," he said, his gaze fixed on my hand. "Especially on your birthday."

"My birthday means nothing to me, Ben," I said, feeling the familiar cloud that always shrouded it. "It's just a day when my father lost one girl and gained a faded version of her."

"Josie Bancroft," he said, his tone scolding. "Don't you dare say that. There is nothing faded about you. And your birthday should be special. It's the day you came into this world, and I for one am damn glad of it."

My heart swelled at his words. "But you don't want me to go."

"I just—" He shook his head. "I hear the other hands talk. They don't see you like I see you. They see this rebellious girl with her smart talk and riding breeches."

"And they would be correct," I said, watching that thumb of his work magic on my palm. "I've grown up with most of them. I've trained them well," I whispered playfully.

"That's only a very small piece of the amazing *woman* I see," he said, meeting my eyes, completely serious. "A woman who's making me crazier every day, and—" He stopped, as if weighing his words. "Other men will see you that way, too. Every party, every gala you have to go to—"

"Wearing silly, frilly dresses, flaunting on my father's arm like a prized calf at auction," I said. "It's not glamorous." He chuckled. "I'd love to see you like that, all haughty with disgust while looking like a dream."

"A nightmare."

"I assure you," he said, letting go of my hand to trace my bottom lip with a finger, "that every man there will trip over themselves to get close to this nightmare."

"Ben, are you jealous?" I said, my heart skipping with delight.

"Ridiculously so," he said, making me laugh again. "Avoid doorways with hanging greenery. I can't stand the thought of anyone else kissing you under the mistletoe."

"I don't suddenly become dizzy with stupidity when standing under silly plants," I said, dramatically putting the back of my hand to my forehead. "Nor do I allow any man's lips to touch mine without permission."

"I wish I could be there with you," he said softly, gazing at my mouth and stealing all the breath from my lungs with his intensity. "Kissing you under that silly plant on your birthday in front of everyone and granting you any wish you'd like."

I stared at him in awe. "That would be my wish."

He brought my hand to his mouth, kissing my palm. Sensations shot all the way to my heart, down to my toes, and straight to a place he'd woken up lately with his ardent kisses. My breathing quickened.

"So soft," he whispered against my wrist, moving up. "Your skin is so soft." The bell sleeve of my blouse was loose, and he moved it up farther, dragging his lips up the inside of my forearm, making me gasp. "Like velvet." He stopped and placed that hand against his face, his gaze heavy with desire. "I love how you feel. How you touch me."

"I love you."

The words were out of my mouth before I realized I'd said

them, and I pressed my lips together as the flush came over my face. It was too forward. Everything with Ben was too forward, too much, too unexpected, too inappropriate. I knew that I had to go to the Mason party, whether he wanted me to or not, because of my father if nothing else. He'd know instantly that something was off if I didn't.

But I'd just declared my love to this man in front of me, knowing that my father would be on a matchmaking hunt. Ben was right. It was insane. And the way he looked at me as I said it made me dizzy with a need I didn't even know I had. It was like all decorum dissolved into smoke when we were this close.

He didn't look put off by my forwardness. Or amused. Or afraid.

A long breath escaped his chest, and his gaze was loaded with every emotion I could ever imagine.

"Oh, God, I love you, Josie," he whispered, as if to himself.

I was all reactive sensation as my hand wound into his hair and pulled his face to mine. Something in the back of my brain said to slow down, not to react to my thighs clamping together over the feel of his stubbled face against my tender skin, over the sound of those words, over the suddenly much deeper kiss we fell into, our tongues exploring desperately. Something said to resist as he pulled my body down to his and I felt all his hard lines and something else very hard pressing right against—oh, sweet Jesus, right against *there*. Something said that his hands on my body and his mouth tasting his way down my neck to the hollow of my throat and unbuttoning my top buttons was wrong.

But nothing felt wrong.

"Josie?" he groaned against my mouth.

"Yes," I breathed.

We were in love. Everything felt incredibly right as I gave myself to the man I loved, body and soul, our murmurs of love and my moans of pain and pleasure being carried off by the sounds of the ever-trickling water below.

Chapter 3

1904

Benjamin

Looking around the large sitting room I rarely inhabited, along with the adjoining parlor and dining room—equally unimpressive to me—now spilling over with a bunch of starched-up people I barely knew, my opinion hadn't changed over the last five years.

I tugged on my too-tight collar and glanced at my uncle's old grandfather clock, mocking me from the corner. He knew. That damn codger knew from whatever direction he was watching that there was little in this world that I despised more than this godforsaken party.

"Benjamin."

I closed my eyes.

Except for maybe that person.

I resisted the urge to roll my shoulders away from him or to duck out of sight the way I'd done when I was younger, but he and this place had sucked the life clean out of me. The only bright light in the whole place—in my whole world—was currently asleep upstairs with a homemade doll tucked under her arm. I wished I could go climb in with her. I felt double my twenty-seven years as I turned for the umpteenth time to see what Theodore needed.

"What?" I asked, knowing that it sounded clipped, and losing the will to care.

Theodore had run this house since long before I came, working for both my uncle and his parents before him. Even before my Uncle Travis made a name for himself in the horse ranching business, his father had run a profitable farm there, and I was pretty sure Theodore was just spawned out of the woodwork or birthed in a stable. I had no illusions of whom the real master of the Mason Ranch was behind the scenes, but right now, I'd just about reached my limit of his hard, emphatic *Ben-ja-mins* at every turn.

"It's seven on the hour," he said, as though that was of vital importance. "It's time to announce—"

"That the food is out," I said, giving a tight smile. "Yes, I know. You've mentioned it. Also, I've done this once or twice."

"Not like this."

Theodore gave me his standard disapproving look, the same one he'd worn since the day my uncle passed and all this glory was shoved into my hands. He never thought I was worthy or able to take those reins, and he was right. I was fifteen shades of green back then, and only cared about the unthinkable manipulation that had just twisted my life.

I liked to think that I'd done it justice. That I'd taken on a ranch I didn't know how to run, a woman I was forced to marry, and the hatred of the one person that ever mattered with some amount of grace. Because in all the chaos, God dropped the sweetest little angel into my arms.

I was bucking the system tonight, however, and Theodore wasn't happy about it. Setting out the food on the long dining table I hated, with the small serving plates my late wife called dessert plates. I figured that guests could serve themselves and continue walking around and talking while they ate. I sure as hell did it all the time. I rarely sat down to eat anymore, except for breakfast with Abigail every morning.

But using dessert plates for regular food evidently *wasn't done* in social settings.

Well, it would be done now.

I couldn't abide another insufferable sit-down with these people, all pretending interest, when we rarely spoke the other 364 days. It was ludicrous, and if I had to have all these damn hypocrites in my house, whispering about my singleness and ability to raise a little girl by myself, then they could be grown up enough to walk, talk, and eat at the same time. If they didn't like it, they could leave. Hell, maybe I was on to something.

"The dessert alone is reason to sit down and savor it," he said, looking physically pained by the thought of not obliging it. "Imported chocolate cake, Benjamin. It's divine. And not something one stands up to eat."

"Why on earth would you import cake, Theodore?" I asked.

"Your sweet wife and uncle would—"

"—say nothing, because they can't," I finished for him. "They're dead. Please go make sure our guests' coats are secure."

Striding away before Theodore could puff up again, I snatched the silver handbell from the sideboard.

"Friends," I said loudly as I rang it, clearing my throat as the word stuck in my throat. "Ladies," I said, nodding to a dapper older woman with a tall, intricate hat. "Gentlemen. Welcome to my home."

There were murmurs and smiles and the rustle of dresses as

people turned to face me from all around the room and the parlor doorway.

"I'm honored that you could all be here tonight," I lied. "I know the weather looks like it could be stirring up something soon, so thank you for braving it. Some of you are new to the event, while others have been coming since my uncle kicked off this shindig in—" I narrowed my eyes toward an elderly man in a topcoat. "What was it, Mr. Alford? Eighteen seventy-five?"

"Before that," the old man rasped with a grin. "After the war. Back before your father left Texas and the Mason brothers would do anything for a party."

I joined the room in amused laughter, in spite of the sour taste the mention of my father left in my mouth. I felt nothing for the man who'd sold me out.

"Well, I'm sure you would know," I said, raising a glass of bourbon, to which the older man smiled among the chuckling with a shrug to his wife. "But seriously, to you all, we're a small community here, and this is one night every year that Uncle Travis loved. Having you all in his home to break bread and mingle for the holiday." The front door squeaked from the other room as the bustling sound of a late arrival reached my ears. I heard Theodore's tone pitch oddly as he asked for a coat or wrap, and I wondered if it was another of my investors from the city. He despised anyone who openly talked about money. "I realize we still have a few days left—"

"Four days," called a young woman I recognized from the feedstore, where she worked with her father. It was her first time here and she was grinning ear to ear. I almost hated to short her of the full experience, but she was young. She'd be fine standing.

"Four days," I said with a laugh, pointing at her and not missing the pink that flooded her cheeks. I hoped that Mrs. Shannon, my daughter's nanny, wasn't watching from a corner somewhere, or I'd never hear the end of that. "So, eat up and enjoy. Theodore will introduce our new dining style tonight," I added, grinning wider at the look of repulsion on his face. "We're going very modern. So, Merry Christm—"

My lips froze as my eyes fell on the newly arrived guest.

Dark hair hung in curled ringlets around her shoulders, grazing bare collarbones as a scalloped neckline and fitted bodice of a burgundy velvet gown hugged curves I could still feel under my fingers if I closed my eyes.

Dark-chocolate eyes met mine, her sun-kissed skin flushed with the cold, perfect brows lifting as she raised her chin haughtily.

"I apologize for being late," she said in a stilted tone, adding with a pause, "Mr. Mason."

My jaw twitched at the formality, and all I could do was tumble back five years since she'd last graced this room, to another night when words had failed me as well. And had turned my world upside down.

Chapter 4

1899

Ben

I tied the tie. Combed my short waves into submission. Pulled on the jacket and rolled my shoulders to let it settle.

This was a bad idea.

For three months, I had stayed incognito at the Lucky B Ranch. Henry Bancroft and Uncle Travis were convinced that someone was stealing supplies from both ranches, and that it might be from the inside. When I first left Colorado to work for my uncle, it was to get away from my manipulative father and his incessant badgering for me to marry a wealthy girl and be set. For *him* to be set was what he really meant. My jaw couldn't take the clenching anymore. While my uncle was pretty much a stand-up guy as far as I knew, his brother would do anything to help himself.

I'd even proposed marriage to a girl I'd tried to love for a year, just to placate him, and finally couldn't stand for it. I had to go. I had to get away. Winifred was pretty and cultured and nice enough, and would probably make someone a very nice wife and give someone's family a very sizable dowry, but that wasn't for me. *She* wasn't for me. Winifred Harwell was spoiled and high-strung and too entitled for her own good.

So, to Texas I went, to my father's childhood home, to the horse ranch their parents and grandparents ran, that was now run by his brother. Uncle Travis had no children and no heir, so he took me in, showed me the ropes, and put me to work straightaway. It was exactly what I needed. Then things started disappearing at his best friend's cattle ranch that bordered his property, and so they devised a plan. I'd go to work for his friend, and keep my eyes and ears open. See if anything sounded off. No one paid much attention to new hands—they were the lowest rungs of any working ranch—and I was new in town, so I'd just blend in.

In return, I'd be paid double wages, and if I listened up and learned well, I'd glean some excellent skills on the workings of two different ranch productions. Because while it wasn't announced or even planned anytime soon, the two ranch moguls were talking about merging their assets. Horse and cattle ranching together in the same business could be hugely profitable for both of them in the upcoming year. The century was turning, and things were happening. Some people in the city had electric lamps lighting their homes, and a handful even owned the new electric automobiles. It was an exciting time.

And then a beguiling creature named Josephine rode up with extra water canteens one day where I was working at the Lucky B, and everything I considered normal in my life blew up. She was breathtaking in a way I'd never seen before, beautiful and confident. Riding full saddle like a man, with breeches and a top shirt and a long duster riding jacket and knee boots. A black cowboy hat sat atop dark hair that she wore in a long braid down her back, with loose tendrils around her face. No makeup colored her dark, expressive eyes or pink, full lips.

There was no pretense or concern with her looks or societal standards. No coyness or games. She was comfortable in her own skin, easy to smile, with an infectious laugh that the other men seemed accustomed to, but that damn near knocked me to my knees. There were no words for the effect Miss Josephine "Just Call Me Josie" Bancroft had on me.

And she was the boss's daughter.

I knew I was doomed.

When she started to come around more often and I knew it was for me, there was no turning back, and when I finally got the nerve to kiss her . . . God help me.

Nothing in this world was better than kissing Josie. Tasting her. Feeling her respond to me as her breathing quickened and she wanted more. It was all I could do to keep my hands to myself and not take what her body kept offering with every close press and embrace. I had no intention of taking advantage or doing anything her father could shoot me over, but then she said those words, and—

Damn it, the second she said them, I knew. I knew it was more than just physical attraction with Josie Bancroft. I knew as the embarrassment took second place to the boldness in her eyes that all the conversations and banter and laughter and getting to know her had shoved me right over the edge. So the cursed words fell out of my mouth, too, and then it was on. Right there under the bridge on that slab of rock, in the most undignified way she could lose her virginity, she gave it to me, heart and soul.

I should have stopped it. I should have been the gentleman who saved her purity for her future husband, but it was out of both of our control. She was all fire, gasping with little moans at every new touch, and it lit me up inside like a volcano. Every taste of her skin as I exposed it was like a sweet dessert. Her body was perfect, soft and tight at the same time. Her muscles were toned from riding, making her movements glorious to watch. Beautiful pink nipples begged to be sucked, and I obliged, nearly losing my own control when she'd arched into me and fisted her fingers in my hair.

This inexperienced girl knew instinctively what she wanted, and wasn't afraid to ask for it. And I was done for.

The next three times—yes, three, over the last two weeks—had only gotten better. Just thinking of her face, now. Her smile, her beautiful body under my hands, her way of giving and receiving with complete abandon . . . unlike other women I'd bedded who remained stiff and compliant, like they were doing me some obligatory service. Like they all attended the same schooling for how to appropriately not enjoy sex. Even Winifred, who was going to be my *wife*, had just lay there sweetly, not daring to like it.

Josie, on the other hand . . . Josie loved to be touched, and to touch me. She was all liquid warmth and breathless moans, shaking violently when she came undone around me. Alive, and exquisite.

Any man would love that. But it was what followed, what came before and every in-between moment. The way she looked at me, touched my hand or my face or my arm, the way her whole face lit up when she'd see me. There was so much love there. So much raw emotion. We'd play a silly lovers' game about who loved who the most, and it was all in fun, but at night when I lay in bed alone, the realization would hit me. It was so much more than just fun. And as that hard reality would wrap around my chest with a mixture of elation and fear, I'd be hit with a dark wall. We'd have the deepest conversations about life and love and the world, talks that shattered all our defenses and boundaries. Except for one.

I was lying to her.

Doubly lying. Not only did she not know that I was Travis

Mason's nephew, but being paid by him and her father to spy at the Lucky B. I hadn't found anything, or heard one negative comment from any of the other hands, but that wasn't the point.

I knew enough about her to know she had a deep sense of integrity. Granted, she didn't yet have any world experience to test it, but still. My instincts told me that she would walk away if I was honest with her. Possibly even lose respect for her father.

I couldn't stand the thought of losing her, but my own integrity was eating me alive.

And now, with my uncle and Theodore insisting that I be at this ridiculous thing—for what? To blow my cover? It made no sense. No hands would be there, but it was a huge risk. Theodore didn't know about the ruse; he just thought I was working elsewhere, but he was nosy and prone to eavesdropping.

I was sure Josie would still come, regardless of my pleas. It was her birthday, after all. Of course, she'd want to come to a party. To try to bring a special memory to a day she dreaded every year. I'd swallowed my pride and the bitter bile that rose in my throat when I'd played the jealousy card, like a lesser man would, but I couldn't think of any other way to get her to stay home. The real kick in the pants was knowing that it was that very streak of wild independence that made me so damn crazy about her.

She would show up, on her father's arm and look directly at me, and the whole room would know. She'd be surprised, and then confused, and then that thing we had would radiate off us and her father would punch me, and my uncle would kick me out, and chaos would ensue, and all the ridiculous Christmas decorations would be for nothing.

But what could I do? Hide in the kitchen?

No.

I met my own eyes in the mirror with acute clarity. *No more.*

"It's done," I murmured.

I would tell her tonight. All of it. As soon as she arrived. She might get mad, but I had to hope that her feelings for me would win and she'd give me a chance to explain. We had no future if I kept up this lie, and no chance of being together at all if we didn't come clean with her father.

He might kill me.

But I'd take that chance. Because—

"Shit," I muttered, realizing with a stab to the chest what came after that *because*. "You want to marry her."

"Ben-ja-min," Theodore intoned outside my door, making my jaw clench.

"What, The-o-dore?" I responded, pulling open the door to his perpetually unhappy expression.

His right eyebrow lifted. "Your uncle asked me to come tell you that guests are arriving and you should come down."

Go down into hell, or the moment of truth. I blew out a breath.

"Tell him I'm on my way."

"I'll rush right to it," Theodore said dryly. "And by the way, one of them is asking for you specifically."

My stomach flipped over. "The Bancrofts are here?"

It was now or never. I'd pull her into the library and tell her everything. And then hit one knee and—God, that was terrifying. I'd done it before, and it was cold and awkward with no love and a lot of giggling, but I hadn't been nervous. I hadn't been anything. I had no idea it could feel like this. Like my whole life depended on her words.

I had no ring, but that could come. Winifred kept hers, and that was a small price to pay for my freedom when I left. I couldn't wait to see Josie now, my nerves shot to hell for a whole different reason. It would be okay. I had to believe that. And then afterward, I'd bring her here, to this room, and make love to her properly, in my bed instead of on a rock, watching her rumple my sheets. Well, no, that would have to come later, too. When her father wasn't here.

"Benjamin!" Theodore said, startling me.

"What?"

"I asked you why on earth the Bancrofts would be asking for you?"

I blinked. "So, it isn't them?" I asked. "Who is it?"

"I believe it was a Miss Harwell," he said, turning and continuing on.

My feet took root in the wooden-planked floor, as his steps moved farther away.

No.

Winifred couldn't have come here. All the way to Texas. Alone. But he didn't mention my father being with her, and he would have known him, even after so many years gone. Suddenly propelled into panicked motion, I sprinted down the long hallway to the stairs.

I heard her high-pitched laughter even before I reached the bottom. Saw her perfectly coifed blond locks and fake smile and head tilt that many perceived as graceful and quaint. I knew how much time she spent practicing that movement with her own reflection, so it was lost on me.

"Winifred," I said, a little more harshly than I intended.

Her green eyes darted to me, her smile faltering a little, just for the span of a second before broadening into a dazzling greeting.

"Benjamin!" she exclaimed, rushing to me. "It's so good to see you!"

I grabbed her hand and held her fast before she could hug me, stopping her show of affection. What I felt on that hand made me glance down. The ring.

"What are you doing here?" I asked, forcing my voice to stay low. "And how did you—"

"My cousin escorted me to Houston," she said. "We arrived last week, actually, but I needed to rest and recover after such a long journey. I can't believe you did that alone."

"Why?" I asked. "*Why* did you make the trip, Winifred? And why is this"—I squeezed her finger discreetly, forcing my words through my teeth—"still on your finger?"

"Because you gave it to me," she said softly. "And I came because we need to—"

Another hearty laugh divided my brain and turned me on my heel, shooting darts of worry straight through my chest. Henry Bancroft clapped Uncle Travis on the shoulder as they laughed mightily about something. As old friends do. All I could see was the vision on his arm.

Josephine. My Josie. In a dress.

I'd never seen her in a dress, oddly enough, and it was more than just an article of clothing on her. It was deep blue and fitted, and covered nearly every inch of skin, save for a frilly collar that she'd left partially unbuttoned. Purposefully, knowing her. The skirt flared out from her waist in a series of layers I instinctively knew she'd despise, but sweet Jesus, just looking at her made me forget my own name.

"Benjamin," Winifred reminded me.

I walked straight past Mr. Bancroft, instead, to the stunning girl with the waterfall curls, and hoped my trousers weren't giving me away as I gazed down into her surprised eyes.

"Ben," she whispered.

Chapter 5

1899

Josie

So many thoughts bombarded at once, tumbling over one another. Contradictions clashing with what I knew as fact. The first being that Ben was here. My heart about leaped from my chest at the sight of him. The second was the automatic response to hide that feeling. Third—wait, why was he here? And looking like—good Lord, he was beautiful in a dark brown suit that made his eyes—but why would he be in a suit? How did he get an invitation?

I glanced up at my father to see if he noticed, but . . . I was quite sure *everyone* noticed.

Because Ben was standing directly in front of me. Holding out his hand. A very odd expression on his face.

"What—I mean—" I stammered, unsure what tack to take.

"Happy birthday, Josephine. May I speak with you for just

a moment," he said, darting a glance toward my father before meeting my eyes again.

"Ben," I said, licking my lips. It was okay. Of course we'd know each other. I knew all of the ranch hands at the Lucky B, but none of them would be at this party. "What are you doing?"

"What's going on?" my father said, his tone low. When I looked up, he wasn't looking at me. He was staring at Ben. Something was strange.

"Josie," Ben said. "Please. Just five minutes."

My hand was off my father's arm in the next second, and onto Ben's. Without another thought. Well, with quite a few thoughts, actually, and with the weight of a million eyes boring into me, but I didn't care. I loved him so much. We'd been declaring our love since that first day under the bridge, when I'd given every part of myself to the only man I could ever imagine loving like this. I told him every time I saw him, and he'd pretend to be insulted and say *I love you more*. Then one day I'd gotten really brazen and told him to prove it. He had. That was quite pleasant.

"I'll be right back," I said to my father, daring to meet his gaze. "It's—fine."

I had no idea if it was fine.

"Benjamin," called a female voice nearby. Something in the back of my brain said it might be relevant, but I was swimming too deeply in the fog.

"Josephine."

My father's voice. And my proper name. Never a good sign from his lips. But it landed at my back as I followed Ben into a library. And we closed the door to the outside world.

Once again, it was just us, the way we knew how to be, but—nothing about this situation felt like us. Above my head, hanging from a hook on the nearest bookshelf, hung a branch of fresh mistletoe. It was the third one I'd seen since I walked through the front doors of Mr. Mason's home. Someone here was a romantic.

"What's going on, Ben?" I asked, echoing my father's question. "This is a bit much to steal a kiss, don't you think? What on earth are you doing here?"

Ben glanced fleetingly above our heads, and then closed his eyes, his hands warm on my upper arms. I felt goose bumps travel from the back of my neck down to the soles of my feet. Something big was happening. Something—possibly not good.

"I love you, Josie Bancroft," he said. "I swear on my life, I will love you until the day I die."

That was ominous. And the way he held me now, the way he looked at me—those goose bumps intensified.

"I love you, too, Ben," I said, winking at him. "I love you more." My hands rested on his suit coat, bringing down my gaze to the fine leather I was touching. Nothing like the work clothes he wore every day. But then, I didn't normally don fancy dresses either, so . . . But maybe it was about my birthday? It felt so off-balance. "Why are you here? How—"

His lips were on mine, stopping my words. Soft. Bold. Incredibly needy, as his hands moved to hold my face as he kissed me as though he were memorizing the feel and taste of me.

This wasn't about a birthday surprise. Or Christmas anything. Something was wrong. Or big. Or both.

I pulled back and looked into his eyes, narrowing mine.

"Tell me," I said. "Whatever it is. Tell me, right now."

Ben took in a long breath and released it slowly, while never breaking my gaze. My last thought as he opened his mouth to speak, was that nothing would ever be the same again.

"Travis Mason is my uncle," he said.

Blinking, I pulled back an inch.

"What?"

"His brother, Lawrence, is my father," he said. "and the long and the short of it is that I came here to work and—"

"Wait," I said, pushing back against the leather suit that suddenly felt foreign under my touch. "You told me—how did you end up at our—"

"The theft at the Lucky B," he said. "The food. The supplies."

"That's you?" I cried, pushing harder against his hold.

"No!" he said, shutting his eyes briefly. "Damn it, this isn't going right," he muttered. "Please just listen."

My mind was going in every direction but in listening mode, but I tilted my head to let him continue.

"I was new in town, so they—"

"They, who?"

He sighed, frustration working on his patience. "My uncle. Your father. *They* sent me to your ranch to see if I could learn anything. Keep my eyes and ears open."

I felt my jaw drop.

"You are at the Lucky B to spy on us?"

"Not you," he said. "The other hands. They think it's someone working there."

"You lied to me," I breathed.

Ben—or whoever he was—stared at me.

"I just told you, my uncle and—"

"I don't care what you did for them," I said, the burn building behind my eyes. "I care that you didn't tell me."

"It was a secret," he said. "Strictly forbidden."

"So was I, but you broke *that* rule with no problem," I said. "You could have confided in me."

"Josie."

"We talk about everything," I said, tears spilling over my lashes that I angrily swiped away. "Everything. Our pasts, our dreams. I gave you—" I sucked in a breath as a heat wave washed over me. "I gave you all that I have. All of me."

"And I love you for that," he said, crossing the space I'd put between us. "I wanted to tell you so many times, but I'm telling you now, love—"

"Only because you're caught," I said, backing toward the door as realization dawned. "That's why you didn't want me here. It wasn't about other men's attention on me. It was about *my* seeing *you* here."

"No," he said. His eyes said otherwise.

How could I have been so stupid?

"I trusted you," I said, my breath hitching.

"Josie, please," he said, his jaw tight. "It wasn't like that."

"No? How was it?"

"It was doing a job and ending up falling in love with the boss's daughter," he said roughly, blowing out a breath. "Yes, I maybe should've told you, but I won't apologize for feeling the way I do." He took my face in his hands again, his large thumbs wiping away tears. "Damn it, Josie. I mean it when I say I'll love you forever."

He dropped to a knee.

"What—what are you doing?" I cried, covering my mouth with my hand. "Get up."

This couldn't be happening. He couldn't possibly be—no—not after everything he'd just told me. Not after knowing that I've been lied to and played for a pathetic fool for months. This man who I gave my heart and virginity to, who I'd loved beyond reason—it was as if a knife kept turning in my chest with every second that passed.

"God is my witness," he said, looking up at me with something so passionate and palpable that the naïve girl of ten minutes earlier would have believed it. He looked like he loved me to his very soul. "I want nothing more than to spend the rest of my life with you, Josie. I know this is smack in the middle of chaos, but I need you to believe me and trust me that *this*—right here," he gestured between us, "is real. You're the other half of me. I don't know what we'll do or how we'll do it. We can stay here on either ranch, or go anywhere you want to go.

Any town. Any state. I don't care, as long as you're by my side."

It was dizzying. Was he actually saying these things in the same breath as the other horrendous sentences?

"Marry me, Josie," he said, his voice almost a whisper as his eyes pleaded with me, so full of everything I thought I knew about him. His hands gripped my hips softly, and he bowed his head against my stomach. "Please be my wife."

Hot tears flowed freely down my face as my every breath trembled and hitched. I gazed down at his beautiful head, my shaking hands touching his hair tentatively. I needed the grounding sensation to balance the horrible twisting ache in my heart.

His fingers tightened on me at my touch, and I felt him exhale a rough breath.

Nothing made sense. Nothing would ever make sense again, but—

"Benjamin Mason!"

I jumped at the shrill female voice and whirled. I'd never heard the door open, or the whispers of the crowd peering in around her. The blond, petite, impeccably put together woman standing in the doorway, her cat-green eyes fixed on Ben. Who was still on his knee.

Then she raised that gaze to me.

I knew instantly who she was. Or some version of it anyway. *Benjamin Mason.*

She knew his last name.

Ben rose to his full height, stepping in front of me protectively. That told me the rest.

"Winifred," he said, shoving the word through his teeth. "This is a private conversation."

"Conversation?" she said on a biting laugh. "Hardly an appropriate one, considering."

"Considering?" I managed.

Her gaze slid to me as though I were a bug on the floor.

"*Considering,*" she seethed, lowering her voice so that the many ears behind her wouldn't hear, "my fiancé is behind a closed door, on his knee, with the likes of you."

"How dare you," Ben said, stepping toward her. "You know—"

"Fiancé."

The word fell from my mouth as it shot through my brain and around the room like a shooting star, bouncing off every surface. The horror that had given way for two seconds as I came up for air was back, shoving me under.

He was—*engaged*?

"No," Ben said, turning to me. "That's a lie."

"Is it?" Winifred said, holding up her left hand. A beautiful square diamond sparkled from her ring finger.

"I allowed you to keep that when I broke things off, Winifred," he said, anger rolling over him now. "And you're using it against me now?"

"I'm not using anything, Benjamin," she said, holding up her chin defiantly. "Just because you throw a fit and leave, that doesn't break our bond."

"We have no *bond.*"

"Oh," she said, lowering her hand to her belly, resting it against the fancy layered fabric of her dress. "But we do."

God himself could have crashed the very roof down on top of us, and it wouldn't have had the crushing blow that that one simple movement delivered.

My feet wouldn't move. It felt as though they'd taken root in the floor, punishing me forever by forcing me to watch this scene. To watch Ben's eyes follow her hand, to see the two of them look at each other, to lock the image in my mind of him making love to her the way he had to me. His desperate growling of my name as he spilled into me—being *her* name instead.

Making a baby. Making a family.

"That's not possible," he breathed.

"Really?" she said under her breath. "Are you unclear on the method?"

"That was months ago."

"*Three* months ago, to be exact," she whispered. "And you need to make this right. Quickly."

"Excuse me," I said, my feet suddenly finding wings. Blinded with mortified tears, I pushed past both of them, past the line of nosy gossips, in search of my father or the door, whichever came first.

"Josie," I heard him say from behind me, but I couldn't get away fast enough. From him, his voice, his pleading eyes, or his lying heart.

He'd deceived me, almost convinced me to forgive him, and then proposed to me while engaged to someone else. A *pregnant* someone else. His surprise didn't matter. His deception did.

A scream from another room halted my anxious steps, and I turned to see the crowd, ever curious for more, move en masse toward the sound. Another shriek, and another, followed by two women in tears, and Theodore, the houseman, looking pale and distraught.

My dilemma slid to the side as worry moved to the forefront. My father was nowhere to be found, and fear sped my steps back through the hordes of hideous busybodies.

"He was just—" one woman was saying through her tears.

"—so still," another one cried.

"—face was like a ghost."

"It's not working!"

I broke through the wall to gasp at the vision in front of me. Travis Mason, sprawled on the floor beside his favorite chair, a half empty tumbler of brandy on a table. My father, coat off, hair swinging free of his oiled-back style as he pumped his fists on Mr. Mason's chest.

His face was red with exertion, his eyes wet as he looked up and spotted me.

Instantly, I moved forward and dropped to my knees, feeling for a pulse like my father had taught me. *Ranch life requires you to know a little of everything, Josie.* I shook my head, looking down at the lifeless face of my father's best friend and pushing back the latest information I had on their little secret scheme.

It didn't matter. Business was business, and the state of my heart was inconsequential. Irrelevant. My father had bigger problems than an irate daughter, especially when he didn't know my role in the whole horrible thing.

He would never know.

There was no purpose to it.

There was movement to my right as the wall of people parted, letting through a wild-eyed Ben. Benjamin Mason. Travis's nephew. His jaw tightened as he dropped to his knees next to my father, and his eyes went red with the burn of telltale tears.

"Uncle," he choked out.

I pushed to my feet, unable to bear the mixture of anger and sadness warring within me, and backed straight into hands holding my arms. Turning, I stared straight into clear green eyes that held not one ounce of sympathy, Theodore, in contrast, hovering behind her like a confused bee, looked ready to collapse.

"Benjamin will be busy," Winifred said stonily. "You may leave now."

"Oh, my Jesus," Theodore said, a hand over his face. "Benjamin gets everything. He's the—he's in charge. This is awful."

Winifred raised a perfect brow, palming her abdomen at the same time, her gaze never leaving mine. "As I said."

Chapter 6

1904

Josie

I clasped my fingers together so tightly they ached, but it was better to stem the tremble that began the moment Benjamin Mason locked eyes with me.

It had been a full five years since we simply stood across from each other and took it in. Yes, I'd seen him here and there, from a distance, but we didn't talk, and one of us always turned away. I didn't leave the ranch much; we had staff for those things. Or we did. So, most of the time, any sighting I had was while I was out riding the perimeter or checking on the herd. And most of the time, that sighting was of him and his little girl, either riding his horse, or in his family's tiny private cemetery.

That, I understood. I'd done that with my own father all my life, visiting my mother via a gravestone. It was the times he was alone that reminded me who he was. *What* he was. A liar

I'd almost trusted with everything. Most of those times, he wasn't visiting his uncle, because I knew where that grave was located. He was kneeling in front of his late wife.

That told me all I needed to know.

Winifred Mason, from the three excruciating minutes I'd shared air with her, had been an abominable, horrid, witch of a woman, and if he loved someone like that, then they'd deserved each other. That poor little girl—I knew what it was like to grow up without a mother, but I had to believe she might have dodged a bullet with that one.

And I was probably going to hell for that.

Now, looking into the face of a man I once thought I knew, I tried not to be affected by him. He was so much the same, and yet different. With no hat to cover his dark blond waves, they were combed neatly back in a gentlemen's style. His face was shaved clean of the stubble I remembered, and his eyes—well, nothing could change that. Except that something had.

There was a sadness there. A hollowness.

I guessed losing his wife had taken a toll.

I held up my head and breathed in a steadying breath. No time for walking memory lane or analyzing the present. I had to somehow get through this interminable party, find a suitor, sell my soul, and maintain some semblance of dignity before I went home and hid in the stable to come undone in private, with my horse, Daisy, and a bottle of my father's whiskey.

That's what I'd done the last time. I'd run on foot from that house, running with no mind to the biting, wet cold on my skin and the bushes and rocks tearing at my gown. I got a tongue-lashing from my father later on the indecency and embarrassment of leaving in such a way, but I couldn't take anymore. Ben suddenly being a stranger, lying to me, then proposing, his fiancée showing up pregnant, his uncle dying in my father's arms, and Winifred's icy hatred . . .

All within the same half hour. It was too much.

I turned away from the flash of his eyes now as I called him by his surname. Let that burn a bit. I wouldn't leave here like a distraught girl this time, but if I had to be here suffering, he could go with a little stab.

No one appeared to notice the pause in his greeting as he continued, or else they were too polite to gawk at the tension between us. And that wasn't likely in this crowd. The rumors of that fateful night's melodrama had not escaped me. I had very much stayed to myself and the ranch in the past five years, purposely avoiding public gatherings and prolonged events like this one that loosened mouths and reminded people of old gossip.

Now, to be back here, in the same place where my life had so publicly disintegrated in front of everyone—it was all I could do not to shake my head at my own ridiculous predicament.

As he finished and the guests began to move and murmur among themselves about the new "modern dining," I drew an easier breath. I could do this. I could be social, and civil, and nice.

"Miss Bancroft."

Then again, this evening's torture might never end.

Falling into step beside me was Benjamin Mason himself. So much for avoiding the gossip. I swallowed hard and kept my fingers intertwined, determined to ignore the foreign yet familiar pull of his body so close to my side. I had no business remembering that.

"I'm sure you have other guests to bother, Mr. Mason," I managed, realizing that that crossed "nice" off my agenda.

"Possibly, but I've already achieved that," he said nonchalantly, facing forward as we walked slowly. "They've had their dose of me."

The rumble of his voice resonated to my very toes, sending goose bumps down my spine.

Stop that.

"How fortunate."

He blew out an impatient breath, but I was saved by the approach of our long-time accountant, Mr. Green. I never cared hugely for the man, finding him a bit smug most of my life, but I smiled in his direction as if he were my closest friend.

"Josie," he said, taking my hand in his and patting it. "Good to see you, my dear. May I help you with your plate?"

I blinked, taken aback. "My plate?"

Mr. Green chuckled, his bald head gleaming in the soft, flickering lantern light that glowed from every few feet. Benjamin had spared no expense for fuel.

"Our host has quite the progressive plan tonight," he said, glancing up at Benjamin. "Kind of a walk and carry."

"Progressive?" I said, not daring to look up to my left, where I could feel the gaze bearing down. "Is that what they're calling moving cattle through the chutes to graze now? I think we've been doing that for some time."

Mr. Green laughed heartily. "She has a point, Benjamin."

"I'm fairly sure I can handle the inconvenience," I said, taking the older man's arm. "But I'll be glad for the company."

With that, the presence to my left stepped away, and I cursed my disappointment. What the hell was wrong with me? Why did I have to fight the urge to turn in that direction and see where he went?

"I have another reason to want a few minutes of your time," Mr. Green said, his voice lowered as we continued our slow progression toward the dining room.

I took a deep breath and released it slowly, thankful for the distraction. "Oh?"

"I know you're aware of the year-end tax deadline," he said.

My gratefulness dissipated, replaced with the despair that had become much more commonplace. Yes. I was aware. As I let my gaze sweep the room and take inventory of the obvious businessmen talking in clusters, I felt so painfully aware.

"Yes. I'm working on some ideas," I said.

He darted a sideways glance my way. "Well, you'll need to work faster," he said, nodding toward those same clusters. "The bank has stated an extended holiday this year, closing next week between Christmas and New Year's. Meaning—"

"No," I breathed, knowing exactly what that meant. "They can't. The holiday is—"

"I know," he said, patting my hand again. "But they can choose to give their employees additional days off, and they are."

I felt my scalp begin to sweat. It was already mostly impossible. Now it was swimming in the land of bleak and hopeless.

"So, I have less than—" My chest ached as my heart clenched inside it. "I have only days left."

"Four," he said. "You have until Christmas Eve."

He clamped his hand down on mine as if that would calm me somehow. As if that would fix the horror that once more rained down on that horrible date.

My mother's death.

Ben's betrayal.

Now, I would lose everything my father created on that day as well.

My burning eyes moved over the room. I couldn't afford to be proud anymore. I had to save my home. The jobs of my last few employees.

"I don't like what you're having to do, Josie," he said as we approached the table and he handed me a plate. "It doesn't set well with me."

I scoffed. "Me either, but what choice do I have?"

"Have you considered asking your grandparents?" he asked. "They have the means."

"To save the thing that took their daughter from them and tainted me?" I responded with a sad chuckle. "They've been waiting for years for this to happen. Especially since Daddy died."

"Even for you?" he asked.

I met his gaze. "If they knew how shaky things were, they'd work even harder to get me there."

Mr. Green rubbed at his jaw as he averted his eyes and appeared to be fascinated with the food spread.

"There is one other option," he said.

"What?" I asked, stopping short and gripping the plate as he placed some kind of meat pastry on it. There was hope? "Tell me."

At this point, I'd do anything, and not having to hand over my life and inheritance to some stranger to bail me out sounded divine.

"Merge with the Mason Ranch," he said under his breath.

The slight flutter my heart had felt for half a second died a horrible death.

"That's not funny," I said.

"I wasn't trying to be."

"Or an option," I continued. "How dare you even—"

"Josie, just listen."

I set down the etched-glass plate with a loud clank, bringing faces already bewildered by the new dinner plan staring my way with curiosity.

"No."

"Josie—"

His voice was a distant, tinny sound as I pushed against the human cattle flow to exit the dining room.

"Excuse me," I said repeatedly as people did their best to let me through. Blindly, I sought the front doors, instinctively wanting out of this house. Wanting away from everything this place represented.

Everything negative from the past five years began . . . here.

Learning about the thefts and the missing food supplies. Mr. Mason's death, followed by the horrible storm that destroyed the island of Galveston the next year. It damaged our stables and cut off our supply connection for months on end. Finally, my father's subsequent decline in spirit and health, his death, and then the illness that wiped out two thirds of our herd and sent what was left of our buyers and breeders running for more reliable cattle sources.

All of it started right there, under that roof, in the beautiful, wooden beamed entryway of the Mason Ranch. And that didn't even include my own personal loss. Finding out that my Ben was Benjamin Mason, that he'd betrayed me with a pack of lies, was engaged to another, and expecting a child.

It was like the portal to hell, and all I wanted was out, but my feet halted at the doors. I shut my eyes tight against the burn that wanted to win, that wanted to make me give up and retreat to a dark corner. I didn't have that luxury now.

Taking a deep breath and turning slowly, I swiped under my eyes and watched the last remnants of the crowd wander through the dining room door, some of them still whispering among themselves as they glanced over their shoulders. I'd reminded them. Glorious.

Let them talk. I didn't care. I had bigger problems.

The library door stood ajar ahead, and a burst of painful laughter escaped my throat before I clapped a hand over my mouth. The irony was almost crazy. But before I knew what I was doing, I found myself inside, raising my eyes overhead. No mistletoe now.

I closed my eyes as I leaned against a shelf and breathed in the quiet. The last time I was in that room, my world turned upside down. I could still see him down on one knee, his head bowed, begging me to—

"Who are you?"

I sucked in a very ungraceful breath, knocking two books from their place as my right hand flailed sideways. They clattered to the ground, and my gaze landed on two little bare feet near where one of them lay open on the wood floor.

A little girl with silky blond hair, a long nightdress, and her father's golden-hazel eyes peered up at me from the corner as she sat cross-legged, a book on her lap.

"Oh my God, you startled me," I said, blowing out a slow breath.

"You aren't supposed to take God's name in vain," she said, holding one finger in her place on the page.

"Well, I'm pretty sure you aren't supposed to be sneaking up on people at a grown-up party either," I said.

"I didn't sneak," she said. "I was reading. You came in *here*."

I bit back a smile. "So I did. What's your name?"

"Abigail Winifred Mason," she rattled off automatically. "Winifred was my mommy's name. What's yours?"

Of course she would have a version of her mother's name to carry around with her. I understood that burden.

"Josephine Elizabeth Bancroft," I said. "And Elizabeth was my mother's name, too."

"Is she dead?"

This girl was direct.

"She is."

"Do you remember her?" she asked, her eyes clear.

I shook my head. "She died when I was born, just like yours did."

Abigail closed her book and leaned forward. "Kind of makes us half orphans, don't you think? Never knowing our mommies? Did you know mine?"

I swallowed at the barrage of questions. "I met her once."

"What was she like?" she breathed.

God, I knew this conversation. I'd had it at least once a week with my father for the first ten years of my life. Any speck of information, of knowledge, of anything that would make me feel closer to the woman I never knew.

"She was very pretty," I said, digging hard for that. "Just like you. Shouldn't you be in bed, Abigail?"

She shrugged. "I couldn't sleep."

"So you came down here to be nosy?" I asked, raising an eyebrow.

She shook her head. "We don't care about the people."

"We?"

"Me and Daddy," she said. "But Uncle Travis did, so Daddy plays pretend once a year to give him a belly laugh in heaven."

I chuckled in spite of myself. "And you? What's your excuse?"

"I like to read," she said. "Books are nicer than people."

"You are absolutely correct about that," I said, dabbing under my eyes to get myself in order.

"You aren't wearing a hat," she said. "Most grown-up ladies do."

"I don't like hats unless I'm riding," I said. "They make my head feel heavy."

"I don't think I'll like them either," she said. "My daddy doesn't like this room." My hands stopped in midmotion. "He says it's a sad room, but I love it. So I come in here to get some quiet sometimes."

A sad room.

I cleared my throat. "I understand that. I have a place like that, too, at my house."

"A library?" she asked.

"The stable," I said. "I like sitting with the horses."

"Me too," she said, her bright eyes lighting up. "Mrs. Shannon doesn't understand that."

"Who's Mrs. Shannon?"

"My nanny," she said. "She takes care of me. Does the mommy things."

I laughed. "I have one of those, too. Her name is Lila."

"But you're a grown-up."

I tilted my head. "I wasn't always."

Her eyes grew wide. "And she still takes care of you?"

I nodded. "More than she should have to."

"Why were you crying?" she asked.

Jesus, this girl.

"I wasn't."

"Daddy says that lying is bad," she said.

I snorted. "I'm not lying."

"I saw you."

"Abigail!" boomed a voice from behind me that simultaneously fired the anger in my blood and made me weak in the knees. "What have I told you about sneaking out of bed?"

I whirled, ready to defend her, but the ire in Benjamin's tone was in full contrast with the mockery in his eyes. Love emanated from him as he gazed upon Abigail, stealing my words.

"I told Josephine I didn't sneak," she said. "This is just the best room in the whole house."

His eyes darted to mine, and the playfulness faded slightly.

"Apologies," I said quickly, turning to move around him before this highly observant, well-spoken *toddler* picked up on the animosity. "I just stepped in here to get a moment of quiet, and—"

"Abigail is good at finding those places, too," he said softly, the low rumble of his voice giving my feet reason to slow. "Tell Jo—*Miss Bancroft* good night, Abigail," he amended. "And go back to bed."

"But—"

"You can take the book with you," he said. "I'll be up to tuck you in *again* in a minute."

Abigail sighed and rose to her feet, padding across the room with her book under her arm. "Good night, Josephine."

"Miss Bancroft," he corrected.

"Actually, you can call me Josie," I said, kneeling to face her and whispering conspiratorially, "We half orphans sometimes have to bend a rule or two."

Her serious little face broke into a grin. "G'night, Josie."

" 'Night, Abigail."

Then she was gone.

And the déjà vu suddenly swam with a vengeance. This room, filled with the smell of old books and older wood, was my permanent memory of the worst night of my life. Along with the company.

His hand was outstretched to help me up, but I rose without it, not needing or wanting anything from him. Not even common courtesy.

"She's quite something," I said, smoothing my skirt. "I know you're proud."

"She's my world," he responded, and something in his tone made me look up.

This close, I saw more than just sadness in his face. Tiny lines fanned from his eyes, and something like anger set his jaw. His full mouth looked hard.

Anger . . . at me?

That was absurd.

"I didn't seek her out, if that's what you think," I said. "I didn't know she was in here."

"Why are you here?"

I narrowed my eyes in confusion. "I told you, I was just looking for a quiet place."

"I'm not talking about the library, but yes, I find it ironic that you'd come here for solace," he said, his tone sarcastic, his eyes darkening. "Of all the choices in this house, you'd come in *here*."

My jaw dropped. "I don't know the other *choices* in this house, Mr. Mason, because I've never been farther than this in the five minutes I've spent here. *Either* time." I felt my blood heating and my mouth was sure to overflow soon. "If you'll excuse me, I have—"

"You have what?" he asked, closing the space between us. I could feel his body heat radiating off him and I curled my short nails into my palms to keep my hands from doing something stupid. "Why are you here?"

"I believe I was invited."

"You're always invited," he said smoothly. "And you've never come. Not once since—"

"Since *when*, Mr. Mason?" I said, lifting my chin defiantly as he leaned closer. "*Please* finish that sentence."

I watched his jaw muscles twitch in response.

"So, why now?"

It took all I had not to avert my eyes. To steel myself against his hard gaze and remain composed with his face just inches away.

"Maybe I came for the exquisite dinner," I said finally, acid dripping from my tone. "Why do you care?"

The question backed him up, as if he'd just realized how dangerously close he was and remembered that we didn't like each other. I tried to focus on that, too, fighting my body's automatic desire to pull him back.

"Do whatever you want," he said, rubbing a hand over his face. "I need to go check on my daughter." He glanced back at the open door behind him. "Do you want to go out first? I can wait a few minutes so the other guests won't talk."

"Please," I said sarcastically, walking past him. "It's a little late to worry about my reputation. If you'll excuse me, I have business to take care of."

Chapter 7

1904

Ben

After doing everything short of making Abigail take a blood oath to stay in her room, I finally left her with her book and a cup of water—and a pastry from the dessert table—and went back downstairs. I couldn't have her wandering around down there with strangers. Call me overprotective, but I didn't know most of the people in my house.

And she was all I had.

She was my miracle baby who survived a premature birth that Winifred had not. As horrible as the woman I was forced to marry could sometimes be, the memory of her huge, terrified eyes as she screamed through her contractions that something was wrong haunted me.

Of course something had been wrong; the baby was too early. The doctor had been summoned, and yes, there was concern, but Winifred was a professional at being melodramatic. Crying wolf was her forte for just about anything. And my mind was distracted with thoughts of betrayal. Being almost a month early—what if my wife had lied to me? What if it had all been a ruse to trick me?

Anger had blinded me to the pain in her eyes. The baby was positioned wrong, and when Winifred went stiff and then limp in the middle of pushing Abigail out, I thought she'd just fainted from the exertion. It wasn't until the doctor cut the cord and tried to rouse her to meet the tiny person needing her attention that we realized her heart had stopped.

No amount of lifesaving measures worked.

I'd finally stared down at Winifred's lifeless eyes as I held our child and realized it was all on me. This was the reason my life had turned inside out. Why I'd had to lose everything. It was because this moment was coming. I had to figure things out, and take care of our daughter. Keep her safe. Keep her happy. Be her father.

Abigail Winifred Mason wasn't full-term; she truly was early and needed to be transported to Houston for care for the first few weeks. It was terrifying, and out of my control, and humbling.

And the reason I went to Winifred's grave every week with Abigail, and sometimes without her, was to silently apologize for my doubt and for not being the husband she needed in her most frightening moment. To tell her about the child she never got to see. I might not have loved my wife, but she gave me an incredible gift that I never knew I wanted. I could swallow my resentment to give her at least that.

Abigail had had a rough start, but my little firecracker was tougher than her petite little frame showed. At just under four and a half years old, she never met a stranger, and had her mother's strong confidence, albeit rooted in grace and sweetness instead of greed. That's why I worried for her. She didn't care for crowds, but she'd talk to anyone, and trusted *everyone*.

And had already made a friend in Josie Bancroft.

Damn it.

I even doubted that Josie had wanted to be her friend. Hell, she'd probably tried to leave the library fifty times once she realized who was in there, but Abigail had that way.

My eyes drifted to where I knew Josie was talking to an older gentleman, a permanent smile affixed to her face as she tilted her head, pretending fascination in whatever he was saying. I knew it was pretending because she wouldn't smile like that, unmoving, not speaking her mind. Josie was animated when she spoke, her whole body coming alive in mesmerizing motion. Or she had been, five years ago.

She didn't even show repulsion when the man—who at second glance I realized was someone I once knew and was a lecherous cad even back then—unabashedly appreciated the view of her perfect cleavage to the point that I thought he might just dive in.

What was she doing? He was the second old asshole I'd watched her corner since she left me in the library. Again.

I'd mostly given Josie a wide berth since that fateful night. I understood her ire and sense of betrayal that I'd kept the truth from her, but what I never understood was her inability to forgive. I'd attempted twice to see her afterward, wanting to apologize, but her father had turned me away. I didn't know what she'd told him about us, but he was cooler with me after that night, cooler with everything, actually. As if losing his best friend in my uncle turned off his spark. He was gone, himself, a couple of years later, and then I stopped trying. I wasn't the only one who had amends to make, after all.

Yes, I was in the wrong, but I'd loved her enough to go to her. She never even tried to come to me. She'd walked away from me in that library and never looked back. What level of love was that?

When the current jackass touched her waist and leered suggestively, I couldn't take it anymore. I scooped a fresh tumbler of bourbon from a passing tray and headed their way.

"Martin, I've brought you a fresh drink," I said, stepping closely enough to force him back from her several inches. "How are you? It's been too long."

It hadn't been long enough as far as I was concerned. Back when I was working at the Lucky B, Martin LaDeen was a senior ranch hand. A senior with an ax to grind and a lot of mouth, but Mr. Bancroft trusted him. He'd been the only one in the stables who was aware of my role.

I knew my actions were rude, interrupting them, but Josie was here unaccompanied. That alone put a bull's-eye on her back for unwanted attention, and the way she looked in that dress didn't help. I didn't know what she was thinking, but I knew damn well what every red-blooded single *and* married man here was.

"Fine," he said, blinking in irritation before covering with a tight smile. "Thank you, I appreciate it."

"Enjoying the move out of the field?" I asked. "Banking, is it? Or—"

"Oil," he said, lifting an eyebrow. "It's a massive wave of the future, Mason. You should look hard at it yourself."

"Got it," I said, dismissing him. "Miss Bancroft, may I have a quick word?" I asked, not wasting a moment, especially when I saw the fire in her eyes. "Martin, be sure to try the chocolate cake. Theodore assures me it's divine."

The words weren't even all the way out of my mouth before I turned her and guided her off. Three steps and she stopped short. I hadn't expected anything less.

"What are you doing?" she hissed.

"I could ask you the same," I said under my breath. "Do you know—"

"What I know and what I do are none of your business," she said sharply, covering the vitriol with a polite smile as an older couple passed us. "I'm a grown woman with no attachment to you."

"Who's acting like a fool right now?" I said. That wasn't going to win me any rounds, but winning wasn't in the cards anyway. "You can't come in here alone and talk to men like that without it going in a direction you won't like."

She blinked at me and shook her head. "Of course. Because men are such spineless, stupid, crotch-ruled creatures that they can't possibly be held to a higher standard."

She moved to walk around me, maybe to chase after Martin, I didn't know. But my hand shot out of its own accord.

"Josie," I said, feeling her warmth against my arm as she walked into it, her breasts heavy and soft. I felt the gasp she bit back at the solid contact, and fire shot straight to my groin.

Dark eyes shot up to meet mine, her cheeks flushed.

"Please let me go," she whispered through her teeth.

"What are you doing?" I asked through mine, echoing her words.

Her breaths were shallow and fast, belying the calm of her face.

"Whatever I have to," she said.

What did that mean?

That question plagued me for the next interminable hour as I watched her chat with Harris Green, our mutual accountant, and then, in turn, make her way to discreetly introduce herself to two well-to-do men he'd pointed out.

There was something nefarious going on, that was without question now. Anyone with eyes and an inkling of suspicion could see that.

"Mr. Mason?" an older female voice belonging to the sheriff's wife was saying. "Do you think so?"

I blinked back to her, clueless as to what she'd asked me.

"I'm sorry?"

"I asked you what you thought of the Lucky B's situation," she said, which continued to tell me nothing. "Do you think she'll let it go to the bank?"

"The—bank?" I echoed.

"Oh, I know I'm speaking out of turn," she said. "But it's no secret the trouble they've been having the past few years, since that disease took her herd. Three of her hands are Charlie's deputies now. They needed jobs. I heard a rumor that—"

"Will you excuse me?" I said as pleasantly as I could. "I need to speak to someone before he leaves."

I made a beeline for my accountant.

"Benjamin!" Harris Green said jovially as I approached, probably looking anything but. He held up one of the little glass plates filled with slivers of meat. "Great idea! Love the modern twist." Lowering his voice, he added, "I was dreading Theodore's seating chart this year. Last year I was stuck next to that taxidermist who always smells odd."

"What's going on with Josie?" I asked.

He looked at me like I was speaking in tongues. "I don't understand."

"Yes, you do," I said. "You've been coaching her all evening. Sending her to various boneheaded fools she'd never give the time of day otherwise. And now I just heard that her ranch might be foreclosing?"

My head started banging out a rhythm against my skull, and guilt had a big role in that. Not so much the distant past anymore—that was done and couldn't be undone—but as Josie's neighbor, I should have known if they were in real trouble. I knew about the cattle disease, or at least that something had hit the herd hard. I'd heard through my men that the loss was pretty bad, and I'd worked out something the year before with her old man to help out after Galveston's supply ports were destroyed. He was pretty frail then, but still wouldn't accept a handout, so I'd purchased a tiny piece of their property. The only part that meant anything to me. I hadn't heard anything more after the cattle debacle, but then, I hadn't gone looking for myself either.

Green sighed and put down his plate, glancing around as if ears were lying in wait to listen in.

"You know that I can't talk about another client with you, Benjamin," he said.

"And you know how little I care about legalities," I responded. "Her father and my uncle were best friends, even almost business partners," I said. "We're neighbors." I wanted to say "friends," but I knew that was pushing it. "She's by herself now, and if she's in trouble, I want to know."

He looked at me wearily.

"She would rather be trampled by her own horse than have you know anything about anything," he said. "You realize that."

"Duly noted," I said. "Now tell me."

Chapter 8

1904

Josie

I hadn't been able to strip out of that dress fast enough.

Yes, it was beautiful and my mother's, and I felt dreamy in it, and all the things that women are supposed to feel upon dressing up, but that all wore thin in the first hour. Actually, I was pretty much done after the library.

So, after more mortifyingly insulting encounters with benefactors than I ever cared to stomach again, smiling and playing the meek and weak female in need of a big, strong man to save the day, I left. Threw propriety to the wind and begged a waiting carriage man to run me home in the then steady mist. Being that it was so close, and whoever he was waiting for would likely never know—and that I probably looked pathetic—he complied. So, I came home, stripped naked, and climbed into my bed, just like that. Rebellious and improper and everything the ridiculous pompous asses at that party would thumb their noses at.

I'd started out thinking I could talk it up as a business deal. Appeal to these men's financial prowess. But none of them were interested in anything a woman had to say that involved more than a few introductory words, an anecdote about my father, and silly laughter at whatever inane thing came out of their mouths. I would have had better luck writing it across my chest, where the majority of the fools' attention was spent anyway. Had I taught my breasts to speak, I could have sealed the deal.

Today was a new day, I told myself as I headed out to check on the herd and make note of some needed fence repairs Malcolm had told me about. He'd given me a list, but I needed to see them for myself. See if costs could be curtailed somehow. He wasn't physically well enough to do them, so with the lack of other hands now, I'd have to hire it done. I cringed at the thought. Fencing was vitally important, but . . . I was running out of funds. Depending on the severity, I might be able to do it myself. I had helped the guys fix a fence or two when I was young, back when I thought it was fun.

So, I dressed in my daily riding breeches and boots, my favorite lace-trimmed white blouse tucked in, with a duster jacket and my hair in a side braid. The rain was soft, but picking up, and it whipped at my face as Daisy trotted the perimeter of the Lucky B. No corset to hold me together. My hat down low. This was me. This was comfortable and practical, and if no one liked that, they could kiss things I was too polite to say. There were no ranch hands left to maintain appropriateness around, but the jacket was enough cover. I could almost ride completely naked and no one would know. The ranch might be limping right now, but it wasn't broken completely. Someone with an eye for business—or just the funds for business—could help me get it all back on track. I knew what to do, from the fences to the breeding to the auctions. I'd done it my whole life. I just needed the money.

I sagged in my saddle as that reality hit me for the fortieth time in the last eight hours.

That horrible party had been my last shot. I was now down not only a week I hadn't planned to lose, but also all the hope for potential marriage candidates. That had been nauseating enough, knowing that my family's legacy would be handed legally to a stranger simply by my marrying him. That it would no longer belong to me. Now, it seemed that even that indignity was beyond my reach.

Four—well, now, *three* days.

Foreclosing with the bank would be my only option.

Save one.

And that thought made me want to vomit.

Especially when I rounded my favorite grove of pecan trees, and saw that option perched atop King, the same big black stallion, dressed like I remembered him in his worn jacket and black hat, and looking every bit as heart-stopping.

I couldn't think about that, though, as my blood sped up for different reasons.

"What the hell?" I muttered, touching my heels to Daisy's soft sides.

She picked up her pace on command, but her ears twitched and she whinnied as we approached, as if she remembered King and was happy to see an old friend.

Great.

He turned at the sound, a scowl already darkening his face.

"Excuse me?" I called out as Daisy's gait slowed. "What are you doing here?"

"How long has it been this bad?" he asked, gesturing with a sweep of one hand.

I didn't have to look. I knew it all too well. The meager herd, if it could even be called that these days. The stables, once so impressive due to constant maintenance, were in serious need of attention and repair since the Galveston storm, one of them listing slightly. The Southeast Texas sun and deep, salty humidity from the nearby Gulf of Mexico was additionally hard on the wood, and we hadn't been able to keep up. The fence—my chest tightened as my quick glance told me volumes—was worse than I'd hoped. Still, I might be able to pull it off alone.

I moved a stray lock of wet hair from where it stuck to my face.

"Better question—again—is what are you doing on my property, Mr. Mason?"

He and his horse turned to look at the fence in tandem, as if that explained it.

"That doesn't give you permission," I seethed. "I assumed you had better etiquette than the simple ranch hand you pretended to be, although no hand I've ever known would breach someone else's property line."

His jaw tightened. Good. Maybe he'd leave and I could get back to the business of breathing at full capacity.

"I'll apologize later," he growled. "What the hell happened over here? And how long has it been this way?"

"Galveston happened," I said, stiffening my spine. "No supplies for months on end. Then the disease that damn near wiped out my herd, which no breeder wants to touch and no buyer wants to get anywhere near, regardless of how many years pass. We're tainted. And what's that other thing?" I said, exaggerating a tap to my temple. "Oh yes, my father died. So what has you suddenly so interested?"

"Maybe just finding out that my nearest neighbor has been going under for some time and hasn't said a word to me," he said.

"Didn't realize that was required," I said. "And Mr. Green has a big mouth. Maybe I need to find a new accountant."

"Well, you might need to after you sell yourself off to the highest bidder," he said.

My jaw dropped, air escaping that I couldn't form into words. I took a deep breath.

"How dare you judge me," I breathed, the cold rain seeping through my clothes. "From your castle on high with a million lamps, a fire in every hearth, a massive table heaped with food you can afford to waste, staff at your beck and call."

"I'm not judging you."

"How far would you go to protect what's yours?" I asked. "To protect Abigail's legacy?"

"This isn't about my daughter."

"No, this is about my property," I said. "That you've come over here yelling at me about, so clearly there are no boundaries."

I slid off Daisy and walked to the nearest section of rotten fencing, picking up the largest piece. I heard him blow out a frustrated breath, followed by the sound of leather and his boots hitting the ground.

"I don't need your help," I said, my back still to him as I weighed one side of a post in my hands.

"Then have your hands come fix this," he said. "Why have they let it slide like this?"

"Because I had to let them go," I retorted, dropping up the post and whirling around to face him. "They likely all came to work for you."

He stopped short, looking shocked. Maybe a little humbled. Ranch owners didn't usually know all the minute details. They had managers for that. *I* used to have managers for that.

"Who's working the herd every day?" he asked.

"Malcolm," I said. "And me."

"You?"

"Yes, me," I said, indignant as I shrugged out of the restrictive jacket and draped it over the fence. I turned to pick up the post again and look down the line. "I'm perfectly capable of it. And with it so small now, it's really nothing." I set the post back down and nodded. "I'll go into town later and get supplies. I can probably fix this tomorrow."

"You?" he said again.

I turned back around, fixing him with a look as I shielded my eyes from the rain. "We've established that."

"You're going to fix the fence." He said it as a statement.

I dropped my hand and crossed my arms, suddenly a little too aware of my state of dress, or lack of it. Especially wet. And white.

"I'm a rancher's daughter," I said. "I've done every job on this land at least once, and fixing broken things is a daily chore."

He wiped a hand over his face.

"You can't go on like this, Josie. You need help to run a ranch."

I snorted. "Really, now? Come up with that all by yourself?"

"So that's why you were interviewing for husbands last night?"

I shook my head. "Are you—do you *mean* to keep insulting me, or is it just your natural charm?"

"I'm sorry, but do you realize the dangerous position in which you put yourself last night? Not all men are gentlemen, Josie."

"Do you realize I don't have a choice?" I spat, stepping up to him just as the rain went a little more horizontal. It didn't matter anymore. There came a point when you couldn't get any wetter. "And I suppose you're calling yourself a gentleman?"

"I try to be," he said, rain dripping off his hat as his gaze burned down into mine. "Every day. I try to be some sort of standard my daughter can use to measure a good man by."

Words stuck in my throat at the sincerity that emanated from him with that sentence.

"Well, here's a tip: Don't be a cad."

His jaw ticked, and being close enough to see that wasn't a good idea. I backed up a step and turned back to survey the damage. *Think, Josie.* If Malcolm and I went into town together, we could probably get enough precut railings to take care of this. He was getting too old to do the physical work. I could do that; I just needed help manhandling the timbers.

"Get the horses out of this," he said behind me, already leading both under a nearby tree.

"Feel free to leave," I said. "You aren't needed—"

"I'll take care of it."

I whirled around. "No, you won't. I just need to get the materials, and I will do this myself. It's not your problem, *Mr. Mason.*"

Anger flashed in his eyes, and that's what I wanted: to make him mad enough to leave. I couldn't keep up this back-and-forth bantering and seeing good in him. I didn't want to see good in him.

"Well, because it borders on my property and your three cows might wander over, it does become my problem," he bit back. "I'll have my men over here in an hour."

I curled my nails into my palms, relishing the burn.

"It's more than three," I muttered. "Did you miss the part about not being an insulting cad?"

"Yes, well, sometimes I fall short," he growled, loosely tying both horses to low branches. Walking back to me, he grabbed my arm and pulled me under the tree before I could register that my feet were moving. "You're soaked. Get out of the damn rain."

I yanked my arm free, glaring up at him. "Don't tell me what to do."

"You—" He blew out a breath and ran a hand over his face again. "God, you are so infuriating." He stepped closer and I backed up the same distance. "You should have said something. To *someone*. Anyone. Let people help you."

"I don't have *people*, Benjamin," I said, hating the hurt that worked its way into my voice at the admission. "I have Lila and Malcolm. That's it. I had my father, and—" I swallowed hard. "And I had you. Both of you are gone now."

I watched that land on him like a punch to the gut.

"I know what I did was horrid, Josie," he said, his voice low, his words slow and measured, as if I might fly off and away at the wrong one. "I can't say that any of my reactions that night five years ago were smart. I was floored."

I scoffed. "*You* were floored?"

"Yes," he said emphatically. "I was spinning out. Uncle Travis dying in front of me. Winifred appearing out of—nowhere. Pregnant." He shook his head, looking off past me somewhere in the distance. "I thought I'd left that chapter of my life far behind me. Like in another state."

"She had your ring on her finger, Benjamin," I said, reminding him. "That's not leaving things behind."

"A ring I let her keep to ease the breakup—I thought," he said. "She loved fancy things. I told you then that she wasn't for me." He stepped forward again, and I backed up, feeling the bark of the tree against my back. My breathing increased, and I cursed in my head. Not out of fear. Out of another response that I had no business having. "That never changed, Josie, not then and not later, but once she was carrying my child, I had no choice. Everything I wanted . . ." His eyes seared me, the gold flecks in them burning like little fires. "It had to wait," he finished softly.

I closed my eyes. "You're a good father, Benjamin."

"Please stop calling me those things," he said, the hoarseness in his voice and the proximity making my eyes flutter back open. My stomach flipped at the rawness in his. "I'm Ben to you."

I shook my head, or it felt like I did. Maybe I didn't move at all. I wasn't even sure I was breathing.

"That was another lifetime."

"Josie."

"And you know damn well that it wasn't just about Winifred," I said hurriedly, my voice pitched oddly. Anything to break the gravity, the draw, the heavy pull that was sucking us down into that place where we used to get lost together. He was right there. Almost touching me as the wind ripped around us. I was on a precipice, about to fall. "That was just the icing on a very sour cake."

"Because I didn't tell you—"

"Because you lied," I said. "There's no pretty way to color that. And nothing has been pretty since."

His brow furrowed. "Let me help you."

I laughed, and his eyes dropped to my mouth, making every one of my nerve endings stand at attention and all things south begin to tingle. *Stay focused.*

"So selling myself to you is better than all the others?"

His eyes narrowed. "Now who is insulting who?"

"And yet—"

"I didn't offer to *buy* you, Josie," he said, so close I could feel the breath from his words. His chest met mine, and my body instantly arced to meet him, betraying me with the need for a man's touch. It had been so long. "I'm saying let me *help* you."

"I don't need you," I whispered, lying. Blatantly, flagrantly lying.

"Oh, I know," he said, removing my hat and dropping it to the ground. "You've made that clear."

I was tumbling down into an all-consuming fire as his mouth got closer, his eyes unblinking as they demanded I not look away.

"So, then—"

"Maybe I need you," he said against my lips.

Chapter 9

1904

Ben

Her soft moan as I cradled her face and took her mouth just about sent me over the edge before it had even begun. I'd been hard as steel since the moment she came riding up in all her angry glory, her breasts bouncing unencumbered and barely covered by that joke of a jacket. The rain soaking her thin clothes to her body, her nipples hard and erect against the fabric, all while she dressed me down like a little general, ire flushing her wet skin.

Jesus, I'd tried to walk away from her, even make her angrier with crazy, ridiculous insults so she'd get on her horse and ride back in the direction in which she came, but she just kept plowing forward. Weakening my resolve. And once I got close enough to feel her heat and her energy, there was no going back. I had to touch her, to taste her, or I'd go mad.

My intention of something soft and searching to cross that boundary went flying away with the wind the second our lips met. Her sweet taste sent my mind reeling through the past and pushing all logic aside. I dove deep, needing more. Her fingers curled into my jacket, tugging me closer before moving up to knock off my hat and scrape through my hair as she pulled me deeper into her kiss.

I felt leaves and grass and God knows what else pelting us as the rain and wind whipped around the tree we were one with. I didn't care. I'd waited five long years to have Josie Bancroft in my arms again this way, and nothing had ever felt more right. I lifted her as she arched into me, and the wild woman I remembered responded, wrapping her legs around my waist, burying my hardness in her soft heat as I pinned her against the tree.

"Oh, God," she moaned, breaking the kiss as I grinded against her, growling against her mouth. Her hips bucked then, her legs tightening around me, and I was gone.

"Josie," I breathed against her skin, my mouth traveling down her neck, licking the rain from her skin like a man starved.

One hand cupped her ass, holding her tightly against me, as the other moved up to fill it with her breast. My thumb squeezed a hard nipple, and she cried out, pulling down my face. God, she still knew what she wanted, and I was dizzy with the need to give it to her. Taking that nipple into my mouth, I sucked her through her blouse, both hands kneading her perfect breasts as she gripped my head and moved against my hard length, her body shaking violently as her orgasm chased her.

Primal noises escaped her throat as she rode the waves down from the fastest and sexiest orgasm I'd ever seen. Especially fully clothed.

When her eyes drifted open and reality dawned, I knew I'd be visiting my own hand later on. The embarrassment and mortification were all over her face. Before I could say anything to soothe her, however, a crack of lightning split the sky and both horses reared, spurring us into action.

"Daisy!"

I set her down and grabbed my horse's lead as she grasped hers, and we bolted from the trees, slinging our bodies onto the animals' backs and heading for the horse stable near the main house, ducking our heads low against the bitter bite of the icy rain.

She was shivering when we made it inside, and I instantly grabbed a blanket from a stack by the door and wrapped it around her. Scoffing, Josie pulled it off herself and draped it over her horse, grabbing another one to rub her down with.

"There are plenty," she said, her voice shaking with cold as she quickly lit a lantern. "Dry him off."

"Dry yourself off," I said.

"We'll go to the house and get dry when we've taken care of them," she said, scrubbing at Daisy's coat. "We need to get out of these wet clothes."

I nearly dried on the spot.

"Yes, we do."

She stood up and gave me a look, her eyes looking huge in the flickering light.

"We can't—" She shook her head and went back to rubbing Daisy's legs like it was her sole mission in life, wavy, dark locks swinging loose from her braid. "That was a mistake. I got caught up in—I don't know what I was thinking."

"You were thinking that things felt incredibly perfect for the first time in years," I said, picking up a blanket and setting to work on King, the regal, nine-year-old stallion that had adopted me when I first got to the Mason Ranch.

Her hands slowed, pausing for a couple of beats before they jumped back to the task. A telltale sign that I'd struck a nerve. Or perhaps a vein of truth.

We worked like that in silence, listening to the rustle of the rough blankets and the howl of the wind around the old stable. Only when the animals were dried and draped with fresh blankets and had been given some oats did she speak again, not looking up.

"You destroyed me, Ben," she said softly.

It didn't escape me that she'd called me Ben, but the pain still evident in her tone cut me to the core.

"I know," I said. "You destroyed me, too."

She turned to look at me then, and I could tell she'd never considered that. I watched the thoughts play over her face.

"You assumed the worst of me and left. Forever."

A shaky breath left her chest. "I did," she breathed. "I'm sorry."

I nodded. "Me too."

Chapter 10

1904

Josie

We were sitting on the big stone hearth, stripped down to our underthings and wrapped in blankets, fire almost licking at our backs, as Lila fussed around Ben and me, and Malcolm came in with two steaming mugs of his spiced tea concoction.

Yes, I called him Ben. After what we'd just done out there ... it seemed frighteningly fitting. My God, I couldn't believe I'd done such a thing. Out in the wide open, humping a man's crotch while he sucked my nipple until I came apart? Against a tree. In a rainstorm. Let's forget for two seconds that the man was Benjamin Mason, the man who'd shattered me into a million pieces five years ago.

Who does that?

Me evidently.

You destroyed me, too. You assumed the worst of me and left.

His words stabbed into me like a hot poker.

Lila's eyes kept meeting mine knowingly, and I couldn't quite read her thoughts. I'm sure I looked a mess, but we were out in a storm, after all. Maybe it wasn't my physical appearance. Maybe I just reeked of animalistic orgasm.

God, I wanted to jump into that fire.

I hadn't been able to stop myself. Every bit of logic that poked at me when it came to Benjamin Mason went zipping off into the raindrops and the driving wind when he got that close, and when he kissed me—I was done for.

Maybe I need you.

Yes. Truly done for. Nothing on this earth tasted as good as him on my tongue. His mouth. His skin. His smell. The feel of his hands on my body as he touched me. Rough and tender. Sweet and scorching. Two people so desperate to memorize every inch of the other that we couldn't get enough. Because yes, I was just as needy.

I couldn't look him in the eye now, and maybe that was what Lila was picking up on. What he'd said in the stable—about things feeling right for the first time in so long—it was exactly what I'd been thinking.

And what I couldn't afford.

But more than that, my heart hurt. What he'd also said—that I'd hurt him, too—my God, I'd never even thought about that. That I'd never given him the benefit of the doubt, I'd just taken it all at the hideous face value in front of me and bolted. Left him to deal with all that landed on him, without even a friend to lean on. Granted, I thought Winifred was that friend at the time, in my haze of anger, but still.

My anger was gone now. Talking to him the last couple of days, meeting his daughter—it helped. Either I was just older and less dramatic, or possibly just more open to listening after all this time, but I understood him better now. I could finally see past my own pain and wrap my head around the choices he'd had to make.

The sacrifices.

But could I chance risking my heart again with him? And with my family's legacy? I didn't know. I didn't think so. I couldn't afford to trust in that. In anything. But at what cost? Losing it all?

I chanced a sideways glance at him, taking in his messy, slightly damp hair that my fingers had twisted in. At the lines next to his eyes and the rough calluses on his hands where they wrapped around his mug. He wasn't cut out to be the big boss. He was a worker at heart. Clearly more than just at heart.

"Good to see you again, Mr. Mason," Lila said, cutting her eyes my way with a subtle eyebrow raise. "It's been a bit."

"Yes, you too, Lila," he said softly, smiling at her, although it didn't quite reach his eyes. There was a sadness there that I'd noticed last night as well. I hadn't recognized it then, but today—today felt like I'd lived a week in this man's presence. Other than with Abigail, he didn't seem very happy. Not like when I'd met him. Back when both of us were . . .

I closed my eyes. That couldn't matter. This was business.

"Last time I saw you was at the funeral, I believe," she said, busying herself with nonexistent dirt on a table as my head snapped her way. "At the back of the crowd."

"Yes, ma'am," he said, his gaze dropping to the floor. "I—didn't want to intrude," he said. "But I had a lot of respect for Mr. Bancroft. He was a good man."

Ben was at my father's funeral? I never knew that. I'd noted his *marked* absence, adding it to his many sins at the time, and Lila had never corrected me. By all appearances, she was saving that little tidbit for some choice moment. Like possibly now.

"He and Uncle Travis were about to merge," Ben continued, lobbing another surprise swing my way. "They were joining forces."

"What?"

"The day my uncle died," he said. "They were making plans."

I shook my head. "I don't believe that."

"Well, you didn't believe they conspired to have me watch things at the Lucky B either," he said. "But I lived it and your father told me that himself. Can't prove it, but you'll just have to trust me." He leveled a sideways look at me that said so many things his mouth didn't. Things that were packed up with old memories that had very recently been shaken out. "Or not."

"What do you mean, joining forces?" I asked.

He looked back down into his mug. "They had a plan. Make the two places into a larger ranch, with the individual specialties benefiting both."

"Why?"

He shrugged. "I don't know. I didn't ask. But now that I'm in this position, and see the numbers on a regular basis, I get it. It makes sense. They were thinking way ahead of themselves, but I'm willing to bet it would have worked."

"It's crazy," I said under my breath. I had to be insane to even entertain the idea.

"Something to think about," he said.

"To think about?" I echoed, standing and wrapping my blanket tighter around my body. "Just yesterday, we hadn't spoken in five years, Ben. Now we're—"

I stopped and swallowed. Hard. He looked up at me with a mixture of the old and new in his expression. The fiery young man who had loved me so fiercely. Or had claimed to anyway. And the present-day ranch owner and father who just looked tired and sad. Who had kissed me into oblivion less than an hour earlier.

"What are we, Josie?" he asked softly.

Malcolm cleared his throat, and we both blinked quickly, remembering we had an audience.

I ran a hand over my face and moved to massage my neck. My hair was tied up on top of my head, and tendrils fell loose over my hand.

"I can't—I can't do that, Ben," I said.

I felt the collective disappointment in the room, and the weight pressed in.

"What else are you going to do?" he said. "Marry Martin LaDeen and be Josephine LaDeen?" Lila snorted, and I cut a look in her direction. "He's in oil, Josie. He's going to put big oil rigs on your land and milk it for all its worth."

I frowned. "He never said such a thing."

"He doesn't have to," Ben said. "All he has to do is get the place in his name and he can do whatever he wants. Why bother you with those pesky little details now?"

I narrowed my eyes. "That's rude."

"That's real," he said. "Forget the cattle. They'll be sold, mark my words. He didn't like them when he worked here."

I was pacing and I stopped and turned back. "Worked here? What are you talking about?"

Ben's brows furrowed. "He—was a senior ranch hand when I first came on."

"What?" I stared at him, "No."

His expression grew more serious. "He didn't mention it?"

"No, and I would remember. I've known every man who worked here." I raised a brow. "I brought the water every day, remember?"

"Well, he never did anything," Ben said. "Never worked any of the outdoor jobs, and found things to sit, stand, or lean on while everyone else worked their asses off. Guys called him Heavy Lean Deen."

I gasped. "Oh my God, I remember that. Or—indirectly anyway. I remember hearing you all talk about him—"

"I do, too," Malcolm said. "I didn't remember his real name, but I remember the nickname."

"You do?" I asked.

Malcolm nodded. "One of only two men I've ever fired in my life."

"You fired him from the Lucky B?" I said, widening my eyes. "When? Why?"

"Right after . . . Mr. Mason left," Malcolm said, pointing awkwardly at Ben. "Caught him stealing tools. Sacking them away in his horse's saddlebags. I had a feeling it wasn't the first time."

I thought of what Ben had told me about their theft suspicions, which, sadly, just helped to confirm all he'd said.

"So, he was the one," Ben said. "He was the only one down there who knew who I was. How convenient. He works for an oil company out of Houston now."

"God, the whole world is crooked," I breathed, closing my eyes. "I can't trust anything."

I heard a sharp release of breath, and I opened my eyes to see Ben drop his blanket and grab his nearly dry shirt.

My throat went just as dry, and Lila turned around and busied herself as Ben made the inappropriate movement of being shirtless in mixed company. But that was the thing with him. It wasn't inappropriate in his world; it was just life. He and I were much alike in that regard, not giving a damn about etiquette, albeit easier for him. Men could get away with that line of thinking, while I sat there not looking away, soaking up every inch of skin and wanting to lick every muscle. His back was even better, but I didn't see much of it as he yanked on his shirt and whirled on me.

"I have to go check on Abigail," he said tightly.

"O—okay," I stuttered, not quite understanding the crisp

coldness coming from him. I stood. "I need to go check on the herd myself."

"I'll do that," Malcolm said, pushing to his feet. "The storm let up. Might even turn to some flurries, as cold as it's getting out there."

"No, Malcolm, I've got it—"

"Let him *go*, Josie," Ben said, his voice booming. I stopped, stone still, as did Malcolm and Lila.

Chapter 11

1904

Ben

I couldn't listen to another word about how she couldn't trust anyone. To hell with it all. I had enough to deal with in my life, with Abigail and the ranch and all the little details of both that kept me running. I didn't need Josie Bancroft's drama.

Not even when I could still taste her sweetness on my tongue.

I didn't mean to raise my voice, but damn it—the constant need to do everything herself made me want to shake her till her teeth rattled. Or until I could shut her up again with my mouth. Which if we were alone, I would do in a heartbeat.

"He's offering to help," I said, pointing at Malcolm.

"But—"

"But nothing," I growled. "Let *him* help you." Yes, let that inflection set in. "I'm going to make sure my daughter is all right, and then I'm coming back with some men to give him a hand—"

"Ben," she began, that chin going up in the air already.

"I don't give a damn what you need or don't need, Josie," I said, making her blink quickly. "I don't care that you don't want my help. I'm doing it." I pulled on my shoes roughly and looked around for anything else of mine that might be lying about. "Be out there if you need to, but I'll be there, too. You aren't alone anymore."

Josie looked away, her jaw tight. "I'm always alone."

"That's a load of bull, Miss Josie," Malcolm said, turning back. Her eyes went wide. "I'm sorry, and maybe it's not my place to say, but look around you right now, young lady. Are you alone in this room? Did you fetch that tea? Did you warm that blanket? Did you stoke that fire?" He shook his head, running veined hands through his silver hair before shoving his hat on top. "We might not be blood, but no one cares for you more than we do." He gestured toward me. "You've been praying for help. Get out of your own way and pay attention."

Malcolm nodded toward Lila as he turned and left the room, touching the brim of his hat.

"Miss Lila."

Both women stared after him, slack-jawed, Lila a little flushed. I guessed they'd never seen that man be a stable boss. He ran a tight ship, once upon a time.

"Miss Lila, thank you so much for this," I said, taking the older woman's hand in mine and covering it with my other one. "If I don't see you, have a very Merry Christmas."

Her eyes warmed, looking a little wistful. "Thank you, Mr. Mason. I'll send some sugar cookies over for your daughter."

I smiled. "Just Ben. And she'd love that, thank you."

When I moved my gaze to Josie, Lila immediately slipped from the room. We were alone. I could have kissed her if I'd wanted, but I had to stop thinking like that. What had happened outside was a fluke and a mistake. There was too much water under this bridge. Right now, things needed to be said. Whether she wanted to hear them or not.

I love you.

I love you more.

Our old banter filled my head and I had to shake it free.

"Josie, I was hired to do a job five years ago, and then I fell for you and handled everything after that like a lovestruck boy. I did nothing right. And I'm sorry."

Her eyes looked distant as she gazed off at nothing. "I still can't believe my father hired a spy to watch his own people. That he did that without telling me. That *you* did the same."

"Things were happening that he felt in his gut but couldn't prove, and no one knew me," I said. "And I was sworn to secrecy."

"From me."

"From everyone," I said. "But I told you that night—"

"Only because you were stuck," she said, her gaze coming back to meet mine. "If I'd never come to that party . . ."

"My hand may have been forced, Josie," I said, stepping forward. "But what you don't know is that I'd already decided that night that I was done with it all."

I could feel the heat radiating from her as I moved closer to her, to see her breathing quicken, her tongue dart out to wet her lips as she worked equally hard to neutralize her expression. I gritted my teeth and focused back on her eyes instead of her mouth.

"Before I saw you, or Winifred, or anyone," I continued. "I was upstairs putting on my coat, practicing what to say to you, how to lay it all out there and ask you to marry me as soon as you arrived. That very night." Those huge, dark eyes widened, her eyelashes fluttering in a way I knew she'd hate but that sent a zing straight to my cock. "There was nothing contrived about that, Josie. Or my feelings for you. I didn't care where we'd go or what we'd do; all that mattered was that you were with me."

Her eyes filled with tears, and when one spilled over, I reached out to brush it from her cheek. The contact was like an electric jolt through my body, but I stayed where I was. All the next choices had to be hers.

"Everything might have blown up afterward, but that was as real as it could be," I said, forcing my hand back down to my side. "That's all there is to my story. There are no more secrets. You can tell yourself you're all you have, but Malcolm was right. You ran from me once and never looked back. If you do that again, it's your own choice. I can't make you trust me. You do what you have to do."

Before I could change my mind and sweep her into my arms, I walked away. Out of the room, out of the house, lifting my collar against the wet cold as I headed to the small horse stable for King.

Chapter 12

1904

Josie

I didn't go.

It killed me, and went against every fiber of my being not to be out there, dealing with my own cattle, my own business, but Malcolm's words kept echoing in my head. All that afternoon and into the night, as I lay in bed until the sun peeked in on the next dreaded day.

Malcolm's, not Ben's.

Malcolm telling me to get out of my own way.

I couldn't think about Ben basically telling me it was all up to me. Or that he'd brought up the marriage proposal from five years ago with as much fervor and passion as he had the night he'd made it, fire burning in his eyes. Or that after just one day of him back in my world, I couldn't stop thinking about kissing him. About how good he'd felt pressed against me, his hands on my body. My hands on his.

How that one singular moment when our mouths met was the happiest and most complete I'd felt in years. Like I'd found my home.

I sat up in bed quickly on that thought. My *home*?

My home was right here. I shut my eyes tight against the burn. "At least for today," I whispered to the walls.

There was a soft knock at my door, and Lila peeked her head in.

" 'Happy Birthday,' " she sang in a whisper, smiling. Pushing the door open, she walked in with a bed tray.

"Lila," I said, standing. "You didn't—"

"Hush, and sit back down," she said, clucking her tongue. "It won't kill you to get a little special treatment today. Sit down and enjoy it."

The tray was set beautifully with a golden-brown croissant, two little tin cups of her amazing canned jellies, two crispy sausage patties, and a small jar of fresh honey.

"Thank you, Lila," I said, catching her around the waist and hugging her before she could get away.

The older woman wasn't one for overt affection, but I felt her soften after a tiny pause, and her arms came around my shoulders as she laid her cheek against my head. I'd had no mother, and she'd had no children, so we'd always kind of filled those spots for each other without saying it out loud.

What would happen to her if I let the bank foreclose? Of course she would come with me wherever I went. Wouldn't she? And we'd do what? I had the tiniest little bit of a personal purse stashed away for emergencies that I hadn't touched since my father died, but it was truly minimal. I, myself, would only last maybe a year if I was frugal, but that didn't take into account finding a new place to live or giving Lila a wage.

But an honest job wasn't out there for me. A woman. With

cattle ranching skills, no less. I could sew a little, thanks to Lila. She took on sewing projects in her spare time and was glorious at it. She would be able to find steady work as a seamstress, no doubt, but no one would pay me for my meager ability.

"You'll be okay, Josie," she said against my hair, as if reading my mind. "You may have to wear a dress every day if you're going to be my assistant, but you'll survive that."

I barked out a laugh and gazed up at her.

"You'd hire me and all my thumbs?"

"In a heartbeat," she said with a wink that I didn't quite believe. "You'd get better, doing it regularly. Before you know it, you'll be measuring, pinning, and threading in your sleep."

That sounded horrid.

A long pause passed between us.

"I know life would be easier if I went with—*any* of the other options," I said. "Things could carry on as normal."

"But it wouldn't be normal for you, my girl," she said, stroking my hair.

I let go of a long breath. "Martin gives me the willies," I said as Lila chuckled, then moved away to pick up a handkerchief from the back of my chair. "He's always leering at my chest, and now the oil thing . . ."

"Mr. Mason's words are weighing on you."

The sound of his name sent warm tingles down my spine.

"Everything is weighing on me," I said, gazing down at the beautiful breakfast in front of me for which I had no appetite. "Could I live with the leering and the uncertainty if it meant the ranch was secure for my employees? That I could actually hire them back?"

"With no cattle?"

I sighed. "Would he really do that?" At her shrug, I averted my eyes. "But I wouldn't have to worry about other things."

"Things that have very little to do with business, I suspect," she said, a knowing tone in her voice.

I met her gaze, shaking my head. "There was a moment," I whispered.

She chuckled. "Oh, there's no doubt about that," she said. "Any fool within five miles knew about that *moment*. It was radiating from both of you, neither of you looking at each other."

I covered my face with my hands. "I'm such an idiot, Lila. I can't let that happen again."

"No, you can't."

I heard the reproach, but it was much less than I expected. I waited for the lamenting of impropriety, but she just opened my wardrobe.

"That's all?" I asked.

She shook her head, her back still to me. "You don't need me to tell you right from wrong anymore, Josie. You're a grown woman." She pulled out a dress, surveyed it, and put it back, where she knew it would likely stay for the next six months. "You just need to be careful."

I sighed. "I know."

"Do you?" She closed the wardrobe, looking back at me. "Because the shattered young woman I pieced back together five years ago is not someone I want to see you wearing again."

I bit down on my lip as I felt the burn begin behind my eyes.

"Protect your heart, Josie," she said. She moved her gaze around the room. "This house, this land—they are just things." She crossed the space to sit on my bed. "He's a good man, I can see that. But this thing between you is—"

"Dangerous," I finished, my voice choked.

The emotion in her face was evident. "And tempting," she said. "I know. And that's a gamble. It could be wonderful, or it could be disastrous, but that's how life is, sweet girl."

"Did you ever—"

"We aren't talking about an old woman now," she said, the mother coming back into her tone as she got up.

"We could be."

"And yet we're not," she said, fixing me with the *look*. There was a flush to her cheeks with the diversion, however, that I didn't miss.

"I don't have that luxury," I said. "Not with him." I swallowed hard. "I can't trust my judgment with him, and that's not good business."

"Business," she echoed, picking imaginary lint off the quilt. "Well, that's a choice."

I frowned. "How is it a choice?"

"Between being the strong person I know, or letting your fears rule you," she said. "If you're afraid of being broken again, Josie, then you will be. And in that case, you're right. You can find other places to live, rebuild your life, but there are only so many times you can rebuild *yourself*."

I just nodded, looking down at my tray through a haze of hot tears, willing them back. When they wouldn't be denied, I blinked them free and swiped them quickly away.

"So one, foreclose and lose everything," I said, pulling apart the croissant. "Or two, marry Martin and keep the ranch, but risk the integrity of it."

"Or three . . ."

I stuffed the flaky bread into my mouth, not even tasting the warm, buttery goodness before I swallowed, shoving everything else down with it. She was right. I was letting my fear rule me. But I couldn't put my ranch down as collateral for my heart. It wouldn't be fair to my employees to hope again and lose. That would be even more disastrous.

I can't make you trust me.

"There isn't a three," I said softly.

Chapter 13

Josie

I was sweeping, pushing, and pulling wet sticks and small debris from the long, wraparound porch when option number two came to call. Martin LaDeen, in all his puffed-up glory and enclosed carriage, rolled up, straightening out his suit as he stepped down.

"Miss Josephine," he said, brushing his hands over his jacket before stepping up to hold one out to me.

I wasn't usually a fan of proper greetings, so the lack of a "Miss Bancroft" was on point, but today, for some reason, it rankled me. Perhaps because this man had no personal knowledge of me, and yet wanted me to saddle up with him in spite of it. It felt presumptuous. Then again, today *was* the day.

"Mr. LaDeen," I said, taking my time resting my broom

against a railing. I turned to let him take my hand in his meatier one just in time to see the disdain color his features.

I had on my daily outfit. Breeches, riding boots, and a top shirt. Sans hat. I had rounds to make shortly, checking on any further damage to the buildings, and I needed to check the herd and double check Malcolm's estimates on fence repairs. In short, I was at work, and this was my work uniform.

Mr. LaDeen had never seen me in it, however. We'd only met twice, once when I was meeting with my accountant in town and again at the party, both times looking much more put together than now. Then again, if he'd worked here at the Lucky B once, when Ben was here, he would have. My daily wear hadn't changed in five years.

"I hope my unannounced visit doesn't offend," he said, kissing the backs of my fingers a little too long. It was all I could do not to yank them back and wipe my hand on my shirt. "Or catch you at an inopportune time," he added, gesturing toward the broom, as if it were the traitorous culprit that had me dressed so offensively.

"Not at all," I said. "I was just doing some chores."

"On your birthday?" he said, a grin pulling at his lips. "Surely one of your help could take care of chores today."

"My help." I chuckled. Maybe too harshly. "Well, one of them is feeding the animals, and the other is in town to pick up food to feed *us*, so . . ." I grabbed the broom handle, needing something in my hands. "I'm it."

He paused, as if about to say something before clearly thinking better of it, placing his other hand over mine on the handle to cover it instead.

"Well, all this will change, I assure you," he said softly. "You won't have to do such inappropriate tasks again—"

"I don't mind," I said, clenching my jaw. "Cleaning makes me feel productive."

"Understandable, understandable," he said, nodding. "But would you like to change and let me take you to lunch for your birthday?"

"Of course," I said. "After you tell me why you were fired from here several years ago."

He withdrew his hand as if I'd burned him.

"Excuse me?"

"I couldn't believe I didn't remember you," I said. "Imagine my surprise. Then again, not everyone is memorable."

His face became a mottled canvas of pinks, reds, and something resembling plum.

"I don't know what you think you've heard," he said, his Adam's apple bobbing. "But you shouldn't listen to gossip, Josephine."

"There was no gossip," I said. "I found my father's notes and ledgers. His shocking revelation right after the big storm that 'Heavy Lean Deen' was stealing from him."

It wasn't a complete lie. There *were* notes and ledgers. Maybe not about *him*, but that was inconsequential. There were also years of teaching me to call a bluff.

The plum color turned positively purple and spread down his neck.

"It was all a conspiracy because Malcolm didn't like me," he sputtered. "He spread rumors about me—"

"Actually, he told no one and fired you quietly," I said, turning to resume my sweeping. "You can go, Mr. LaDeen."

"Josephine . . ."

"Sorry you wasted your day," I added.

I heard a huff of breath behind me. "You don't understand just how profitable our relationship could be."

Profitable.

I looked back at him over my shoulder.

"I'll survive the disappointment," I said. "Goodbye."

The front door opened as his carriage jerked and sped away

like his horse wanted away from him as well. Lila stepped out onto the porch.

"I take it you heard?" I asked.

"I might have," she said quietly.

I swallowed, gripping the broom handle as I watched the dirt cloud behind the carriage.

"Can you find me something appropriate to wear, please?" I asked, the words thick on my tongue as I shut my eyes tight against them. My heartbeat was loud in my ears. "For a ride into town?"

I felt the pause. "Would you like me to try to ring up Mr. Green?" she asked. "The line may be full today, but I can try."

I shook my head. "The town will know soon enough," I said. "I don't need a bunch of nosy blowhards speculating beforehand."

"Josie." I turned at her tone. Firm. Expectant. "It's okay, sweetheart. We'll be okay. All three of us. You're making the right choice."

The hot tears burned my eyes. "Am I?"

I arrived at the office of Harris Green, Accountant, at one o'clock in the afternoon, driving solo in the small buggy Malcolm used for supplies. It wasn't the best we had, but it rode smoother than the silly little carriage, and, also, I didn't care. I'd dressed appropriately feminine in a simple ankle-length dress with laced boots and conservative gloves, and that was enough. I refused to wear any of the hats Lila put out. Hats didn't belong on me unless I was riding a horse. For pleasure. Or work. Not for going into town alone on my birthday to sign my very life's work away. They didn't deserve me in a damn hat. I conceded to an updo. That was all I could stomach.

It wasn't really *town*, per se. The places we frequented—the market, the butcher, the bank, and Mr. Green's office—these were all in a small subset of Houston proper. All within a two-block radius, and not inside the city itself, which was fine by me. Much less hustle and bustle, and less pretentiousness as well.

The sound of my booted feet on the worn wood of the steps leading to his door sounded ominous. Like I was walking to my demise.

In a way, I was.

I shut my eyes tight against the burn, as I lifted my hand to the doorknob.

"I'm sorry, Daddy," I whispered. "I'm so, so sorry."

The knob squeaked as I turned it, and the door gave way to the musty smell of old paper as I walked in. The room was dimmer than the last time I'd been there, a testament to the layer of dust coating the windows.

"Josephine," Mr. Green bellowed jovially, entering from a back hallway. "Happy birthday, my dear." He crossed the room as I removed my gloves and took one of my hands in both of his. "What brings you all the way here?"

I blinked, confused. "What—what brings me?" I chuckled bitterly. "What do you think *brings* me? You said that my deadline was today."

It was Mr. Green's turn to blink and be taken aback.

"Yes," he said.

I widened my eyes. "And so here I am." I took a deep breath and forced out the words. "I'm letting the bank foreclose. I only ask for a couple of weeks' grace to get the animals placed and our furniture—"

"Josie."

The way he said my name stopped me. With fervor and curiosity. Possibly alarm.

"What?"

"The debt has been paid," he said. "Yesterday evening, before closing. I—I thought you knew."

My skin prickled with his words. "Yesterday? What—how?" My quickening breaths echoed in my ears. "Who?"

"Benjamin," he said, as if that was perfectly logical. "Mr. Mason. He—" A shake of his head preceded a worried look in his eyes as he passed a hand over his face. "Josie, I thought you and he had agreed upon this."

My chest went tight. "Agreed on *what*?" I managed to wheeze out. "Were there—are there papers? Does he own the Lucky B now? Did something transfer to—" My head went dizzy as the thoughts hit me at lightning speed. "Does he own *me*?"

I knew that last one wasn't legitimate. We'd have to marry for that. But what had he done? What did he go behind my back and do *now*?

I can't make you trust me.

Well, no damn wonder.

Turning on my heel, I ran from the room, the door swinging open behind me and Mr. Green's voice calling my name. It was all a distant haze, covered by the ringing in my ears and my blood rushing through my brain. I had one mission, and one destination.

He had tricked me with his pretty words. Again. Let me think he cared for me, when all he wanted was my property. Well, I wouldn't be obligated to someone who spent his life thinking of new ways to rip my life apart, and I would not be played for a fool. I would find a way to fix this, to get out from under him in every way. And by God, this would be the last conversation I had with Benjamin Mason.

Chapter 14

1904

Ben

"Daddy?"

The sweet little voice called my name again, breaking through the pounding in my skull. I knew I needed to haul my butt up from the chair and go to the tree and see which present she was pointing at this time. Because it would be different from the other fifteen times, and each one was vitally important to her.

"Daddy, did you hear?" she said, padding across the room in her tiny, soft little slippers, a shiny, red-wrapped box cradled in her arms. "Is this the one I get to open tonight?"

"Whichever one you want, sweetheart," I said, leaning on the arm of the chair as I massaged my right temple. "You can open one gift tonight before Santa comes. One gift from me. You decide."

"Do you get to open one, too?"

I chuckled. There wouldn't be one for me. Not yet. Not till after she went to bed and I filled our stockings with gifts from Santa Claus. Then there would be the new knife I'd been eyeing at the tannery and finally bought, and the small tin of strawberry tarts from the bakery. My favorite. Because obviously, Santa had to bring me something, too.

"I'll wait till tomorrow, bug," I said. "Tonight is all for you."

"What did you ask for, Daddy?" Abigail asked. I met her beautiful, innocent hazel gaze.

That was a good question.

Until a few days ago, the answer would have been the same as it had been for the last four years. Peace and love and happiness for her. I was just Abigail's father. I didn't need anything for myself. But now . . .

I rubbed at my eyes as I pondered the *but now*.

Now, I couldn't get a pair of dark eyes out of my head. Again. The same ones I fought so hard to forget the first time around. Opinionated, sharp words that flowed from a mouth I had devoured just yesterday. I hadn't been able to stop myself once I'd started. Her taste drove me mad, and her hands on me—God, they were intoxicating.

And not just because she had felt divine under my touch, all responsive and reactive and warm. Not just because my dick knew exactly where it wanted to be as it nestled against her hot core. But because being in her radius yanked me back in time to the twenty-two-year-old I'd been, hanging on her every word and wanting to listen for hours. Falling hard for the one person I had no business even thinking about.

I didn't have the luxury of being that guy again. I was a father, and a rancher. I didn't have time for that. But, God, the way Josie looked at me—nothing woke up the man in me more than one glance from her. And nothing made me crazier than any of the random conversations we'd had in the last few days.

In short, she'd awakened the beast I'd buried. The damning, burning need for the love I'd found, lost, and would never have again. I'd come to terms with that, and made peace with it. I was good, wasn't I? Content. Then she'd shown up out of nowhere, and I had to go and cross that line as if no time had passed. I'd tasted heaven again, and damn if I could untaste it now.

What did I want for Christmas? Josie Bancroft. In every way.

So, what did I do? The one thing that would royally piss her off and ensure that she'd never want me back. Help her.

"Daddy?" Abigail's voice brought me back from my torturous ride through hell.

I sighed. "I'm sorry, baby, what did you say?"

"What did you ask Santa for?" she asked.

I twisted one of her blond ringlets around my finger and tugged, making her giggle.

"It's a secret," I whispered conspiratorially. "I sent him a secret wish, and I'll just have to wait till tomorrow to see if he grants it."

"Why wouldn't he?" she breathed.

"Well, those are rare," I said, gazing toward the beautiful tree that she and I had decorated together, all the ornaments clustered at her level. "So all I can do is send the wish, and not be disappointed if it doesn't happen."

I was babbling my way down an impossible hole. What the hell was wrong with me? Secret wishes? Now my daughter would grab onto that idea next year and not tell me what she wanted, thinking this secret thing was something special. *Good job, Dad.*

"Do those come wrapped in sparkly white packages that glow?" she asked.

I nodded. "Sure."

The deep sound of the heavy metal knocker landing against the hard oak of my front door rescued me from spiraling further into lunacy, and Theodore was there before I could get all the way to my feet.

I knew who it was.

It was just a matter of time.

"Miss Josie!" Abigail exclaimed, stopping Josie in her tracks as she rounded into the living room ahead of Theodore. "Did you know that today is Christmas Eve?"

I bit back a smirk. Any other time, Josie's expression at being waylaid by a four-year-old would have doubled me over with laughter, but I had to restrain. She looked just this side of enraged.

Everything she had on her lips, ready to throw at me, she swallowed back at the sight of Abigail, grinning hugely up at her.

"I—do," she said stiffly, gripping her coat tighter around her when Theodore caught up and offered to take it. "Hello, Abigail."

"Merry Christmas Eve!" Abigail sang, bouncing on her toes.

I should have stopped her, but her antics were both entertaining and diverting, and just laying eyes on Josie left me with the need for the extra few seconds. Even angry and windblown, Josie was breathtaking. Hell, yesterday she'd been a drowned rat, and I'd damn near taken her against a tree. I was doomed.

"Happy birthday, Josie," I said, resting my hands in the pockets of my trousers, as if I wasn't wound tighter than a drum.

Abigail sucked in a melodramatic breath.

"It's your *birthday*?" she breathed. "Happy birthday, too!"

Josie smiled gratefully, but I noticed that it didn't reach her eyes, nor did it slow the shallow rises and falls of her chest.

"Thank you, sweet girl," she said. "Can I have—"

"So, do you get double presents?" Abigail asked. "Because you have to wait all year?"

Josie's gaze met mine, and I knew her ire wasn't going to be thwarted with more questions.

"You paid my debt," she whispered under her breath, her lips barely moving.

"Happy birthday," I repeated, just as softly.

She scoffed. "I can't be indebted to you."

"You aren't indebted to anyone," I said. "It was a gift."

"A gift," she echoed.

"A present?" Abigail chimed in. Josie smiled down at her again, and reached out to stroke her cheek. My heart squeezed so painfully I had to clench my jaw.

"No," Josie said, answering her but looking at me. "It's not. I can't take a gift like that. It comes with strings."

"Like bows?" Abigail asked.

Josie's head was shaking. "No," she said. "Like reins. You can't do this, Mr. Mason."

I felt my eyebrows shoot up. "*Mr. Mason* is it again?"

"I don't care what I call you," she said, attempting in vain to keep the smile affixed. "You cannot do this—"

"I can, and I did," I said, stepping closer.

The fury in her eyes was mesmerizing.

"You are infuriating," she said through her teeth, raising her chin defiantly as I stepped closer again.

"I—" I clamped my mouth closed and flexed my fingers, knowing that what I wanted to do and what I had to do didn't match. Spinning on my heel, I knelt in front of Abigail. "Baby girl, I need to have a very grown-up conversation with Miss Josie for a minute," I said, squeezing her tiny hands in mine. "Can you go help Mrs. Shannon with the cookies?"

"Can Josie stay for Christmas, Daddy?" she whispered. Loudly.

I searched my daughter's eyes, and leaned forward so that we were head to head and nose to nose, my heartbeat thundering in my ears.

"Would you be okay with her being around for more than

that?" I whispered very low, so only she could hear. "Like maybe all the time?"

Abigail nodded, her curls bouncing. She giggled as she skipped out of the room, and I took a deep breath as I pushed back to my feet. I knew my daughter only recognized the excitement of the moment and her permission wasn't weighted in anything. That I needed to think of her first and probably much more in depth—but this wasn't a fleeting thing. This wasn't someone I'd just met or hadn't already gone through this thought process about in painstaking detail.

"Benjamin Mason," Josie said, her words heavy with impatience as I stepped closer to her. "You are by far the most—"

Whatever I was the most of, it was lost when my mouth landed on hers.

Chapter 15

1904

Josie

I couldn't breathe as the lips I'd fantasized about since yesterday claimed my mouth, cutting off my words, my thoughts, my logic. His hands framed my face, holding me as he kissed me again. And again.

But wait . . .

"Ben," I said, my voice husky, drunk on his taste.

All the reasons I'd come here danced over my head, just out of reach. Anger. I was angry. He couldn't just shut me up with—with—

I pushed against his chest, curling my fingers into his shirt at the same time.

"I love you," he said, his voice thick and gravelly.

Everything froze. My hands, my breathing, my heart.

I leaned back a fraction and peered up into eyes so fiercely passionate that goose bumps peppered my entire body.

"What did you say?" I whispered, the words barely forming. He didn't blink, didn't flinch, didn't look for one microsecond like anything got away from him. My insides had gone rogue, my heart threatening a coup.

"You heard me," he said softly, his fingers trailing over my face as he slowly let me go and backed up a step.

Pulling free of my grip on his shirt. Instantly missing the contact, I stepped forward to follow, cursing my body's reaction to him. I forced my feet to stop, and I shook my head.

"Don't say things like that," I said, my fingers going to my lips before I yanked them away and clasped my hands in front of me. "You don't—that's not love you feel, Ben. That's chemistry."

"Oh really?" he said on a chuckle I wanted to smack right off his face.

"And guilt."

The laughter faded from his eyes. "Still, with that?"

"I'm not talking about history," I said, the blood returning to my brain, logic within touching distance again. "I'm talking about this thing you call a *gift*, that's just another pretty word for manipulation."

He crossed his arms over his chest. "Do tell."

I raised an eyebrow. "Buying out my tax debt so that I'm indebted to you. So that you can what? Win me over? Marry me so that my property goes to you?"

"Let me tell you something," he said, dropping his arms and stepping back into the space between us. His eyes flashed. "I'm perfectly fine over here. I don't need anything of yours to complete my business or pad my land rights. I don't give a shit about your ranch, Josie. And I don't have time to win anyone's affections with money." He flung an arm in the direction Abigail had skipped away. "She's everything," he said. "My whole world. Everything with me and you might have gone to hell that day five years ago, but Winifred could have stayed in Colorado and never told me about her. I have my daughter *because* she came here and tore our world apart."

My hands shook at the palpable love that came over him at the mention of Abigail. It was a phenomenal thing to see on a man, and so beautiful. And he was right. In spite of all the drama with her mother, Abigail was no mistake or casualty of battle. She was the prize.

"Then why did you—"

"Help you?" he said incredulously. "My God, Josie, are you that jaded? That distrustful of me?"

I wanted to say yes. To call on the days and weeks and months of anger and resentment that had built up these horrible walls. But the last two days with him had made those walls weak. Made me see a different perspective.

"You apologized for not telling me what was going on back then," I said. "For keeping it from me. And then the very next minute, go and do another thing *that involves me*—without telling me. Again. How would you feel?"

He sighed wearily, nodding as he dropped his gaze to the wooden floor beneath our feet.

"I helped you because I have never stopped loving you, and I have the means to do it," he said with a slight shrug. "It's just that simple."

That simple, and yet the words falling out of his mouth stole my breath. I reached for the nearby wingback chair to ground myself and keep my knees from giving way.

"There are no complicated twists or hidden agendas." He blew out a breath. "I'm not a complicated man. But I see your point, and I'll try to do better."

I lifted my chin and gripped the chair's fabric a little tighter. "Better?"

He reached over to a nearby shelf at the same time, and plucked something from a basket, holding up a sprig of mistletoe. A bitter taste filled my mouth.

"I started a conversation back then that I never got to finish."

It was my turn to sigh wearily. "Promises made under a silly plant mean nothing, Ben. Our lives have proven that."

"I proved exactly what I said," he responded. "I promised you that I would love you for the rest of my life, and I will do exactly that. I don't want your ranch," he continued. "Yes, we can make something truly special by merging them if you ever want to, but that's inconsequential."

His gaze was intense as he stared down at me and shrugged.

"What's yours would still be yours, Josie. I'd deed it right back to you."

I blinked. "You're—talking about—"

"I want *you*," he said, so close to me again now that we were almost touching. "I want to be the one to kiss you good night every night, and wake you up every morning." He touched the mistletoe to my lips and then tossed it aside, lowering himself to one knee before me.

A gasp escaped my throat, as my eyes burned and my mind raced back to the last time. His last proposal, also made on the fly, before his fiancée walked in.

"What are you doing?" I whispered, the déjà vu of the moment making me dizzy.

"I don't need that thing to say what I want to say," he said. "I asked you a question back then, before we were interrupted."

"Ben—"

"I love you, Josephine Bancroft," he said, looking up at me with an adoration I knew in my heart was a once-in-a-lifetime thing.

Suddenly, all that was spinning just—stopped. The noise cleared. The fog lifted. Regardless of all the heartache and chaos, I knew that nothing had ever, or would ever, be more amazing than that moment, as I gazed down at this man.

"I've loved you from the first day I watched you ride up on

that horse, bringing us water," he said. "And you have owned my heart from the first time I kissed you. We may have been broken and lost, but we're being given a second chance to—"

"I love you."

The words tumbled out with no warning, no plan, as if my heart shoved them out to make room for all the emotion blowing up in there.

Ben's composure faltered, a rush of breath escaping his chest as he blinked rapidly and fought it back.

"Will you be my wife, Josephine Bancroft?" he asked, his voice breaking on my name.

A sob stole my breath, and I clapped a hand over my mouth. How had it—I came over here to blow my top and now—now my entire brain felt like it was going to explode, and yet nothing in my whole life had ever felt more right and more real than this.

"Please, Josie," he said. "Marry me. Today. On Christmas Eve."

Warm tears fell over my fingers, and a crazy bark of laughter choked out of my throat.

"Today?" I squeaked.

Because *that* was clearly the strangest part?

"I'll get the preacher here before dark—hell, I'll go pick him up myself," he said, rising to his feet, his eyes never leaving mine. Rough hands touched my cheeks and wiped away my tears. "I'll marry you this very day and make Christmas Eve a day to make you smile. For once."

My thoughts jumbled over one another, screaming resounding yeses for every no I searched for.

"But—Abigail," I began. "Replacing her mother isn't—"

"She never knew her mother," he said. "Any more than you did. She—" He spun quickly. "Abigail!"

I jumped, startled. "Oh my, I—"

Little feet bounded from the kitchen.

"Yes, Daddy?"

"Come here, bug," he said, scooping her up with one arm and letting out a deep sigh. "I never thought I'd ever find anyone to live their lives with us," he said, looking at her seriously as she matched his expression. "That anyone would ever be worthy of you. But what do you think of Miss Josie? Not just for Christmas, but in our family for real?"

"Forever?"

"Forever," he echoed.

Abigail slid her gaze to mine, full of so much personality, then back to her dad.

"She didn't know her mommy, either. She's a half orphan, like me," she said, making me dig my nails into my palms to keep it together. Oh, this girl would surely break my heart, too.

He looked at me and swallowed, hard. "Trust me, Josie," he said quietly, pleading with his eyes. "Trust this."

In front of me was what could be my future. My family. Ben looking at me so intently, my skin felt like it might catch fire.

"Will you share your secret place with me?" she asked. "In the stable?"

I chuckled and swiped under my eyes. "If I can come sit in the library with you sometimes?"

Abigail nodded, her curls making it a full-motion activity. "Deal."

I started to laugh nervously, blinking more tears free and thinking I hadn't cried this much in years, but the anxious, expectant look on his face was priceless. I shrugged at the sheer simplicity of it.

"Deal," I whispered.

"Can I go back to the cookies, Daddy?" she whispered loudly.

He set her down and crossed the space to me in seconds as the sound of her steps pattered away, and my hands could finally go up around his neck and into his hair.

"Yes?" he breathed.

"Yes."

Chapter 16

1904

Josie

"Josephine Bancroft Mason," I whispered, testing the sound of it on my tongue. "Josie Mason. Mrs. Benjamin Mason."

It was all very bizarre and exciting. This morning, as I'd awakened on my birthday to Lila bringing me breakfast, I'd hardly expected to be married by evening.

I gazed down at my left hand, where my mother's wedding band now resided. At the still beautiful white satin and lace dress that now lay across the chaise in Ben's—in our bedroom.

Our bedroom. In Ben's house, that was my home now, too.

Married.

Me.

On Christmas Eve.

The very second I'd said yes, the day had turned into a whirlwind. Ben sent people to attend to every need. Theodore went for Lila, who then went back and forth twice more for my mother's ring and wedding dress, not allowing me to help her in the name of my birthday. Another went to find someone to marry us. Yet another brought us food to stay in and snack on all day, and Mrs. Shannon—who I could already tell was Abigail's very special version of my Lila—whipped us up a wedding cake. A simple one, granted, but in the midst of Christmas baking, I called it a miracle.

Then I'd married Benjamin Mason.

And he'd married me.

What?

I laughed out loud at the irony of it. At the crazy culmination of everything this day had ever represented. Death, birth, sadness, stress, and heartbreak, now rounded out with unspeakable joy and the love of a lifetime.

And a daughter I'd never expected, tossing rose petals at our feet.

Bizarre didn't even begin to cover it.

Now, after their Christmas Eve night tradition of opening a gift, and watching Abigail's squeals of joy and anticipation at waiting for Santa Claus . . . I was the one waiting.

For Ben.

"Wait for me in our room, love," he'd said before heading off to tuck Abigail in and read her a story.

I hadn't even been back to my house since leaving for Mr. Green's office that morning. It was like living in a dream. I didn't know how daily life was going to roll out going forward, but we would figure it out.

"Our room," I'd echoed. "That sounds so . . ."

"Delightful?" he said under his breath, dropping a kiss on my lips. "Decadent?"

"Both," I said. "Shall we wait for Santa as well?"

He raised an eyebrow. "I'm hoping to get my present early."

I laughed softly. "I do believe you already opened one under the tree. Plus gained a person."

"Well, see, there was this chat that my daughter and I had today about secret wishes and how they'd be sparkly or something," he said.

"Oh?"

"And we were just getting to the crux of that when this woman came over and started yelling at me."

I clamped my lips together and then grinned. That felt like a year ago. Now, my ranch was safe, new plans were in the works, I could hire back all the old hands to help Malcolm, and my heart—it was soaring for so many reasons.

"I see. How did you handle that?"

"I married her," he said simply. "So, I'm going off incomplete information, but I'm thinking that the sparkly stuff is still to come tonight," he said, pulling me to him and kissing me as I giggled. "I want very, very, *very* much to make love to my wife," he whispered against my lips. "Sparkles or not."

Tingles of lightning-hot heat went straight to all things south.

Wife.

God, nothing sounded better. I had been worked up into a frenzy since he'd kissed me into a proposal that morning. Watching him in action today was like an aphrodisiac.

"You know, technically, we could have made that happen while all the people scattered at your command like you were the voice of Zeus," I said to his already shaking head.

"I said *wife*," he clarified, glancing around for little ears. Pulling me to him again, he brushed his mouth against my ear. "I've loved you on a rock, in a field, and made you come against a tree," he whispered, sending shivers of desire down my neck. "The next time I touch you, love of my life, I want you in my bed, calling me your husband."

Hence . . . now I waited. Staring at his huge four-poster bed.

Because I couldn't wait to do just that.

When he finally strolled in, boots in hand, latching the lock behind him, my breath caught in my chest. Gone was the black jacket he'd worn to say his vows. Gone was the tie. His shirt was open at the neck, pulled a little loose at the waist—probably from tickling Abigail. His shirtsleeves were unbuttoned and rolled up on his forearms.

More than any of that, it was the expression he wore. A look of pure happiness mixed with a driving carnal need that intensified as his eyes raked my body.

I was dressed in *only* a dressing robe that Lila had brought over. A long one, made of fine black silk, that I'd found in Houston years ago. My grandmother bought it for me when I'd eyed it longingly at a boutique, probably thinking she was adding to a soon-to-be-needed boudoir.

Well, she did. Just much later, and not to whom she expected.

My hair was down in waves, and the robe was wrapped tightly around me and belted, showing all my curves. It was sinful and decadent, and completely unladylike, and I didn't care. If I couldn't show up this way for my husband, what was the point of taking his name?

"You look—stunning," he said breathily.

"You look too far away," I said, crossing to him.

I didn't have a need for etiquette either.

Ben's hands went into my hair as our mouths met, moaning as I pressed myself against him.

"God, I've waited so long for you, my love," he growled against my mouth.

Pulling his shirt free from his trousers, I made quick haste with the buttons. I needed it gone. I needed him.

Yanking it off his body, he pulled away from me for a moment and dropped it on the floor. He grabbed my hand and tugged me to him, and in one quick swoop, swept me off my feet.

I squealed and wrapped my arms around his neck, laughing.

"Pretend that's a threshold," he said, walking over it and carrying me straight to his bed, looming over me as he laid me down and kissed me, deeply and thoroughly.

When my robe magically came loose, and he worshipped my body with his kisses, angels sang in my head. When my hands relieved him of his trousers and stroked his heavy length, he cursed and fisted the sheets underneath me.

"Josie," he growled as he finally slid inside me, making all my muscles tighten around him.

"I love you, Mr. Mason," I said on a gasp.

"I love you more, Mrs. Mason."

I rolled my hips and relished his quick inhale. My lips curved upward.

"Prove it."

For more from Sharla Lovelace, check out the first in
her Charmed in Texas series . . .

A CHARMED LITTLE LIE

*Charmed, Texas, is everything the name implies—quaint,
comfortable, and as small-town friendly as they come.
And when it comes to romance, there's no place
quite as enchanting . . .*

Lanie Barrett didn't mean to *lie*. Spinning a story of a joyous
marriage to make a dying woman happy is forgivable, isn't it?
Lanie thinks so, especially since her beloved Aunt Ruby would
have been heartbroken to know the truth of her niece's sadly
loveless, short-of-sparkling existence. Trouble is, according to
the will, Ruby didn't quite buy Lanie's tale. And to inherit the
only house Lanie ever really considered a home, she'll have to
bring her "husband" back to Charmed for three whole
months—or watch Aunt Ruby's cozy nest go to her weasel
cousin, who will sell it to a condo developer.

Nick McKane is out of work, out of luck, and the spitting
image of the man Lanie described. He needs money for his
daughter's art school tuition, and Lanie needs a convenient
spouse. It's a match made . . . well, not quite in heaven, but for
a temporary arrangement, it couldn't be better. Except the
longer Lanie and Nick spend as husband and wife, the more the
connection between them begins to seem real. Maybe this modern fairy tale really could come true . . .

Published by Kensington Publishing Corp.

Chapter 1

*"Take caution when unwrapping blessings, my girl.
They're sometimes dipped in poop first."*

In retrospect, I should have known the day was off. From the wee hours of the morning when I awoke to find Ralph—my neighbor's ninety-pound Rottweiler—in bed with me and hiking his leg, to waking up the second time on my crappy uncomfortable couch with a hitch in my hip. Then the coffeemaker mishap and realizing I was out of toothpaste. Pretty much all the markers were there. Aunt Ruby would have thumped me in the head and asked me where my Barrett intuition was.

But I never had her kind of intuition.

And Aunt Ruby wasn't around to thump me. Not anymore. Not even long distance.

"Ow! Shit!" I yelped as my phone rang, making me sling pancake batter across the kitchen as I burned my finger on the griddle.

I'm coordinated like that.

Cursing my way to the phone, I hit speaker when I saw the name of said neighbor.

"Hey, Tilly."

"How's my sweet boy?" she crooned.

I glared at Ralph. "He's got bladder denial," I said. "Possibly separation anxiety. Mommy issues."

"Uh-oh, why?" she asked.

"He marked three pieces of furniture, and me," I said, hearing her gasp. "While I was in the bed. With him."

I liked my neighbor Tilly. She was from two apartments down, was sweet, kinda goofy, and was always making new desserts she liked to try out on me. So when she suddenly had to bail for some family emergency with her mom and couldn't take her dog, I decided to take a page from her book and be a *giver*. Offer to dog-sit Ralph while she was gone for a few days.

"Oh wow, I'm so sorry, Lanie," she said.

"Not a problem," I lied. I'm not really cut out to be a giver. "We're bonding."

"I actually kind of hoped he'd cheer you up."

What? "Cheer me up?"

"You've been so—I don't know—forlorn?" she asked. "Since your aunt died, it's like you lost your energy source."

Damn, that was freakishly observant of her. Maybe *she* got the Barrett intuition. She nailed it in one sentence. Aunt Ruby *was* my energy source. Even from the next state over, the woman that raised me kept me buzzing with her unstoppable magical spirit. When her eyes went, the other senses jumped to the fight. When her life went, it was like someone turned out the lights. All the way to Louisiana.

I was truly alone and on my own. Realizing that at thirty-three was sobering. Realizing Aunt Ruby now knew I'd lied about everything was mortifying. Maybe that's why she was staying otherwise occupied out there in the afterlife.

Then again, *lying* was maybe too strong a word. Was there another word? Maybe a whole turn of phrase would be better. Something like *coloring the story to make an old woman happy.*

Yeah.

Coloring with crayons that turned into shovels.

No one knew the extent of the ridiculous hole I had dug myself into. The one that involved my hometown of Charmed, Texas, believing I was married and successful, living with my husband in sunny California and absorbing the good life. Why California? Because it sounded more exciting than Louisiana. And a fantasy-worthy advertising job I submitted an online resumé for *a year ago* was located there. That's about all the sane thought that went into that.

The tale was spun at first for Aunt Ruby when she got sick, diabetes taking her down quickly, with her eyesight being the first victim. I regaled her on my short visits home with funny stories from my quickie wedding in Vegas (I did go to Vegas with a guy I was sort of seeing), my successful career in advertising (I hadn't made it past promotional copy), and my hot, doting, super gorgeous husband named Michael who traveled a lot for work and therefore was never with me. You'd think I'd need pictures for that part, right? Even for a mostly blind woman? Yeah. I did.

I showed her pictures of a smoking hot, dark and dangerous-looking guy I flirted with one night at Caesar's Palace while my boyfriend was flirting with a waitress. A guy who, incidentally, was named—Michael.

I know.

I rot.

But it made her happy to know I was happy and taken care of, when all that mattered in her entire wacky world was that I find love and *be taken care of.* That I not end up alone, with my ovaries withering in a dusty desert. Did I know that she would then relay all that information on to every mouthpiece in Charmed? Bragging about how well her Lanie had done? How I'd lived up to the Most-Likely-to-Set-the-World-on-Fire vote I'd received senior year. Including the visuals I'd sent her of me and Michael-the-Smoking-Hottie.

My phone beeped in my ear, announcing another call, from

an unknown number. Unknown to the phone, maybe, but as of late I'd come to recognize it.

"Hey, Till," I said, finger hovering over the button. "The lawyer is calling. I should probably see if there's any news on the will."

"Go ahead," she said. "I'll call you in a few days and see how my Ralph is doing."

So, not coming back in a few days.

"Sounds good," I said, clicking over. "Hey, Carmen."

"Hey yourself," she said, her voice friendly but smooth and full of that lawyer professionalism they must inject them with in law school. She warmed it up for an old best friend, but it wasn't the same tone that used to prank call boys in junior high or howl at the top of her lungs as we sped drunk down Dreary Road senior year.

This Carmen Frost was polished. I saw that at the funeral. Still Carmen, but edited and Photoshopped. Even when I met her for drinks afterward and we drove over to the house to reminisce.

This Carmen felt different from the childhood best buddy that had slept in many a blanket fort in our living room. Strung of course with Christmas lights in July and blessed with incense from Aunt Ruby. That Carmen was the only person I truly let into my odd little family circle. She never made fun of Aunt Ruby or perpetuated the gossip. Coming from a single mom household where her mother had to work late often, she enjoyed the warm weirdness at our house. It wasn't uncommon for her to join us to spontaneously have dinner in the backyard under the stars or dress up in homemade togas (sheets) to celebrate Julius Caesar's birthday.

Returning for the funeral and walking into that house for the first time without Aunt Ruby in it broke me. It was full of her. She was in every cushion. Every bookcase. Every oddball knickknack. Her scent was in the curtains that had been recently washed and ironed, as if she'd known the end was near and had someone come clean the house. Couldn't leave it untidy on her exit to heaven for people to talk.

We sat in Aunt Ruby's living room and cried a little and told a few nostalgic stories, trying to bring back the old banter, but it was as if Carmen had forgotten how to relax. She was wound up on a spool of bungee rope and someone had tied the ends down. Tight and unable to yield.

Still, we had history. At one time, she was family. Which is why Aunt Ruby hired her to handle her will and estate.

A word that seemed so silly on my tongue, as I would have never associated *estate* with my aunt or her property. But that was the word Carmen used again and again when we talked. Her *estate* involved the house and some money (she didn't elaborate), but it had to be probated and there were complications due to medical bills that had to be paid first.

Which made sense. It had taken almost two months, and I had almost written off hearing anything. Not that I was holding my breath on the money part. I was pretty sure whatever dollars there were would be used up with the medical bills, and that just left the house. I figured that would probably be left to me. I was really her only family after my mom died young. Well, except for some cousins that I barely knew from her brother she rarely talked to, but I couldn't imagine them keeping up with her enough to even know that she died.

I didn't know what on earth I'd do with the house. It was old and creaky and probably full of problems—one being it was in Charmed and I was not. But it was home. And it had character and memories and laughter soaked into the walls. Aunt Ruby was there. I felt it. If that was intuition, then okay. I felt it *there*. But only there.

So I'd probably keep it as a place to get away, and spend the next several months going back and forth on the weekends like I had right after she passed, cleaning out the fridge and things that were crucial. Mentally, I ticked off a list of the work that was about to begin. That was okay. Aunt Ruby was worth it.

"How's it going over there?" I asked.

"Good, good," Carmen said. "How's California?"

Oh yeah.

"Fine," I said. "You know. Sunshine and pretty people. All that."

I closed my eyes and shook my head. Where did I get this shit?

"Sounds wonderful," she said. "It's been raining and muggy here for three days."

"Yeah," I said, just to say something.

"So the will has been probated," Carmen said. "Everything's ready to be read. I wanted to see when you'd be able to make it back to Charmed for that?"

"Oh," I said, slightly surprised. "I have to come in person?"

"For the reading, yes," she said. "You have to sign some paperwork and so do the other parties."

"Other parties?"

"Yes—well, normally I don't disclose that but you're you, so . . ." she said on a chuckle. "The Clarks?" she said, her tone ending in question.

"As in my cousins?" *Really?*

"I was surprised too," she said. "I don't remember ever even hearing about them."

"Because I maybe saw them three times in my whole life," I said. "They live in Denning. Or they did. I don't think you ever met them."

"Hmm, okay." Her tone sounded like she was checking off a list. "And you'll need to bring some things with you."

"Things?"

"Two, actually," Carmen said, laughing. "Just like your aunt to make a will reading quirky. But they are easy. Just your marriage certificate—"

"My what?"

Carmen chuckled again, and I was feeling a little something in my throat too. Probably not of the same variety.

"I know," she said. "Goofy request, but I see some doozies all the time. Had a client once insist that his dog be present at the reading of the will. He left him almost everything. Knowing Aunt Ruby, there is some cosmic reason."

Uh-huh. She was messing with me.

I swallowed hard, my mind reeling and already trying to figure out how I could fake a marriage certificate.

"And the second thing?" I managed to push past the lump in my throat.

"Easy peasy," she said. "Your husband, of course."

Christmas Road

SCARLETT DUNN

Special Thanks

Much respect and appreciation goes to John Scognamiglio—always professional, always generous with his time, and responds to emails faster than anyone.

Many thanks to Elizabeth Trout, and the invaluable staff at Kensington who work diligently to see the projects come to fruition—you make everything possible.

A heartfelt thank-you to the readers. My goal is to write stories that will take your mind away for a few hours. Your reviews, comments, and emails are genuinely valued.

Also, to the special people in my life who tolerate me, encourage me, and give me their unending support—thank you. I love you more than you can imagine.

Chapter 1

Slumped over in the saddle, Clint Mitchum jerked awake when his horse stumbled. Born from years of experience on the trail, Clint whipped out his pistol, leaned low over his horse's neck, making himself a smaller target until he gained his wits. He listened for any threatening sounds lurking in the darkness. Seconds passed, but hearing nothing amiss, he holstered his pistol and stroked his horse's neck. "Everything okay, Reb?"

Reb turned his head to the side, giving Clint *the look* and snorted.

As tired as he was, Clint still managed a chuckle. The evil eye was Reb's way of letting him know he was the smart one in this group of three. "You're right, we've ridden too long." It was one thing for him to push himself past exhaustion, but he needed to take care of his horses. Reb and Champ had given all they had on this journey and they deserved a nice, long rest.

Wasting no time, Clint made a deft maneuver from the trail, and within minutes he found a suitable place to make camp. After he cared for his horses, he built a fire to ward off the nippy night air. Deciding to forgo dinner, he settled for a cup of coffee he had warming over the fire. Once he tossed his bedroll near the fire, he settled back against his saddle, lit a cigar and pulled the worn piece of paper from his shirt pocket. He'd already read the letter so many times since he'd received it at the post office in Santa Fe that he could almost recite it word for word, but he felt a need to read it again. With eyes burning from lack of sleep, he held the letter to the flickering firelight and read the fine script.

October 1, 1867
La Grange, Texas

My Dearest Son,

It is with the heaviest heart that I write to tell you that your two brothers, and now your father, succumbed to yellow fever. Dr. Sims did his best, but even he couldn't prevent me from contracting this dreaded disease. Sadly, I am too weak to pen this missive, but my lovely neighbor, Amelia, is seeing to this one last chore for me. Though she lost her parents to the fever, she has not abandoned me in my time of need. Son, I fear I may not have many days as this fever runs its course, no matter how much I have tried to cling to life just to see your face one last time. It has been my most fervent prayer to have one more Christmas together before my time here came to an end.

Dr. Sims told me 20 percent of our neighbors have died since the fever came to our town in August. Many of those not afflicted have fled their homes out of fear. It's been weeks since we've received mail, and most businesses have closed with the exception of Stanton's mercantile. The situation here is dire indeed.

I've worried Amelia has stayed too long caring for me. She has promised me she will leave with the Nelson family once she can do no more for me. Mr. Nelson gave me his word that he would wait for her. It breaks my heart that we have lost so many children, and the ones left behind have little to look forward to this Christmas season. What should be a time of joy and thanksgiving is now filled with dread and sadness.

I am uncertain if this letter will reach your hands, but your last letter said you were headed to Santa Fe, and I pray you made it there. There is much I wanted to say to you, Son. Just know how much I have missed you and how much I love you. We understood your difficulties since the war, but I know you are in the palm of God's hand, and He will see you through. Remember we cannot judge ourselves harshly by the trials of war, nor should you carry the horrors with you the rest of your days. Time is fleeting and life quickly passes you by, so you must appreciate each day. I hope you will return home and train horses one day. I am certain you will learn to love the ranch again, and caring for God's creatures will renew your soul and help you to find your purpose. Find someone to love and share your life, and give thanks for every breath.

Have faith, my beloved son, and always believe in the magic of Christmas.

I love you,
Mother

P.S. Mr. Mitchum, please come home, your mother needs you desperately. Amelia

Clint removed his hat and tossed it on his saddle horn. He leaned back, clutched the letter to his chest and closed his eyes. Thankfully, he'd been in Santa Fe when the letter arrived at the post office three weeks from the date it was written. Even though his mother said they weren't receiving mail, he'd immediately sent a telegram, encouraging her to hold on until he arrived. He needed to see her again. He *had* to see her again. It was important to tell her how sorry he was that he hadn't been there for her when she needed him most. The postscript written by his mother's friend, Amelia, heightened his sense of urgency. Though it was only one sentence, he felt the panic in those few words. *What had he been thinking to stay away so long?* Before he'd received his mother's letter, he'd been planning to return home for Christmas this year and stay to run the ranch for his father. Now it was too late. What a cruel twist of fate.

Tears threatened as he thought about the precious time he'd wasted, all because he couldn't come to terms with the past. The last time he'd shed tears was the day his childhood friend was shot dead as he rode beside him during the war. Clint was a sharpshooter in the war, always proficient at his duties—until that fateful day. He'd failed to see a man ready to waylay him and his fellow sharpshooters. His best friend died in his arms. Like so many men who returned from the war, Clint couldn't understand why he'd survived when so many were killed. What was the purpose of neighbor killing neighbor? When the answers didn't come, Clint buried his feelings so deep that nothing, and no one, touched his heart. Until tonight. Tonight he cried. He cried for the loss of his family, his friends and for the loss of precious time. *Time is fleeting.* His mother's words were haunting.

Hours later, Clint was still wide awake, with his many regrets playing over and over in his mind, when he heard his horses restlessly moving about in the makeshift corral. He knew their habits as well as his own, and they were signaling something was not as it should be. Listening intently, he heard horses slowly approaching. *Two horses.* He heard a man's voice in the stillness, which told him the riders weren't trying to surprise him. Still, he was a cautious man. Moving to a sitting position, he silently pulled his Colt from the holster and held it by his side.

"Hello to camp," came a deep voice from the brush.

"Come ahead."

A man leading two horses came into view. As the man drew closer, Clint saw two children sitting atop one horse.

"We saw your fire," the man told him.

Clint holstered his pistol, stood and raked his gaze over the newcomers. Judging by their disheveled appearance, he figured they'd been traveling for a few days.

"You got any food?" one child asked.

"Hush, Son, that's not polite," the man reprimanded.

The hopeful sound in the boy's voice forced Clint to direct his attention to the children. He was surprised to see the two boys were exact replicas of each other, with thick red hair and freckled faces. "I think I can find something for you to eat."

The man lifted the boys from the horse. "That's not necessary; we'd be happy sharing your fire and company."

Clint recognized the telltale sound of a tired man . . . tired of worry . . . tired of shouldering burdens alone . . . just plain tired of existing. He'd been there. "I was just thinking about rustling up some grub for myself. No trouble." He pointed to his horses nearby in his makeshift corral. "Let's get your horses settled first."

"I'm Whitt Newcombe." He pointed to the boys who were staring at Clint's large black horse. "These are my boys, Bo and Boone."

Clint extended his hand. "Clint Mitchum." He glanced down at the boys. "Nice to make your acquaintance, boys."

One boy looked up at Clint and said, "You got a big horse."

Clint chuckled. "Yep, he's a big one."

"What's their names?"

"The black is Reb, and that buckskin is Champ."

The same boy pointed to their horses. "That one is Sugar, and the gray is Britches."

Clint smiled at the names they'd given their horses. "Those are fine names." He noticed they didn't have much in the way of provisions, but their horses were well-tended. He opened his sack of grain and offered it to the boys. "Give Sugar and Britches some of this grain."

After the horses were settled, they walked back to the fire, where Clint pulled out some food for a meal. Once he'd tossed fresh coffee beans in the pot along with more water, he opened the cans of beans and emptied them in a pan. In another pan, he warmed the bacon and biscuits he had for dinner the prior night.

Clint saw the boys eyeing the food. "It's not fancy, but we'll make do."

"We're thankful. It's more than we've had recently," Whitt replied.

"Where are you headed?" Clint asked.

"To a spot on the Llano River, a place called Honey Creek. We're going to try our hand at panning for gold. A lot of folks from La Grange are headed there, hoping to change their luck. Did you hear about the yellow fever hitting our town and towns to the south?"

Before Clint responded, one of the boys spoke up. "Our ma died of the fever."

Clint eyed the boys, thinking they were about six or seven years of age. Too young to have lost their mother. Here he was, a full-grown man, and he couldn't bear the thought of losing his ma. The sadness in their big brown eyes told Clint they had already experienced too much sorrow in their short lives. "I'm real sorry to hear that."

"Just about everyone who hasn't caught the fever has left town. Where are you headed?" Whitt asked.

"La Grange."

Whitt looked at him with concern in his eyes. "You don't want to go there, Clint. They say a peddler brought that disease to town. Too many folks are dying there."

"I've heard, but my mother is there," Clint answered soberly.

Whitt realized Clint had said his last name was Mitchum. "Your ma is Ingrid Mitchum?"

Clint nodded.

Whitt dropped his head. "I'm sorry. I heard she was real sick. But we left town before . . . well, I don't rightly know how she fared."

Trying to ignore the feeling that his heart was being squeezed inside his chest, Clint said, "A lady by the name of Amelia was caring for her."

"It's a blessing she had someone to look after her. After my wife died, we left town. I didn't want to wait for my boys to get sick. I even heard Doc Sims was ill by the time we left. It's so bad, they were burying folks in mass graves." Whitt shook his head, as if he still couldn't believe what he had witnessed. "It was a bustling town, but now the businesses have closed up. There was no way for us to survive. We had nothing left except for a couple of cows."

"We don't have much food. Pa shot a rabbit and we ate that yesterday," one of the boys added.

Clint didn't know if it was Bo or Boone talking. "Times are hard." Looking at their small faces, Clint thought they shouldn't even know what that phrase meant. Another worthless expression when an adult could offer no explanation for what they couldn't control. He didn't like that helpless feeling—he never did.

"We really appreciate sharing your meal," Whitt said. "I'm a pretty good shot, but you have to see game to shoot it."

"I can give you some provisions that should last until you get to Honey Creek. I'll be in La Grange in a few days, and I have more than I need." Seeing the beans were steaming, Clint loaded the tin plates and passed them around.

"That's good of you to offer your food, but I have nothing to pay you in return. I wish you would turn around and go with us. Your ma wouldn't want you to go there knowing the risk."

"I need to go, and the provisions are a gift. I want nothing in return." Clint offered Whitt a cup of coffee.

"Thank you. Your ma and pa were fine people, as good as they come. I didn't know them well . . . wish I did."

Clint caught his reference in the past tense, but he didn't comment.

"Have you seen other folks on this trail?" Whitt asked.

"Yeah, several families. I stopped long enough to talk to a few, and they were coming from La Grange."

Whitt nodded. "I heard that the fever has ended in a few towns, people are returning and things are getting back to normal. I hope that happens in La Grange. We only lived there five years, but we considered it our home and we'd like to go back." Whitt glanced at his boys. "I want them to be near their ma so they never forget her."

"We'd never forget Ma," Bo replied.

"Show Mr. Mitchum her likeness, Pa." Boone looked up at Clint and said, "Our ma was real pretty."

Clint smiled at him. "I bet she was."

Pulling his watch from his pocket, Whitt snapped it open and held it out to Clint.

Clint stared at the yellowed image of a young, unsmiling woman with dark hair and average-looking features. She wasn't a raving beauty, but Clint figured she must have been a won-derful mother to raise these two fine boys. "You sure were lucky to have such a good mother. I know you will never for-get her."

Clint thought Whitt was a few years older than himself, and while they'd lived different lives, he admired Whitt for settling down and having children. Actually, he envied Whitt, even though it was going to be tough for him raising two boys with-out his wife. There was a time Clint thought he would be mar-ried by now with a couple of children. That seemed like an eternity ago. Clint glanced at the boys and saw they were star-ing at him as they gulped their food. He winked at them. "Now, how do I tell the two of you apart?"

One of the boys pointed to himself. "I'm Bo. I have a cowlick on this side." He pointed to the left side of his head. "Boone's cowlick is on the other side."

"We don't care if you get us confused; everybody does," Boone added. "Sometimes we even fool Pa."

Clint chuckled. "I can see how that would be easy to do." Clint listened to the boys chatter as they finished their meal. Answering all their questions took his mind off his own trou-bles. He enjoyed seeing smiles on their faces as he told them stories about rounding up wild horses and training them for the military.

"Pa's good with horses," Boone stated proudly. "He taught us how to take care of Sugar and Britches."

"It's important to take good care of your animals." Clint gave Whitt a thoughtful look. He imagined Whitt had been through so much heartache that he couldn't see a brighter fu-ture right now. But Clint knew how important it was for a man to keep his dreams. Thinking about what his mother had writ-ten in her letter—*Working with God's creatures is good for the soul.* Clint thought he could share her wisdom by offering

Whitt a ray of hope. "Maybe when the fever is gone from La Grange, you could come back and work with horses on your ranch."

Whitt chewed his biscuit as he thought about Clint's remark. "Maybe so."

"It's a decent living, and I never ran out of horses to train. Of course, it might be a nice change of pace to pan for gold. You never know, you might strike it big."

The boys finally came to the end of their questions, settled down on their bedrolls and quickly fell asleep. Clint stoked the fire as Whitt covered the boys with blankets. "I'm sure they're a handful, but they are fine boys."

Whitt smiled wistfully at his boys. "They are good boys. They were crazy about their ma. She was a wonderful mother and wife. I don't know what we are going to do without her."

Clint felt a lump growing in his throat listening to Whitt describe his loss. He didn't imagine one would ever get over something like that, particularly when you had two little reminders with you every day.

By daybreak, Clint had already packed most of his provisions on Whitt's horses. When Whitt and the boys awoke, Clint had a warm meal prepared for them. "We have fresh biscuits and bacon for breakfast this morning."

Bo rubbed the sleep from his eyes. "It smells good."

"It sure does," Boone agreed.

Whitt helped himself to some coffee. "I don't know how we can thank you for what you've done for us."

After the boys finished their breakfast, Whitt cleaned the pans and tucked them in a pack. He thanked Clint again for the provisions. "If things aren't better in La Grange, why don't you come find us? We can pan until we see how things turn out at home."

"I'll see. But if the disease is over in La Grange, I'll get word to you," Clint promised as he lifted the boys onto the horse. He pulled Whitt aside so the boys couldn't hear his next question. "Do you have plenty of ammunition? You never can be too careful on the road."

Whitt nodded. "Yes, that's one thing I have. I'm a good shot with a pistol and a rifle. And I've been teaching the boys to shoot."

"Good. Take care, Whitt."

The men shook hands, and Clint walked back to the boys to say goodbye.

"Mr. Mitchum, I wish you would come with us. What if no one is left in La Grange and you're there all alone?" Bo asked.

Clint reached up and ruffled his hair. He found the young boy's concern touching. "If that happens, I'll find you."

"Don't forget we'll be at Honey Creek. You'd be welcome," Whitt reminded him.

Clint told them goodbye and they rode off in opposite directions. Looking back, Clint saw two tiny hands waving to him. He lifted his hat in farewell.

Chapter 2

Reining in at the front door of his ranch, Clint jumped from Reb and bounded up the stairs in two long strides. Grasping the door handle, he hesitated long enough to take a deep, bracing breath, preparing himself for whatever he might find on the other side. Opening the door slowly, he walked inside, the thump of his boots echoing around the silent room. "Ma?"

No response. He walked through the front room to the back bedroom. The door was slightly ajar, and when he pushed it open, he saw the bed was empty. His mother's favorite hand-stitched quilt embroidered with lilies of the valley was neatly draped over the feather mattress. Glancing around the room, he saw nothing out of place. It looked exactly as he remembered, neat and tidy, just as his mother left it every morning. Clint swiped his hand over his face. He didn't want to think about what he would find outside.

He ran from the room, not stopping until he reached the small knoll a hundred yards from the back of the house. Clutching the gate leading to the family cemetery, Clint stood with his heart in his throat, scanning mounds of earth beneath the massive white oak tree. Grass had not yet covered the four freshly dug graves. He slowly opened the gate and walked inside, remorse heavy on his shoulders. Unlike the other graves of past generations, there were no markers—no one left to see to that last task of memorializing a life. Clint reminded himself he hadn't been there to handle that chore. Removing his hat, he stood silently, not praying as much as regretting. He glanced up at the old oak spreading its strong limbs as if protecting those buried beneath. That old tree had seen a lot of death. He was the only Mitchum left. He'd been so selfish, thinking only of what he needed while his mother had to face the loss of those dear to her all alone. His regrets were too many to count.

Much later, Clint fed and brushed his horses before he stabled them. He walked back to the house, hung his hat on the hook inside the door and looked around at what once had been a vibrant household. The stillness of the room made him feel more alone than he'd ever felt. He wished he could sleep for a week and awake to find this had all been a nightmare. Yet, he knew sleep would evade him again tonight. After making some coffee, he walked to the rocking chair by the fireplace. Seeing something in the chair, he reached down and picked up an old, tattered cloth doll. He sat down in the rocker with the doll in his hand, wondering who had left it behind. The poor thing had seen better days. The doll's threadbare dress, made from an old flour sack with faded yellow flowers, might have been pretty a long time ago. One button eye was missing, and the other eye was broken, leaving only a small fragmented piece behind. That eye reminded him of his life.

Leaning back, he drank his coffee as he thought about the many times his mother sat in that chair sewing when he was a young boy. She was an excellent seamstress and often made dresses for other women. Glancing back down at the doll in his hand, he thought someone had probably asked her to make a new dress for the sad little figure. After he finished his coffee, he stood and returned the doll to the chair. He roamed around the house until he finally made his way back to his mother's bedroom, where he sat on the side of the bed and picked up her Bible from the bedside table. He smiled at the memory of her quoting a scripture or two when she thought he needed to hear something in particular. A strip of old leather was sticking out between the pages, marking what he assumed was a passage his mother had been reading. He recognized the old, worn bookmark he'd made for her when he was five years old. On one side, he'd written the verse, *Honor thy mother and father. I love you Ma.* A folded piece of paper tucked between the pages drifted to his lap. He picked it up and recognized the note was written in his mother's hand.

> *Son, if you are reading this I know you have*
> *found your way home. Please do one last favor for*
> *me and find Amelia Wakeland. I want you to help*
> *her if she is in need. I have never met a sweeter soul,*
> *and I'm worried about her.*
> *Your loving mother*

Clint read the note several times before tucking it into his shirt pocket. He placed the bookmark back in the Bible and returned it to the table. Walking from the room, he thought he'd done little over the last few years to show his mother how much she meant to him. What a fool he'd been. He'd do this one last thing she'd asked of him.

Feeling as if the walls were closing in on him, Clint walked outside to look over the ranch. He thought about his future without his family. Even though he'd been far away, he always knew he had a place to call home. But could the ranch be a home without his family? He didn't think so. He walked until he was exhausted, mentally and physically. That night, after he checked on his horses once last time, he returned to the house and tossed his bedroll on the floor in front of the fireplace. But sleep didn't come.

The next morning before dawn, Clint was on his way to the Wakeland ranch. As he approached the house, he looked over the land. Like his ranch, it appeared desolate, no cows or horses grazing in the pasture. It felt like every person and animal had disappeared from the face of the earth. He was just about to rein in at the house when a man walked from the stable.

"Can I help you with something?"

"Hope so." Clint took the man's measure. He looked to be younger, but he was almost as tall as he was, just not as muscled. He looked none too pleased by the interruption. Clint pushed back his hat on his head and rested his hands on the saddle horn. "I'm Clint Mitchum. I'm looking for Amelia Wakeland."

If the man recognized Clint's name, he gave no indication. "She left with Tom Nelson two weeks back. Headed to the Llano River."

"That river covers some territory," Clint replied.

"That's all I know," the man responded curtly.

Clint could tell he didn't want to offer more information. "Thanks." He turned Reb back in the direction of his ranch. His mother had asked one last thing of him. He'd failed her when she was alive; he wouldn't fail her in death. He'd find Amelia Wakeland no matter how long it took.

Returning to his ranch, Clint walked to his mother's bedroom, picked up her Bible and headed for the door. He stopped in the front room, his eyes drawn to that raggedy little doll in the rocking chair. Something seemed to be telling him to take the doll with him. It was just a brief thought that made no logical sense, but he walked to the rocker and grabbed the doll. After he stuffed both items in his saddlebag, he loaded his packs on Champ and rode out. He didn't know if he was leaving the ranch for the last time. He didn't want to think about the future now. It might take a few weeks, a few months or a few years to find Amelia. After that, maybe he would be in a frame of mind to plan his future.

He rode at a slower pace because his horses hadn't had time to recuperate from the grueling ride on the way home. Riding always helped him sort things out in his mind, but it also gave him too much time to think. He wished he'd asked the man at the Wakeland ranch more questions. Grief had taken hold of his every thought, and he hadn't been thinking straight at the time. He realized he didn't have much information to go on. He wondered why that man had stayed behind at the Wakeland ranch when the place looked to be abandoned. He'd have to focus on what he did know. Amelia Wakeland was alive two weeks ago, and she was headed to the Llano River. He decided to ride to Honey Creek to find Whitt and the boys. The odds of finding Amelia in the same location were not in his favor. Although Whitt had told him several families from La Grange were headed to Honey Creek, so it was as good a place as any to start looking for Amelia.

Days later, Clint arrived in Honey Creek at dusk. It didn't take him long to find Whitt Newcombe once he described the boys to a family he'd passed camping on the river.

Whitt saw Clint as soon as he reined in at their campsite. "I can't believe you're here."

"I left the day after I arrived in La Grange," Clint said as he dismounted.

Whitt understood what Clint was saying. He gripped Clint's shoulder. "I'm sorry the news wasn't better."

"Me too." Clint looked around for the boys. "Where's Bo and Boone?"

"Over by the stream where we're panning. They think looking for gold is fun." Whitt laughed. "I hope after a month they still enjoy it." Whitt poured Clint some coffee. "I just came to grab some grub and coffee."

"Any luck yet?"

Whitt reached in his shirt pocket, pulled out a small pouch that held gold flakes along with several tiny nuggets and held them out for Clint to see. "I remember my pa always told me gold will follow a certain path in a streambed, from inside bend to inside bend, so I looked for slow-moving water that ran in that direction. He also told me when I found black sand, that was a good sign. I searched all day for what I thought would be the best spot. When I saw the logjams and idle pools of water here, I thought it was the perfect place to start."

Clint inspected Whitt's findings. "It does look like you found a promising location."

Whitt tucked the pouch back in his pocket. "You're more than welcome to join us here if you're interested. Come on; the boys will be excited to see you."

As soon as Clint and Whitt reached the streambed, Bo and Boone dropped their pans and came running to Clint. He picked up both boys and swung them around. "I hear you men are working hard."

Bo nodded. "Yeah, this is a lot of fun. Did Pa show you the gold?"

"Pa said if you came here, you could pan with us," Boone told him.

"Please stay with us," Bo pleaded.

It touched Clint's heart that the boys wanted him to stay with them. "If your pa is sure he doesn't mind me joining you."

"I think more and more people will be coming, so it'll be

safer as a team. We can take turns sleeping," Whitt replied. He didn't want to scare the boys by saying their safety could become an issue if word got around about finding gold.

Clint nodded his understanding of what was on Whitt's mind. He agreed with Whitt about safety in numbers. He'd heard stories about greed overruling common sense when men had gold fever. With two boys to protect, it made sense that Whitt preferred to have another man around. Clint placed the boys on the ground and shook Whitt's hand. "I'll stay, but I have one thing I need to do before I start working. I need to find Amelia Wakeland."

"Is she the woman who cared for your mother?" Whitt asked.

"Yes. My mother left me a note asking that I find her. I think she must have been worried that Amelia might become ill. I need to see her and make sure she's well."

"I think I know where she is. You told me she was planning to leave with the Nelson family. I saw Ben Wilburn a few days ago, and he said the Nelson camp was less than a half mile from his." Whitt told him how to get to their camp. "But don't stop at Ben Wilburn's camp. Ben's son is sick with influenza. At least Ben said it was influenza, but there's a chance it could be yellow fever. They need to keep him away from everyone until they know for sure."

The wagon at the Nelson campsite was well-hidden behind a row of pecan trees, not far from the water. Clint saw a woman cooking over the fire a few feet from the wagon. Hearing his horse, the woman stopped working and watched him approach with a wary look on her face.

Dismounting, Clint politely removed his hat, hoping to put her at ease as he kept some distance between them. "Morning."

The woman gave him an almost imperceptible nod.

"Whitt Newcombe told me I could find Tom Nelson here."

"Yes."

"I'm Clint Mitchum . . ."

Her expression registered her surprise. "Ingrid's son?"

Clint nodded. "Yes, ma'am, and I'm looking for Amelia."

"I've heard about you."

Clint wondered if his mother had told her how disappointed she was that he hadn't come home in years. No, his mother wouldn't tell anyone that her eldest son had caused her grief. She'd always given him much more understanding than he deserved. He watched the woman as she turned back to the fire and lifted the coffeepot.

"This is fresh coffee." She picked up a cup from a makeshift table near the firepit. The woman pointed to some stumps that had been conveniently situated around the fire. "Please have a seat."

"Thank you, ma'am." Clint settled his hat back on his head and gratefully accepted the cup of coffee. As he took a drink of his coffee, he thought about what he wanted to say to her. He didn't know what he expected Amelia to look like, but she was considerably older than he thought she would be. She was also almost as round as she was tall, and he was gratified to see she looked healthy. "My mother . . ." Clint halted when he heard voices approaching.

The woman looked at him and smiled. "Here's Amelia now."

Clint's brow furrowed in confusion. His gaze shifted to two young girls running toward them. The smaller girl ran right to him, while the older girl hung back a few feet. Clint thought they were two of the cutest little girls he'd even seen. They both had long, curly, dark hair and big blue eyes.

"Who are you?" the younger girl asked.

"Remember your manners, girls," a woman trailing behind them instructed.

"Yes, ma'am," the girls stated in unison.

Clint glanced up at the woman admonishing the little girl for her question. A beautiful young woman returned his scrutiny. Clint quickly jumped to his feet and removed his hat again. Like the little girls in front of him, the young woman had long, dark, curly hair, lighter blue eyes and porcelain skin.

When Clint felt a tug on his shirtsleeve, he forced his eyes from the woman to the little girl in front of him. She was staring up at him with an impish smile revealing two dimples. "I'm Annie. Who are you?"

Clint chuckled, amused by her direct manner. "I'm Clint Mitchum."

"Amelia, Mr. Mitchum is looking for you," the woman he'd mistaken for Amelia announced. She glanced at Clint, giving him a slight smile. "I'm Sophie Nelson, Tom's wife."

Clint knew she'd intentionally wanted him to believe she was Amelia. "Nice to meet you, Mrs. Nelson."

"Call me Sophie."

Clint nodded. His eyes move to Amelia again. "Amelia?"

"Yes." She placed her hand on the older girl's shoulder. "This is my daughter, Katherine, and you've met Annie."

"Everyone calls me Katie," Katherine told him.

Clint inclined his head. "Hello, Katie."

Three more children walked toward them, a boy and two girls, and Sophie made the introductions. "This is my youngest grandson, Mark. We lost the eldest, Matthew, to the fever. These are my granddaughters, Hannah and Bonnie."

Clint judged the boy to be about twelve or thirteen years of age, and the girls were a little younger. "Nice to meet you."

"We'll give you some privacy." Mrs. Nelson motioned for her grandchildren to follow her away from the camp.

"Please sit down, Mr. Mitchum." Amelia sat on a log near Clint with the girls at her side. She glanced at him, waiting for him to speak first. Ingrid Mitchum had told her that her son was a handsome man, but Amelia hadn't expected him to be such a large, imposing man. And she certainly hadn't expected him to be quite *so* handsome. Dark hair, dark eyes, a strong chiseled jaw, wide shoulders and a trim waist—no, he was not lacking in masculine appeal. The pistol he wore low on his hip didn't escape her notice. Most of the ranchers of her acquaintance carried rifles.

Clint cleared his throat, buying time to find the words without becoming emotional. "My mother asked me to find you. She wanted to make sure you were doing well." He wanted her to know how much he appreciated how she cared for his mother. "I also wanted to meet you to thank you for staying with my mother."

"Oh my! You rode all this way just to see if I was well?" Amelia could hardly believe he'd come so far to check on her. "How is your mother?"

Clint stared at her, trying to make sense of her question. "You weren't there when . . ." He couldn't bring himself to finish his sentence.

Amelia looked at him quizzically. "Did something happen to Doc Sims?"

"Doc Sims?" Clint repeated.

"Yes, he was very ill when we left. I wanted to stay to help nurse him, but Mr. Nelson wanted to leave."

Clint shook his head. "I don't know how the doctor is doing."

Amelia gave him a questioning look. "Your mother didn't have a relapse, did she? Does she need me?"

"I don't understand," Clint responded. "Did you not stay with my mother to the . . . to the end?"

"The end?" When she realized what Clint was saying, her lips started to quiver. "You're not saying that Ingrid . . . that Ingrid . . ." a tear slid slowly over her cheek ". . . died?"

Chapter 3

"I thought you knew . . . since her grave was . . ." Clint swallowed hard. Seeing Amelia's tears freely flowing was nearly his undoing. He stood and walked to her. His first thought was to comfort her, but he hesitated because they were complete strangers. He started to place his hand on her shoulder, but to his surprise, she jumped up and threw herself into his arms. A heartbeat later, the girls were clinging to him, all three crying as if their hearts were breaking. Clint put one arm around Amelia and one arm around the girls. "It will be okay." His own emotions were so raw that he could hardly speak. He clenched his jaw, trying to maintain his composure and stay strong for the grief-stricken females in his arms.

Minutes later, Amelia pulled away and swiped at her tears with the back of her hand. "I'm sorry, Mr. Mitchum; we should be the ones comforting you."

Clint pulled his bandanna from his pocket and handed it to her.

Katie dried her tears on her sleeve. "We loved Miss Ingrid."

Annie pulled up her skirt and wiped her face. "She was going to make Lucy pretty again."

Clint started to ask who Lucy was, but Amelia said, "Mr. Mitchum, we were all very fond of your mother." She picked up Clint's forgotten cup, filled it with fresh coffee and held it out to him. "Girls, why don't we let Mr. Mitchum sit and drink his coffee?"

His arms now empty after the brief moment of sharing his grief, Clint took the cup from Amelia and sat down again. The girls dutifully sat down beside their mother and silently stared at him. Their forlorn expressions broke his heart. It gave him comfort to know they loved his mother. At least she'd had people surrounding her who cared about her during her illness.

"Did anyone tell you what happened? Ingrid was doing well when we left. I never considered she might have a relapse."

"I didn't see anyone until I rode to your ranch. I asked the man at your ranch where I could find you."

After a few moments, Amelia asked, "How did you know your mother wanted you to find me?"

"There was a note in the family Bible."

"Who told you that your mother . . . had passed? Casey?"

"Casey?" Clint didn't know who Casey was. "No, I saw her grave."

Jumping to her feet, Amelia stood before Clint. "But that grave was dug a long time ago. Your mother asked Casey to dig the grave when she contracted the fever. But I told him to fill it in, because I didn't want her to think she was going to die." Seeing Clint's confused expression, she added, "Your mother recovered before I left town. She insisted that I leave with the Nelsons while she stayed behind to care for Doc Sims. She told me because she had survived the fever, she would probably be immune. If you didn't go to town, how do you know she wasn't there caring for Doc Sims?"

Clint studied her face, trying to make sense of what she was saying. Was it possible his mother was still alive and in La Grange, nursing the doctor? "Are you saying my mother was completely well when you left La Grange?"

"Yes, but when the doctor became ill, she insisted on staying with him. Doc lost his wife several years ago, so there was no one to help him. He had done so much for everyone else and your mother wouldn't desert him."

Clint looked off into the distance. He didn't want to get his hopes up, only to have them dashed once again, but at that moment he felt a spark of faith. "Then it's possible she's alive."

"A family passed this way two days ago and told us that the fever had stopped spreading, and some families were already returning to La Grange," Amelia told him.

"Was Mr. Nelson thinking of returning?" Clint asked.

"Not yet. I would like to go home as soon as possible, but I think he wants to stay here for now. I understand why he wants to wait, after losing one grandson. We all want to protect the children."

"Ma left because of us. She didn't want us to get sick," Katie commented.

Clint thought Katie sounded too old for her age, much like Whitt's boys. "Your mother did the right thing." Clint remembered his mother's letter mentioning that Amelia had lost her parents to yellow fever, but she hadn't mentioned Amelia's husband. "Did your husband come with you to Honey Creek?"

"My husband is deceased," Amelia replied softly.

Clint assumed he must have died from yellow fever. He hadn't expected Amelia to be a young widow with two children to care for. Staring at her, he thought again how beautiful she was, with her dark hair and pale skin. He imagined her husband fought that disease every step of the way so he could stay with her and their children. If she was his wife, and these beautiful little girls were his, it would take more than yellow fever to take his life.

Amelia sat down beside Clint. "Mr. Mitchum, I believe your mother is in La Grange, caring for the doctor. She was determined to stay alive to see you, and I can't see the fever taking her life after what she had been through. She is a strong woman."

Clint knew his mother was a determined woman of faith. He hoped it wasn't wishful thinking on his part—he'd been disappointed too many times—but Amelia's words rang true in his heart. He had to find out as soon as possible if his mother was in La Grange. "I'll have to let my horses rest for a couple of days before I go back. They've been pushed to the limit."

"Did Casey know you were Ingrid's son?" Amelia asked.

"Who is Casey?"

"The man you saw at my ranch."

"I introduced myself, but he didn't seem to want to divulge much information," Clint replied.

"That sounds like Casey," Amelia retorted with a frown on her face.

Mrs. Nelson walked back to camp accompanied by her husband. After introductions were made, and Amelia explained the situation to Mr. Nelson, he told Clint he was welcome to stay at their camp.

"I'm sharing a campsite with Whitt Newcombe and his two boys. Our camp is less than a mile away."

"Is he having any luck finding gold? I haven't found a flake," Tom Nelson said.

"Some. You folks should ride back with me and set up camp there."

"I would rest a lot easier if there were others nearby," Sophie Nelson admitted, looking at her husband.

Clint didn't think Whitt would mind having them. He'd prefer that two men be on hand to protect the women and children while he was gone. "There's a spot for your family. It would be a wise decision to stay close to one another."

Tom Nelson readily agreed. "We'll pack up and go with you."

Bo and Boone ran to Clint when he returned to the camp with the newcomers. Whitt welcomed everyone, and told the Nelsons to set up camp right next to his. Clint had an opportunity to talk to Whitt alone while the Nelsons were getting settled.

Clint discussed with Whitt what Amelia told him about his mother. "I'll be leaving in two days for La Grange. I didn't think you would mind having another man around."

"I'm glad you brought them here. I know they lost one grandson to the fever, and they lost both their son and daughter-in-law a few years ago to cholera. It's been rough on them." Whitt offered Clint a cup of fresh coffee. "I hope you find your ma alive and well. That would be a Christmas miracle indeed."

Whitt voiced what Clint had been thinking. Having taken his family for granted for so many years, he didn't think he was deserving of such a miracle, but he was asking anyway. "I can't think of a greater blessing than to see her again."

Later that day, Clint decided to try his hand at panning. It wasn't an occupation he would have chosen; he preferred more active work from the back of a horse. He thought about what his mother had written in her letter about coming to love the ranch again. He did love the ranch; he always had. He should have recognized that a long time ago. He'd spent too much time thinking of himself instead of doing what was best for his family. Seeing Whitt's and Amelia's children made him realize how fortunate he had been as a young man. These children had either lost a parent or grandparents or siblings. He'd had a family he'd taken for granted. Yes, he'd seen his share of horrors during the war, but it was nothing he could change. If the last few weeks had taught him anything, he'd learned not to waste another minute on reliving a past he couldn't change. He felt an overwhelming need to do something for these children who were much too young to face the harsh, cold realities of life.

Walking down the bank, Clint found a peaceful spot where the stream was slowing. It was a good area for him to keep an eye on the children, who were on the bank several yards away. Bo and Boone yelled at him and waved. The boys were teaching Katie and Annie how to pan for gold at the water's edge. Clint could hear Bo explain to the girls how to tell if they had gold in their pans. He saw Amelia join the children, and Bo and Boone gave her the same instructions they'd given the girls. Bo demonstrated how to scoop some gravel and silt into her pan.

"You have to shake it like this," Boone told her, demonstrating by vigorously shaking his pan.

"Like this?" Amelia asked, swirling her pan.

"Yeah, that's pretty good for a girl," Bo replied.

Clint grinned at Bo's comment, thinking Whitt better teach that boy how to talk to a woman or he may never get married. Clint couldn't keep his eyes off Amelia as he continued to swirl his own pan. He wasn't thinking about gold as he watched her. Not only was she uncommonly beautiful, she was patient with the children. Boone said something that Clint couldn't hear, but the sound of their laughter carried along the bank. Clint smiled, thinking how nice it was to hear laughter again. He thought about Amelia saying she wanted to return home. For a brief moment as he watched her, he thought of what it would be like to have dinner with her and the children at the ranch with his mother. Like a family. He shook his head and looked down at the water he'd sloshed on his pants while he was daydreaming. He questioned his sanity, dreaming of such a thing. Amelia was probably still grieving for her husband. And what made him think she'd be interested in having dinner with him anyway?

Hearing a masculine voice, Clint glanced back toward Amelia and saw Whitt had joined them. It occurred to him that Amelia and Whitt had a lot in common. Both understood the pain of losing a spouse and having two children to raise alone. It seemed logical they would be drawn to each other.

Turning his attention to the task at hand, he picked up his spade and shoveled some river sediment into his pan. He shook the pan, swirling the contents, allowing the black sand to settle at the bottom. Tipping his pan into the water, he moved it back and forth in the slow-moving current to lift away the first layer of sediment. He repeated the process, but his thoughts drifted back to one particular woman.

"You've swirled that a long time."

Clint nearly dropped his pan at the sound of Amelia's soft voice. He'd been so lost in his thoughts that he hadn't heard her approach. So much for keeping an eye on everyone. He glanced down the stream and noticed Whitt had waded into the water to pan by a large boulder. The children were now playing a game on the bank, gold forgotten for the moment.

Amelia sat near Clint on a fallen log and leaned forward to watch him agitate his pan. "I'm afraid I don't have the patience for this."

"I was thinking the same thing," Clint admitted.

Amelia inched closer to him and lowered her pan into the water. "The boys were trying to teach me, but I may be hopeless."

"Here." Clint picked up his spade and scooped the river contents into her pan. "It helps to have a spade."

Amelia imitated Clint's actions, swirling and dipping her pan into the stream.

Clint reached over, placed his hands over hers and tilted up her pan a few degrees. "Don't let too much flow away at once. Gold is heavier and it will settle at the bottom of your pan."

Amelia laughed. "I see now what I was doing wrong." She

glanced into Clint's pan. "Mr. Mitchum, I think I see gold in your pan."

Clint was so busy staring at her flushed cheeks that he'd forgotten his own pan. Just having her so near made his heart skip a beat. When her eyes met his, he quickly turned his gaze to the contents in his pan. He was surprised to see shiny, gold flakes mixed in with the dark sand covering the bottom of the pan. He moved the black sand around with his fingers. Not only did he have gold flakes, there were several small nuggets of gold. "I never expected to find anything like this." He held his pan for Amelia to see.

Amelia's eyes widened. "Oh, Mr. Mitchum! I've never seen nuggets that size!"

Clint grinned at her excitement. "Call me Clint. It's rare to get so lucky the first time you pan a place." Clint pulled the nuggets out of the pan and held them in his palm.

Amelia looked around to see if anyone was watching. "Mr. Nelson told me you shouldn't let anyone know if you make such a find."

Clint chuckled. "I think we can trust our group."

Amelia nodded her agreement. "Of course. But more and more people are arriving here every day. Mr. Nelson advised that it's best to keep our business quiet."

"Good advice." There were many things Clint wanted to ask her, but it wasn't about finding gold. He wanted to know when her husband died, and what her plans were for the future. Yet he didn't want to broach the subject if her feelings were still tender. Instead of talking, he reached over and helped her swirl her pan. "Let's see if we can find you some gold."

Amelia smiled up at him. "Thank you. It would be wonderful if I could purchase gifts for the girls this Christmas. They've faced too much sorrow, and I would love for them to have some joy, particularly during Christmas."

Clint looked into her eyes, wishing he could replace the sadness with some hope. "The children have had a rough time. Bo and Boone lost their mother."

"Almost every family I know lost someone. It's been a terrible time for so many families."

Clint thought now might be the right time to mention her own loss. "I'm sorry for your loss."

"Thank you. I miss my parents terribly."

Clint glanced down at his large hand covering hers. He noted she hadn't mentioned missing her husband. "Here's how you do it." He gently dipped the pan at an angle in the water and allowed the water to remove some of the debris. He released her hand as she repeated the process. "I think you've got it."

They worked side by side for several minutes before Annie and Katie joined them.

"Look at what we found." Annie opened her small hand.

Amelia and Clint looked down to see a few flakes of gold in her palm.

Katie opened her palm for them to see. "I found some too."

"Oh my! You girls did a good job." Amelia hugged them to her.

"You can buy my dinner," Clint teased.

"Bo and Boone told us you can buy things with gold. Is that true, Mr. Mitchum?" Katie asked.

"The boys are right. It might take a bit more flakes than you have so far to buy things at the mercantile, but it's possible," Clint answered.

"We'll work every day to find more because we have something we want to buy," Annie responded.

"What do you want to buy?" Amelia asked.

The girls exchanged a look, then replied in unison, "It's a secret."

"I see. Well, you shouldn't tell a secret." Amelia stood and placed her hands on their shoulders. "Let's go help Mrs. Nelson with dinner."

"Can we stay here with Mr. Mitchum and pan some more?" Annie asked.

When Amelia glanced at Clint to see if he was agreeable, he smiled at her. "They can stay with me if you don't mind."

"Stay with Mr. Mitchum and don't wander off, and don't ask him a thousand questions." Amelia didn't know if Clint knew what it was like trying to keep up with two girls, so she gave him fair warning. "They can ask a ton of questions."

Clint laughed. "No problem. I've already been the target of Bo and Boone's inquisitions."

As soon as Amelia was out of earshot, Annie moved closer to Clint and whispered, "We'll tell you our secret. We want to buy something for Ma."

Clint looked at their earnest little faces. "What do you want to buy?"

Before the girls could tell their secret, Bo and Boone joined them. Boone handed Clint a cup of coffee. "Mrs. Nelson told us to bring you this, and to tell you supper will be ready in thirty minutes."

"Thank you, boys." Clint smiled when he saw the cup was only half full.

"We're going to tell Mr. Mitchum our secret," Annie announced to the boys.

"They already told us their secret," Bo told Clint.

"Well, we don't want Ma to know, so don't tell her," Katie instructed.

Bo and Boone nodded. "We won't."

Clint took a sip of his barely warm coffee just as Annie said, "We want to buy Ma a husband for Christmas."

Clint choked on his coffee and started coughing.

Katie slapped him on the back. "Are you okay, Mr. Mitchum?"

When he finally stopped coughing, he sputtered, "I thought I heard you say you wanted to buy a husband for your ma."

Katie and Annie nodded in unison. "That's what we want to do," Katie confirmed.

Clint dropped his pan on the bank, his eyes bouncing from Katie to Annie. "That's your secret?"

Annie grinned at him. "Yes, we want to surprise her. Isn't it wonderful?"

Boone sat down beside Clint. "We heard Mrs. Nelson tell Pa lots of men send money for wives, but I don't know where they send the money. Do you know where to send the money, Mr. Mitchum?"

"Why don't you buy our pa for your ma?" Bo asked the girls before Clint could respond.

"Yeah. Your ma is real pretty. I bet our pa would like her. He's really been missing our ma," Boone agreed.

Clint held his hand in the air. "Now wait a minute. You can't go buying a husband for your ma, girls."

Annie stuck out her lower lip, and Katie frowned at him, saying, "That's how Mr. Collins got his wife. He wrote a letter and sent money for a wife to come meet him."

Clint was stunned how much the children knew about the affairs of adults. "Who told you that? And who is Mr. Collins?"

"I heard Mrs. Nelson tell Ma. Mr. Collins owns the boardinghouse in La Grange," Katie answered. "His new wife does all the cooking."

"Mrs. Nelson said she would make a better floozy, because she can't cook," Annie stated.

Bo furrowed his brow at Annie. "What's a floozy?"

Annie shrugged and shook her head from side to side. "I don't know, but I guess she does it better than she cooks."

Katie looked up at Clint. "Mr. Mitchum, do you know what a floozy is?"

"Ah . . . it's ah . . ." Clint didn't know how to answer that question for children's ears, so he quickly thought of something else to say. "I don't think your ma would want you to find her a husband. She can do that all by herself, when she's ready."

"But we heard Ma tell Mrs. Nelson she didn't know how she would care for us since our pa died. We want to stay with her, so we need to find her a husband," Annie replied.

Clint thought the girls were just missing their pa. "Of course you'll stay with your mother. I know you miss your pa, but it might take some time for your ma to want to marry again."

"Mrs. Nelson said a lot of men don't want no one else's children. We'd be good, and he don't have to like us," Katie added.

It seemed to Clint that Mrs. Nelson had a whole lot to say on the subject. "Girls, there's not a man I know who wouldn't be happy to have two girls like you."

"I guess Ma could always marry Casey," Annie mused.

Casey. Clint remembered that was the man at Amelia's ranch.

"We'll talk to our pa. I'm sure he'll want your ma," Boone offered.

Clint didn't like the sound of that. "You children need to leave things like this up to the adults."

Boone looked up at Clint. "You don't think Pa would like their ma?"

Clint couldn't lie to the boy. "That's not what I'm saying. But in situations like this, women like to make up their own minds if they want to marry again." Clint questioned his own motives for objecting to a hypothetical union between Amelia and Whitt.

"Do you have a wife, Mr. Mitchum?" Boone asked.

"No, I don't."

"Then why don't you marry their ma?" Bo asked.

Chapter 4

Throughout dinner, Clint thought about Bo's question. Thankfully, the Nelsons' grandchildren joined them at the creek and the conversation turned from marriage to Christmas. The children reminisced about past Christmases, when times were not so dire. Clint could hear the excitement in their voices as they recalled happier times in their homes on Christmas morning.

"Ma told us we'll celebrate this year having dinner with good friends," Katie stated.

"We're lucky we still have family, even if none of us can afford presents this year," Mark, the Nelsons' grandson, commented.

Clint asked the children what they would ask for if they could have one present this year.

"No one gets presents this year," Bo reminded him.

"I know, but I'd still like to hear what everyone would want if they could receive one present." Clint thought he would get them started by saying, "I'd like to have new martingales for my horses if I could have a present this year."

"I'd just want Lucy back, even if your ma couldn't make her beautiful again," Annie told him.

"Who is Lucy?" Clint asked.

"My doll."

Until that moment, Clint had forgotten about the doll he'd stuffed in his saddlebag when he'd left his ranch. It was Annie's doll.

"I'd like a puppy," Katie shared.

"Have you ever had a dog?" Clint asked.

Katie and Annie both shook their heads. "Casey always said we couldn't afford to feed one."

Clint refrained from commenting on what he was thinking. If they were his girls, they'd have a dog no matter what. He wondered if Casey had plans to replace their father.

Clint ruffled Bo's hair. "And what would you dream about having?"

Bo chewed on his lip for a moment before he responded. "I want a billy goat."

The girls seemed to like Bo's response, saying they had never seen a goat before.

Boone agreed with his brother. "I want a goat, too."

Clint looked at Hannah and Bonnie. "And what about you two pretty little ladies?"

Hannah wanted a new dress and Bonnie wanted a doll.

"Mark, what would you like to have?" Clint asked.

"A new pair of boots. All I ever had was my brother's hand-me-downs, and they are too small now. Maybe next year we can ask for a present."

Clint had already noticed the condition of Mark's well-worn shoes. "My ma always told me that we should always believe in the magic of Christmas."

Annie furrowed her forehead. "What does that mean?"

"I think the magic of Christmas means many things. It's

having a family who loves you and friends to share a meal. When you are older, you will have fond memories of family and friends and the times you spent together. Sometimes dreaming of things you want is the fun part. It also means that anything is possible at Christmas."

"But everyone is so sad now," Katie remarked.

Clint understood how difficult it was to think of anything but what was lost. "That's true, honey. But you still have people who love you, and you are making more friends now. We all have so much to be thankful for."

Annie placed her small hand in Clint's. "Mr. Mitchum, I hope you get the nightingales for your horses."

Clint chuckled and gave her tiny hand a gentle squeeze. "Martingales. I'll show you what they are later."

During dinner, Clint sat near Amelia and the girls. He listened to Annie and Katie tell Amelia about their conversation that day. To his surprise, they remembered what all the children wanted if they could have one present for Christmas.

"And what did you wish for?" Amelia asked.

"I miss Lucy. All I want is Lucy," Annie replied.

Amelia touched her daughter's cheek. "I know you do, honey."

"I want a puppy," Katie added.

"A puppy would be nice," Amelia agreed.

"Mr. Mitchum wants nightingales for his horses."

"Nightingales?" Amelia glanced at Clint, and he grinned at her.

Katie corrected her sister. "They are martingales, and Mr. Mitchum is going to show us what they are after dinner."

Amelia patiently listened as Annie and Katie recounted their entire conversation with Clint. Instead of sounding disappointed there would be no presents this year, they seemed content to believe in the magic of Christmas. As the girls prattled on about Clint, Amelia found herself glancing his way. All the boys were now surrounding him, asking him question after question and hanging on his every word. Like the girls, the boys were just as smitten with the tall cowboy. And who could blame them? Clint was the type of man she'd dreamed of meeting one day. Of course, that was before she'd married, before her fanciful dreams had faded away. While she didn't regret the choices she'd made, she still wished she'd known the love of a man. A man like Clint. Everyone told her that few men would want to marry a woman with a ready-made family. She loved the girls with all her heart, and if she had to spend the remainder of her life without a husband, she would still have her girls.

The magic of Christmas. How nice that sounded. She was thankful that Clint had given the children hope. If she believed in those things now, she'd dream of a man like Clint falling in love with her. A man who could put a smile on the faces of children; a man who encouraged children to dream regardless of the discouraging facts of their situations; a man who made the children feel safe. Clint managed to do this in a short period of time even though he was dealing with his own worries about his mother. Men like Clint were few and far between in her opinion.

Katie and Annie didn't really know their father. Amelia doubted if he'd ever spent more than five minutes alone with the girls in their lives. It wasn't his fault; he'd been away at war, and when he came home, he was ill until the day he died. The girls hadn't known a man like Clint, a man who would take the time to really talk with them. Amelia smiled to herself, thinking about Clint walking back from the lake tonight with Annie sitting on his shoulders, laughing as though she was having the best time of her short life.

Annie and Katie were helping Amelia clean the pans after dinner when Clint approached them, his saddlebag slung over one shoulder. "Miss Annie, I have something in my saddlebag you need to see."

Looking up at him, Annie's eyes widened in surprise. "What is it?"

Clint opened the flap on the saddlebag and held it down for her to look inside.

"Lucy!" She reached into the saddlebag and pulled out her doll. "Where did you find her?"

"She was sitting in the rocking chair in front of the fireplace at my home."

Annie clutched Lucy to her. "Thank you for bringing her to me, Mr. Mitchum!"

"How did you know the doll belonged to Annie?" Amelia asked.

"I didn't, until Annie mentioned her earlier today. I had forgotten I put the doll in my saddlebag when I left the ranch."

Amelia gave Clint a warm smile. "She's really missed her doll."

Later that night when it was time for the girls to go to bed, Amelia found them with Clint, watching him care for his horses.

When Amelia joined them, Annie pointed to a well-worn leather strap hanging across a log. "Ma, that's a nightingale."

"Martingale," Katie corrected.

Amelia smiled, replying, "I know." She stayed with Clint and the girls a few more minutes before she told them it was their bedtime. "It's time to say good night to Mr. Mitchum."

"'Night, Mr. Mitchum." Annie walked to him and yanked on his shirtsleeve. When Clint looked at her, she whispered, "Can I kiss you good night?"

A lump formed in Clint's throat as he leaned over. "I'd be honored."

Annie kissed one cheek and Katie kissed his other cheek.

"Good night, girls. I'll see you in the morning."

Clint finished with his horses and walked to the fire. He saw Amelia and the girls placing their blankets near Bo and Boone, who were already asleep. Whitt was sitting by the fire, drinking coffee.

"The boys must have worn themselves out," Clint commented to Whitt as he poured himself some coffee.

Whitt laughed. "I'm surprised they haven't worn out your ears."

Clint sat down near Whitt. "I'll admit I've never been asked so many questions."

While Whitt talked about the gold he'd found that day, Clint tried to hear what the girls were asking Amelia. One question in particular from Annie caught his attention.

"Ma, will we ever have another pa?"

Clint wished Whitt would be quiet for a moment so he could hear Amelia's response. As it was, he only caught her last few words.

". . . count our blessings that we have one another."

In the next instant, Whitt walked to the fire and poured himself more coffee, and Clint heard Katie say, "Mr. Mitchum doesn't have a wife."

"Hmm," Amelia murmured.

Clint wondered what "hmm" meant.

"We heard Mrs. Nelson say that Mr. Mitchum is real handsome. What do you think, Ma?" Katie asked.

"Girls, where do you get these questions?" Amelia glanced Clint's way.

"We just thought you might want another husband, so we can have food and stuff. Mrs. Nelson said a woman needs a man's help to survive out here," Katie explained.

"Well . . ." Amelia couldn't finish her reply because Annie spoke up.

"Mr. Mitchum would make a good pa. He talks to us."

"What about Mr. Newcombe? He's nice, and Bo and Boone are really nice too—for boys. Do you like him better?" Katie asked.

Clint glanced at Whitt to see if he was listening to their conversation. He was.

Amelia leaned over the girls and covered them with blankets. "They are all very nice. Now, it's time for you to get some sleep. Enough questions for one day."

Exchanging a look with Whitt, Clint shrugged and lowered his voice. "We're *nice.*"

Whitt laughed. "But you're handsome and nice." Whitt eyed Clint, trying to gauge his reaction to Amelia. "You seem mighty interested in what she had to say."

Clint took a drink of his coffee. "Aren't you?"

"She's a fine woman, but I just lost my wife."

"Don't you think the boys will need a mother?"

"Maybe one day, but not right now. It's not that easy to get over the loss of the woman I've loved since I was sixteen years old."

Clint thought of his parents and how in love they had been. It had to be tough on his mother to lose not only the love of her life, but her children as well. "I'm sorry, Whitt."

"Me too." Whitt glanced Amelia's way, then smiled at Clint. "Besides, it seems to me that she looks your way fairly often."

Looking across the fire at Amelia, Clint shook his head. "She's probably going through the same thing you are, losing her spouse."

"According to Mrs. Nelson, she lost her husband a few years back."

Clint turned to look at him. "You mean he didn't die of the fever?"

"I don't think so."

* * *

Once the girls fell asleep, Amelia walked to the fire and poured herself a cup of coffee. She held the pot out to the men. "Would you like some more?"

Whitt declined, but Clint held out his cup to her. After she filled his cup, she sat down near him.

"Did you think they were going to stay awake all night?" Clint teased.

Amelia laughed. "They've had an exciting day."

Whitt excused himself to check on his horses, leaving Clint and Amelia alone.

Clint figured Whitt left on purpose to give him time alone with Amelia. He'd have to thank him for that later. "Those girls are something special."

"They think highly of you. It seems you have won two hearts today."

Clint was just about to say he'd lost his heart to them, but he heard horses approaching. He held out his hand to Amelia, indicating she should stay seated as he stood and gripped the butt of his pistol.

Three men reined in opposite the fire, but they didn't dismount.

"Can you spare some of that coffee?" the man in the middle asked.

The first thing Clint noticed was that the strangers were all wearing sidearms. They didn't have packhorses, which told him they were either outlaws on the run or had a camp somewhere else and were out looking for trouble. Either way, they were up to no good. He'd spent a lot of hours on the trail, and he often had to make quick decisions about men who approached his camp late at night. Some strangers he'd invite to stay and have coffee, others he didn't. He didn't like the looks of these characters, and he particularly didn't like the way they were staring at Amelia. "Sorry, we just finished the last of the coffee."

"Can't you make some more?" The stranger pointed to the man on his left. "My friend here don't feel too good."

Clint spared a quick glance at the sickly man. It was a cool evening, but the man was sweating profusely. "Why are you out here at this time of night looking for coffee?"

The man doing the talking stared at Amelia and grinned. "What are you two doing out here?"

Clint glared at the man. "Mister, I suggest the three of you ride on out of here."

"Is that your wife?" the man asked.

Clint took a step forward, blocking the man's view of Amelia. "Maybe you didn't hear me. You need to ride out."

"Why don't you introduce us to the little lady?" The leader's eyes darted to his men.

Quickly calculating which man would be the first to draw his weapon, Clint chose the right man. The leader reached for his pistol, but Clint was much faster, pointing his gun at the man's head before his pistol cleared his holster. "I think that would be a big mistake."

"There's three of us and one of you," one of the other men reminded Clint.

"Mister, if you're looking for trouble, you just found it," Clint told them.

The three men exchanged a glance before the leader smirked at Clint. "You can't take three guns."

"He probably can, but I'm here if he needs me." Whitt walked from the brush with his rifle pointed at the men.

The leader glanced at his companions and holstered his pistol. "Let's ride, boys." Before they turned their horses around, the leader gave Clint a hard look. "I'll see you again."

Whitt lowered his rifle and joined Clint by the fire. "What do you think they had in mind?"

Clint holstered his pistol. "Nothing good. I think we need to sleep in shifts in case they return. If you think you can sleep, I'll take first watch."

"Sounds good." Whitt stretched out on his bedroll and covered his eyes with his hat.

Amelia stood and poured two fresh cups of coffee. "I'm so nervous, I don't think I can sleep. Do you mind if I keep you company for a while?"

Clint couldn't think of a better way to stay awake. "Not at all. I'll pull over my bedroll closer to the girls' so we don't disturb Whitt."

After placing his bedroll near Amelia's blanket, Clint gathered more wood for the fire. Once he had the fire blazing again, he saw Amelia had a blanket wrapped around her shoulders. "Cold?"

"A little, but the fire feels wonderful." She watched Clint check his rifle and position it within easy reach before he sat down. "What do you think those men wanted?"

"Probably looking for someone to rob. I'm sure word is out that people are panning for gold here."

Amelia shivered. "I didn't like the looks of them. I'm glad we're here with you and Mr. Newcombe. I think Mr. Nelson is too trusting; he might have invited them into our camp."

Clint stared at her, thinking she looked so lovely by the light of the fire with her flushed cheeks and her long, beautiful hair draped over one shoulder. When his gaze moved to her lips, he had an almost irresistible urge to kiss her. He reminded himself that she may not have recovered from the loss of her husband. His eyes drifted back to hers. "I'm glad you and the girls are here with me."

Their eyes remained locked for a few seconds more before Amelia nervously glanced away. "Do you think we should warn the other families in the area to be on the lookout for those men?"

Clint immediately regretted that he'd allowed the moment to pass without making a move. He thought of the old proverb; *fortune favors the bold. It won't happen again*, he promised himself. "I'll ride to tell the other folks in the morning. When I'm not around, I want you and the girls to stay close to the men."

Chapter 5

Early the next morning, Clint was saddling his horse when Amelia joined him. "Please be careful, Mr. Mitchum, and give my best to the Wilburn family."

Clint cinched his saddle and turned to face her. "Please call me Clint, and I'll be careful. Do you know how to use a pistol?"

"My father taught me to shoot a long time ago, but I don't have a gun."

Clint pulled an extra gun from his saddlebag and checked to make certain it was loaded. He held it out to her, and was somewhat surprised that she wasn't fainthearted about handling the firearm. He liked that about her. It told him that she had the courage to protect the girls as well as herself if necessary. "If you have to use it, don't hesitate. Aim at a button and pull the trigger."

Amelia nodded her understanding before she tucked the pistol into her pocket.

Clint jumped in the saddle. "I'll be back as soon as I can."

* * *

Anxiously awaiting Clint's return, Amelia wouldn't allow the girls out of her sight. Along with Mrs. Nelson, they joined the children at the creek to pan for gold. The children were not aware of the three men who'd rode into their camp the previous night. The women didn't want to frighten them, but they stressed the importance of staying together.

On Clint's return to camp later that day, Amelia thought the men were as relieved as she was to have him back. She didn't want to think about him leaving for La Grange, but she understood he had to go. For the remainder of the day, Clint panned for gold, keeping Amelia and all the children within his sight at all times. He panned in the same location where he'd had some luck the prior day. Within a few hours, he'd found several small nuggets.

After they took a break to have something to eat, the children rested along the bank under the warmth of the afternoon sun. Clint watched Amelia pan at the bank for a while, but the next time he glanced her way she was lying in the grass with a blanket covering her. The three strangers had unnerved her last night, and Clint knew she hadn't slept well. It wasn't until Mrs. Nelson brought him some coffee at the lake that he learned the real reason Amelia was resting.

"Amelia's not feeling well. I told her to go to our wagon to rest, but she wants to stay near the girls. I've worried about someone getting sick ever since Ben Wilburn came to our camp and told us his boy was sick. Ben said the boy had influenza, but the symptoms are the same as yellow fever. And Amelia told me one of those strangers last night looked sickly."

"Ben said his son has improved when I saw him earlier today," Clint replied.

"Maybe we're all on edge because of the fever. We don't want anyone bringing it to our camp."

* * *

Later that evening, Mrs. Nelson insisted Amelia go to the wagon to rest.

"I'll be fine right here by the fire," Amelia replied.

"You're as pale as an apparition. Now go on to the wagon so you can get some sleep. We'll look after the girls."

Clint agreed with Mrs. Nelson, Amelia was very pale, and that worried him.

"Ma, Annie and I will help Mrs. Nelson," Katie offered.

"Thank you, girls. I think I will lie down for a few minutes." Amelia stood, took one step toward the wagon and slumped to the ground.

Clint tossed his cup of coffee aside and ran to her. Turning her over on her back, Clint gently shook her. "Amelia!" When she didn't respond, he propped her upper body against his thigh and shook her again. "Amelia!" By this time, everyone had gathered around him, and Clint heard the girls crying behind him.

Slowly, Amelia's eyes opened, and she was surprised to see Clint was holding her in his arms. "What happened?"

Mrs. Nelson leaned over and felt her forehead. "Honey, you fainted. You've worn yourself out from worry and taking care of everyone else. You're burning up." Mrs. Nelson turned toward the wagon. "Mr. Mitchum, give me a few minutes to get some things from the wagon, then take her inside. The girls and I will sleep out by the fire tonight."

"I'm fine, girls," Amelia assured Katie and Annie when she saw their tears.

Clint saw Mrs. Nelson whisper something in her husband's ear. Mr. Nelson nodded and followed his wife to the wagon. Once they removed some belongings from the wagon, Mrs. Nelson motioned for Clint to carry Amelia inside.

Despite Amelia's protest, Clint carried her to the wagon and gently laid her on a stack of blankets Mrs. Nelson had arranged for her.

"I'm fine now, Mr. Mitchum. I just remember getting a little dizzy."

"Would you like some coffee or water?" Clint asked.

"No, thank you. I think all I need is some rest. Please tell Mrs. Nelson to keep the girls with her."

As soon as Clint jumped from the wagon, Katie, Annie, and Mrs. Nelson were waiting for him.

"Is Ma going to be okay?" Katie asked.

"You're ma just needs some rest. She wants you to stay with Mrs. Nelson."

"Does she have the fever? We don't want to lose another ma," Annie cried.

"Your ma will be fine. Now go help Hannah and Bonnie clean up. Don't you worry, your ma will be as fit as a fiddle by morning," Mrs. Nelson assured them.

The girls walked away, and Clint looked at Mrs. Nelson. "What did they mean that they didn't want to lose another ma?"

Mrs. Nelson took Clint by the arm and pulled him away from the wagon. "Amelia's sister was their mother. You see, Amelia's sister was married to Mr. Wakeland, and when he was away during the war, she died not long after Annie was born."

Clint listened intently as Mrs. Nelson explained further. "I'm afraid Mr. Wakeland wasn't well when he came home from the war. He asked Amelia to marry him so the girls would have a mother. You might say Amelia's marriage to Mr. Wakeland was one of convenience, for the sake of the girls. Mr. Wakeland was much older than Amelia."

Clint was quiet, absorbing what Mrs. Nelson was saying. She interpreted his silence for disapproval. "Please don't think harshly of Amelia for her choices. She loves those girls as though they are her own. She thought it was the best decision for everyone, and she didn't want any of Mr. Wakeland's relatives laying claim to the girls. Not only that, but even before the war, there weren't many matrimonial prospects for young women in La Grange."

Clint appreciated Mrs. Nelson's plain speaking manner. "I'm not passing judgment on anyone. I think she's a fine woman, and knowing the responsibilities she's taken on, I admire her all the more."

"Mr. Mitchum, Amelia's marriage wasn't one of . . . well, it wasn't a typical marriage. Mr. Wakeland was very ill when he returned from the war, and he never left his bed. He died just days after they were wed. Then, this last year, she had to nurse her parents during the fever only to lose them. That girl has sacrificed so much, and she deserves some happiness in her life."

Clint stared at her, trying to read between the lines for what she wasn't saying.

Mrs. Nelson put her hands on her hips and looked expectantly at him. "I've seen how you look at her. Are you interested in that gal, or do you think she is just another pretty face?"

Clint glanced away. He wasn't sure he was in any position to say what he wanted. Amelia was a beautiful woman, no doubt, but she was much more than that. *What do I want?* He'd found himself daydreaming about having a wife and children over the last couple of days. *Who am I kidding? I haven't been thinking about just any woman; it's Amelia's face I see, and those precious girls.* "I don't have much to offer any woman."

Mrs. Nelson gave a loud harrumph. "If all men waited to have something to offer a woman in these hard times, there wouldn't be any marriages at all." Mrs. Nelson turned to walk away after one parting comment. "Don't turn her head if you're not interested in something permanent. She has too much to lose to give her heart to the wrong man. Besides, Casey is waiting on her to come home. He wants to marry her."

* * *

Clint waded into the water to do some panning before darkness descended, hoping to find some privacy to think. He leaned against a large boulder while he unconsciously worked his pan and thought about what Mrs. Nelson had told him. He knew in these hard times many people married out of necessity instead of love. Unless he was mistaken, Mrs. Nelson had hinted that Amelia's marriage was not an intimate one. It was obvious that Amelia loved the girls dearly, so he could understand if she married for their benefit. *Could he marry a woman because she needed him for the sake of children?* Amelia's face flashed before his eyes. He smiled, thinking it would be no hardship to see her every morning and night. Not only that, but any man would be proud to be Katie and Annie's father. There was no question in his mind that he would marry her to help secure a more prosperous future for the girls. It was heartbreaking that the girls had lost both parents. Now he understood why they wanted to buy Amelia a husband—they wanted a secure family. But he wanted love in his marriage— not simply a marriage of convenience. *Could Amelia come to love me? Or is she in love with this Casey character?*

Though light was fading, Clint was still in knee-high water swirling his pan when he saw what he thought was a stone at the bottom. He plucked it out, and just as he was about to toss it back in the water, he looked at it more closely. *Gold!* It was much larger than the nuggets he'd found earlier in the day. He knew what he was holding in his hand was of such value that it could change everything. His excitement at finding the large nugget was tempered by the uncertainty of what he would find once he returned to the ranch. Nothing could really make him happy until he knew his mother was alive. He rolled the nugget around in his hand. That one nugget meant he could help Amelia and the girls, as well as Whitt and the boys. If they didn't want to return to La Grange, he could help them get settled somewhere else. Tucking the gold in his pocket, Clint continued to search the bottom of his pan. He couldn't believe it when he saw several smaller nuggets, along with gold flakes covering the bottom of the pan. Before he left the creek, he decided to try his luck one last time and dipped his pan into the water. This time, he found ten small nuggets.

After he made his way back to the bank, he pulled out his bandanna and gently placed all the nuggets and flakes inside. Once he folded the cloth tightly, he stuck the bandanna in his back pocket and walked back to the camp.

Mrs. Nelson approached Clint around midnight, while he was still awake, drinking coffee and thinking about his mother. Leaning over to his ear, Mrs. Nelson whispered, "I need to speak to you."

Glancing around at the sleeping children, Clint stood and quietly followed Mrs. Nelson away from the fire. They were just a few feet from the wagon when she turned to face him.

"Mr. Mitchum, I'm afraid Amelia is very ill." She motioned for him to come closer to the wagon. "She asked that you stay out here while I go inside, and you can listen to our conversation."

Clint frowned. "Why can't I go inside and talk to her?"

Mrs. Wilson looked around, as if she was afraid someone would overhear them. "We're afraid she may have yellow fever. She has a very high fever, has been vomiting and has a terrible headache—all symptoms of yellow fever."

Clint pulled the lantern from the hook, pushed the flap aside and climbed inside the wagon.

Hearing the commotion, Amelia's eyes snapped open. "Mr. Mitchum, you shouldn't be in here! Didn't Mrs. Nelson tell you that I may have yellow fever?"

Clint leaned over, holding the light so he could see her face.

He was shocked how her appearance had deteriorated in a few short hours. She was also shivering, even though she had beads of perspiration on her face. Clint placed his palm on her forehead. Feeling how warm she was, he tried to keep his expression neutral so she couldn't see his concern. "Don't worry about me. I'll be fine."

The flap opened and Mrs. Nelson peeked inside. Clint held out his hand to assist her inside the wagon. Mrs. Nelson added another blanket to the stack already covering Amelia. "I fear her fever is getting worse."

"Mr. Mitchum, I have all the symptoms. I need to get away from everyone before it gets worse. I don't want to endanger everyone," Amelia explained softly.

Mrs. Nelson touched Clint's arm. "We have a plan. I'm going to speak to Tom about taking the wagon away from here, and I will care for Amelia until she's well."

"No, that's not what we discussed," Amelia responded. "I want you to return to camp with Tom. You must take care of the children in case . . ."

Clint's gaze slid from Mrs. Nelson to Amelia. He knew what she was thinking even though she didn't voice her worst fear.

"I'm not leaving you alone," Mrs. Nelson stated.

Amelia smiled up at Mrs. Nelson. "You must, for the sake of the children. And we must act quickly, before others nearby find out I'm ill. They will want all of us to leave."

Mrs. Nelson sat down beside Amelia. "You can't care for yourself if you get worse. You, of all people, know what will happen if this takes a turn for the worse."

Amelia was quiet for several minutes. She looked at Mrs. Nelson, her eyes pleading. "Please, I can't infect the children. And . . . they couldn't bear to see me succumb. . . ."

They knew what she was thinking. Clint admired what Mrs. Nelson was willing to do for Amelia, but the children also needed her. Amelia was right about that. He quickly formulated a different plan. "Tell me how this disease progresses."

Mrs. Nelson explained her experience with yellow fever. "If the symptoms haven't improved in a few days, and if the fever and vomiting persists, that's when many do not . . ."

"Survive," Amelia finished Mrs. Nelson's sentence.

"You told me that the symptoms are similar to influenza. Could this be influenza?" Clint asked.

Mrs. Nelson thought about Clint's question. "I guess it could be influenza, but if the other families hear she is sick, they will assume the worst, just like with Ben Wilburn's boy."

Glancing at Amelia, Clint asked, "Amelia, do you think you could travel?"

Mrs. Nelson's mouth dropped open. "You don't think she should go off alone, do you?"

"No." Clint's eyes shifted from Amelia to Mrs. Nelson. "I think she should go with me back to La Grange. You can tell me how to care for her. If the doc is still alive, he will know what to do once we arrive in LaGrange."

Mrs. Nelson frowned at him. "Mr. Mitchum, I know you have nothing but the most honorable intentions, but she will not even be able to change her clothing by herself."

Clint arched his brow at her. "I assure you, I've seen a woman's body before, Mrs. Nelson. I have no intention of taking advantage of Amelia."

Flustered by his comment, Mrs. Nelson's face turned a rosy pink. "I'm not suggesting . . ."

Clint's expression and his voice softened when he looked at Amelia. "You know this is the only thing that makes sense. You can trust me."

Amelia's gaze met his. "I trust you, but I can't let you do this. I don't want you to get sick because of me."

"I'm not going to get sick. And you don't actually think I would let you go off by yourself, do you? Even if Mrs. Nelson convinced you to allow her to go with you, I couldn't let that happen." Clint quickly decided he would not listen to more objections. "Mrs. Nelson, please be kind enough to get together what I'll need for her and we'll leave at dawn." His tone let them know that the decision was made. He knew traveling with Amelia was going to slow him down, but that didn't sway his decision. He couldn't leave her behind, not knowing what was going to happen to her. He didn't wait for her to respond; he walked to the back of the wagon.

Tears filled Amelia's eyes. "Please don't do this. I would rather stay alone than risk you becoming ill."

Clint turned and walked back to her, leaned over and cupped her cheek. He spoke softly to her. "Stop worrying about me. I told you, I will be fine. I'm too darn mean to catch anything. I want you to rest now. We'll leave at dawn."

A tear slid from the side of Amelia's eye. "Say goodbye to the girls for me. Don't let them come in here. Make sure they understand I don't want to leave, but I must."

Clint reached down, picked up her hand and held it in his. It felt so small and delicate in his grasp. He hoped her will to survive was stronger than she looked or felt. He'd learned in the war that a man's will to make it home to his loving family increased his chance of survival when faced with a life-threatening illness or injury. Those men had a reason, a purpose to make it through any hardship. "I promise I will explain the situation to them. Now you must promise me you will get well."

When she didn't respond, Clint gently squeezed her hand. "Promise me."

"I promise," she whispered as she looked into his eyes.

Before dawn, Tom Nelson helped Clint carry some supplies to the wagon. "Clint, this is good of you to take Amelia to La Grange, but do you know what you're in for?"

"I can't say I've seen yellow fever, but I saw just about everything else in the war." Clint had been exposed to more diseases and injuries in the war than he cared to recall. He felt he could handle yellow fever. Only problem was, he'd never cared for a woman. There might be situations where he would shock Amelia's delicate sensibilities if she was coherent. But it couldn't be helped. She couldn't stay in camp and endanger the others, and in Clint's estimation, there was no one equal to the task of caring for her, or protecting her in case there was trouble—like dealing with two-legged varmints.

Mrs. Nelson joined the men at the wagon. "Mr. Mitchum, you must make her eat to keep up her strength. Most likely she'll refuse food, but she needs to eat and drink as much as possible so she doesn't become dehydrated."

"Yes, ma'am, I'll see to it."

"The girls are awake, and they are asking about their mother."

"I'll go talk to them."

Chapter 6

Clint absently stoked the fire as he thought about what he was going to say to the girls. Once his thoughts were in order, he asked Katie and Annie to sit next to him.

"Girls, your mother wanted me to tell you that she has to go back to La Grange to see the doctor there."

"She's sicker, isn't she?" Katie asked.

"Is she gonna die too, like our other ma and pa?" Annie asked.

"I'm taking her back to see the doctor so he can help her."

"Why can't she stay here, so we can take care of her, like she took care of your ma?" Katie asked.

"She doesn't want to make anyone else sick." Clint saw tears forming in Annie's eyes and he pulled out his bandanna.

"She's gonna die and we'll be all alone," Annie whimpered.

"I promise I'm going to take good care of your ma," Clint told her.

"Most people die with the fever." Katie wasn't showing her emotions like Annie, but Clint thought she was trying to be brave for her younger sister.

Clint put his arms around their shoulders. "I'm not going to let her die."

Annie looked up at him, and through her tears, she asked, "You promise, Mr. Mitchum?"

"You have my word on that." Clint didn't allow himself to think of all the things that could go wrong having made that promise. But he couldn't let these girls down.

Katie jumped up and stared Clint in the eye. "You can't say that! She's probably going to die, just like everyone else."

Clint reached for Katie and pulled her in his arms. He felt her small body trembling, and she finally lost control and started sobbing uncontrollably. Annie stood and nudged her way under one of Clint's arms until he was holding both of them. "I promise you girls I will do everything I can to help your mother. Will you trust me?"

Both girls nodded.

After a few moments, Katie whispered, "Can we go say goodbye?"

"Your ma doesn't want to take any chances you might get sick. She loves you too much to do that, but you can stand outside the wagon and talk to her that way."

Annie sniffled. "Okay."

"I want you girls to remember this is hard on your ma too. She doesn't want to leave. Don't let her think you won't see her again, because you will see her when she's better."

"Okay," they answered together.

Clint hugged them tighter, hoping he could live up to their faith in him. "I think you should tell your ma you will see her for Christmas." Clint released them and bent down to look at their faces. "Stop the tears; we don't want her to know you were crying. As a matter of fact, why don't you tell me what you would buy your ma for Christmas . . . besides a husband . . . if you could?"

The girls wiped away their tears. "You mean a real present, like we could get at the mercantile?" Annie asked.

"Yes. What do you think she would like?"

"Ma saw a pretty locket at the mercantile," Katie told him.

"A locket. Now that sounds like a fine present," Clint responded.

"But we don't have money," Annie countered.

Clint smiled at her. "Remember, I told you about the magic of Christmas. You have to believe anything is possible. Tell your ma you will have her Christmas gift waiting for her."

"Do you think the gold we found would be enough to buy that locket?" Katie asked.

"I think if you girls look for more gold while we are away, you might have enough by Christmas. But promise me that you will stay close to Mr. and Mrs. Nelson or Mr. Newcombe at all times."

"Yes, sir," they replied.

When they reached the wagon, Clint opened the flap and peeked inside. "Amelia, the girls wanted to say goodbye. They are standing right by me."

"Oh, girls, I'm going to miss you." Amelia was making an effort to sound cheerful.

"We're going to miss you too," Annie whispered with trembling lips.

"Mr. Mitchum says we will see you by Christmas," Katie stated.

Amelia was quiet for a moment, then replied, "We shall celebrate together. Mind Mrs. Nelson and always stay within her sight."

Clint heard Amelia's voice cracking as she tried to hold her emotions in check.

"Yes, ma'am, we will. We already promised Mr. Mitchum."

"Remember how much I love you," Amelia told them.

"We love you, Ma."

"And we'll have your Christmas present waiting for you," Katie remembered to say.

Tears started falling over their cheeks, and Clint knew Amelia was also crying. "Amelia, we will be leaving soon."

"Thank you, Mr. Mitchum, I'll be ready."

Mrs. Nelson handed Clint a cup of coffee, along with a plate of biscuits and bacon. After he gulped his breakfast, Tom and Whitt helped him with the horses.

"This is a fine thing you're doing. Come back as soon as you can," Whitt told him.

Clint told Whitt about the gold he'd found. "It might be a good spot for you to try."

"I'll pan there today." Whitt shook Clint's hand. "I wish you well."

"Keep a sharp eye out. Those men might come back."

"I will."

"We'll sleep in shifts," Tom Nelson told him.

Bo and Boone ran to Clint before he reached the wagon.

"You will come back, won't you?" Boone asked.

"Yep, I'll be back." Clint bent down and added, "Will you boys look after the girls for me?"

"Yeah. Pa already told us that we have to take care of the ladies. We'll look after them," Bo promised.

"I knew I could count on you."

Katie and Annie ran to him and hugged him goodbye one last time.

Clint drove the wagon slowly, not wanting to cause Amelia more discomfort than she was already feeling. He stopped once every two hours to check on her and to make sure she had plenty to drink. Each time, he tried to persuade her to eat, but she refused food, and that worried him.

"Mr. Mitchum, I'm sorry, but I don't have an appetite. I'm afraid my headache is making me dizzy."

"I think you need to call me Clint. Does riding in the wagon make your headache worse?" Clint noticed the dark circles under her eyes.

"I don't think so. But Mr. Mitchum, I think you should stay outside the wagon instead of coming in here each time you stop."

Clint smiled at her as he held the back of her head, urging her to take another sip of water. "Yeah, you told me that the last time we stopped."

"I think you are a stubborn man, Mr. Mitchum."

"So I've been told. And my name is Clint."

Amelia closed her eyes. "Of course . . . Clint."

"We can stop for the day."

She shook her head from side to side. "No, let's keep going."

"Okay, but let me know if you need to stop. Do you need more blankets?"

"No, I'm fine. I know you are going slower for me, but I don't mind if we go faster."

Clint thought she might be saying she needed to get to La Grange as fast as possible to see the doc. "Yes, ma'am."

When Clint stopped for the night, he had a nice fire going before he carried Amelia from the wagon to a pallet he'd arranged close to the fire. He tried to hide his concern about her deteriorating condition throughout the day. "I thought you might be tired of being in that wagon."

"It's nice to be outside, and the fire feels good."

Clint warmed some biscuits, and he was pleased when she ate two small bites. After she drank some water, she leaned back against Clint's saddle, which he'd placed behind her and closed her eyes.

Thinking she wanted to sleep, Clint poured himself another cup of coffee.

"I want to thank you for doing this for me."

Glancing her way, Clint noticed her eyes were still closed. "My pleasure." Again she was silent, and he sat quietly and drank his coffee. He was feeling a little more optimistic about her condition. Two cups of coffee later, he decided he'd check the animals one more time while she was resting.

He'd just placed his rifle down by his bedroll when Amelia mumbled something. He walked over and kneeled down beside her. The optimism he'd felt earlier about her condition quickly dissolved. She was shivering, and as soon as he touched her forehead, he knew her fever was much worse. After throwing another blanket over her, Clint added more logs to the fire and dampened a cloth to place on her forehead.

"So cold," Amelia muttered.

Pulling his bedroll beside her pallet, he pulled her into his arms and covered them both with another blanket. After a few minutes, he was sweating, but she was no longer shaking. "Better?"

"Better." She snuggled close to him and buried her face in his chest.

She finally fell asleep, but sleep evaded Clint. He spent the night watching over her, afraid he wouldn't hear her if she needed him.

The next several nights were a repetition of the first night, with Amelia alternating between freezing and sweating. Clint was more discouraged because she absolutely refused to eat. He could barely get her to drink, and he felt somewhat guilty that he was forcing water down her. To make matters worse, the entire day Clint thought someone was following them. He hadn't seen anyone, and it was difficult to see if he was being trailed while he was driving the wagon. Over the years he'd developed a sixth sense on the trail. This wasn't a feeling he could ignore. When he stopped for the night, he carried his rifle with him as he cared for the horses and prepared their meal over the fire. If he'd been traveling alone, he would have forgone a fire tonight. That feeling he'd had all day about being followed remained with him, and he knew a fire could be spotted for miles.

Later that evening, Amelia's fever seemed to be higher than before, and once it broke her clothing was drenched. He carried her inside the wagon and he'd just removed her dress when he heard the snap of a twig. Clint covered her with some blankets, grabbed his rifle, lifted the canvas and slid over the side of the wagon. Crouching low, he silently made his way to the trees. He'd intentionally arranged his bedroll to look like someone was sleeping in it because he was halfway expecting company. And he had a feeling he knew who the visitors would be.

Just as he positioned himself where he could see the fire, he saw three men walk into the camp. As he expected, it was the same threesome he'd encountered in Honey Creek.

"Look at what we have here." The leader of the group had his pistol drawn, and he used the toe of his boot to kick Clint's bedroll.

Clint walked from the brush with his pistol pointed at the man. "Yeah, look here."

The man laughed and pointed his gun at Clint. "We know you and the little lady are traveling alone. Where is she?" His eyes darted to the wagon. He glanced at one of his men and inclined his head toward the wagon. "Check it out, Alvin."

"If Alvin takes another step, I'll shoot you," Clint stated resolutely to the man who was giving the orders.

"If you shoot me, my boys will still have a fine time when we're dead."

When Alvin took another step, Clint and the leader fired their weapons at the same time. The stranger's gun hit the ground and he dropped to his knees grasping his hand. Clint had shot his gun hand, but the man's bullet had grazed Clint in the side.

"Take him, Marv," the leader on the ground commanded as he clutched his hand.

Suddenly a blast came from the wagon. Alvin stumbled backward, hopped around on one foot and screamed, "My foot! My foot! Someone shot my foot!"

Marv was so busy watching Alvin hop around like a fool that he didn't see Clint move until he felt his pistol at his temple.

Clint pulled the hammer back. "Unless you want to end up missing an important body part like your friend on the ground, you'll ride out and not come back."

Alvin and Marv stuck their hands in the air as Clint took their weapons, tucking them in his gun belt.

"Now grab your boss and ride out. If I see any of you again it won't bode well for you."

When the men were out of sight, Clint hurried back to the wagon. He found Amelia lying on top of the blankets with the pistol he'd given her gripped in her hands. "Amelia?"

"I heard them," she replied, her voice sounding stronger than it had in the last couple of days.

"I thought you were unconscious." Clint reached over and felt her forehead. She was much cooler than she had been before their unwanted guests had arrived.

"At first I thought I was dreaming. Then I recognized that man's voice. I remembered your pistol was under my blankets."

"That was one heck of a shot."

"I was aiming at a button on his shirt," she replied weakly.

Clint couldn't help but let out a hearty laugh. It felt good to laugh, and seeing Amelia smile up at him lifted his spirits.

"I told you my pa taught me how to shoot. I didn't say I was a good shot."

Clint shook his head, but he was still smiling. "I hope you never shoot at me," he teased as he took the gun from her hands. He reached for a clean dress and said, "Let's get you dressed."

Amelia looked down and saw that she was dressed in only her camisole and bloomers. "Oh my! Where's my dress?"

Clint held it in the air. "Right here. Now we just have to put you in it."

She wondered how many times he'd undressed her. "What day is it?"

When Clint told her the day, she was surprised she could hardly remember what had happened since they'd left Honey Creek. "Thank you for taking care of me. I know I've slowed you down."

"We've made pretty good time. It didn't seem to bother you how fast I drove." Clint helped her pull her dress over her head.

Amelia gazed at his large hands as he buttoned the bodice, thinking he had a gentle touch for such a large man. "I thought Mrs. Nelson was going to faint when you said . . ."

Clint knew what was on her mind. He waited for her to finish her thought, and when she didn't, he said, "That I'd seen a woman's body before."

"Mmm-hmm. You're very good at this, Mr. Mitchum. I didn't know you were married."

"I'm not, never have been." Clint wondered if she would remember this conversation in the morning.

She didn't respond for the longest time, and he realized she had fallen asleep again.

Chapter 7

Clint lay down beside Amelia, intending just to rest a moment. He was so exhausted that he didn't think he had the strength to carry her to the fire. His side was hurting where the bullet had grazed him, and he knew he needed to see to it before it became infected. He looked at Amelia; she seemed to be resting peacefully, so he closed his eyes for a moment.

"You were shot!" Amelia exclaimed. She had awakened to see Clint lying beside her with blood on his shirt.

Clint's eyes snapped open. He jumped up from Amelia's cot, and pain shot through his side, causing him to look down at his blood-soaked shirt. "It's just a graze."

"That's a lot of blood for a graze." Amelia moved to a sitting position. "We need to see to it."

"I'll take care of it. Do you want to go out by the fire?"

"I don't want you to carry me, I can make it," Amelia told him.

Jumping out of the wagon first, Clint held up his hands to assist her. When she leaned over, he picked her up in his arms and carried her to the fire.

"You shouldn't be carrying me."

"It's not that far to the fire and you don't weigh much."

"But you're injured," Amelia countered.

"It's nothing but a scratch."

When Clint lowered her on the pallet, she instructed him to remove his shirt.

Clint smiled at her authoritative tone. "Yes, ma'am."

When Clint stripped off his shirt, Amelia found herself staring as his muscled chest.

When she continued to stare, Clint asked, "What's wrong?"

Amelia shook her head. "Nothing. Would you boil some water?"

Clint poured fresh water in a pan and placed it over the fire. While he waited for the water to boil, he pulled his bandanna from his pocket and dabbed at his wound.

"Do you have some clean bandannas? If not, I can tear some cloth from one of my petticoats." She glanced down at her dress and lifted the hem. "Oh, I'm not wearing one right now."

Clint arched his brow at her and grinned. "They're too much trouble to put on and take off."

Amelia felt a blush rising over her cheeks. "You seem to have intimate knowledge of women's clothing."

Clint chuckled. He pulled out another clean bandanna from his saddlebag, dipped it in the boiling water and then started to clean his wound.

"Let me do that." Amelia's eyes met his as she held out her hand for the bandanna. "It's the least I can do after all you've done for me."

Clint relinquished the cloth to her, raised his arm and leaned to one side, allowing her to easily reach his wound. As soon as she braced her free hand on his chest and applied the cloth to his bleeding wound, Clint sucked in his breath. He wasn't certain if it was because the cloth was hot or the mere fact that her soft hand was resting on his chest.

Pulling back, Amelia glanced up at him. "Did I hurt you?"

Clint shook his head, but his eyes were on her hand. He needed to think about something else, so he asked, "Do you think you can eat something tonight?"

"I'll try." After she finished cleaning the wound, Amelia asked him to retrieve one of her petticoats from the wagon. She watched him walk away, admiring his wide-muscled shoulders. When he returned with the petticoat, she asked him to tear off a strip of cloth to wrap around his torso.

"I don't think it is necessary for you to ruin your petticoat," Clint told her.

"We don't want that wound to get infected. I can repair the petticoat." After he tore the strip of cloth, she helped him wrap it around his waist. Once the task was completed, she leaned back on her pallet, exhausted from that little effort. Within minutes she was sound asleep.

Clint covered her with a blanket and sat down and watched her for a while. He thought about her illness, wondering if everyone who contracted yellow fever was subjected to the erratic nature of the illness. Amelia would feel better for a short period of time before having another relapse. Did his mother and siblings suffer in the same way? As a man, it was his nature to want to fix things, and it was frustrating that he couldn't do more for her. Staring at her beautiful face, Clint questioned whether his mother had asked him to find her because she knew he would be attracted to her. How could a man not be attracted to her? She was everything a man could ever want in a woman.

Clint cared for the animals before he cooked dinner, allowing Amelia time to rest. Once everything was ready, he kneeled down beside her and touched her forehead. He was pleased that she felt cool. Her eyes fluttered open, and Clint smiled down at her. "Do you think you can eat something now?'

"It smells wonderful." She made an effort to move to a sitting position, and Clint put his arm behind her back to lend his assistance. Once she was sitting, Clint reached for a blanket and wrapped it around her shoulder.

"How's that?"

"Perfect. Thank you."

Amelia's face was mere inches from his and their eyes locked. He didn't hesitate or question his next move. His lips found hers and he kissed her, gently at first, then longingly. It had been too long since he'd given and received affection. He felt Amelia lift her arms around his neck, and in the next instant, her fingers were curling through his hair. At that moment, Clint realized he'd found what he had been searching for— Amelia. He wanted her, not for a night, or a few weeks, but forever. He wrapped her in his arms and pulled her close. When he finally pulled his lips from hers, he was still lost in a haze of desire. After a few moments passed, he remembered his promise to her before they'd left Honey Creek. He'd told her she could trust him. He didn't want her to think he was taking advantage of her tenuous situation. *I don't even know if she loved her dead husband, or if she is still mourning him. She could be interested in Casey.* All he knew at that moment was that she was totally dependent on him for her very survival. Though he struggled with his next move, he released her. "I'm sorry. I shouldn't have done that."

Amelia's arms slowly slid down his chest when he pulled away. She looked up at him and blinked, stunned by her reaction to him. Even though he apologized for kissing her, she wasn't sorry she'd kissed him back.

Clint walked to the fire, where he ladled some food on their plates. "I want you to eat as much as you can."

Amelia had regained her composure, and even managed to give him a slight smile when he sat beside her. "I will."

"You're as weak as a newborn."

"I'll get back my strength." She took a bite of a biscuit as she glanced his way. He was looking off in the distance and seemed to be lost in thought, making her wonder what was on his mind. Her mind was on that kiss. No man had ever kissed her that way. The only kiss she'd ever shared with Richard was a light peck on the cheek when the pastor married them. No matter what happened in the future, she didn't think she'd ever again experience anything as exciting as that one kiss.

Clint was debating whether to ask her about her husband and her marriage. Since Mrs. Nelson told him about their "convenient" marriage, he'd been wondering if she'd been in love with her sister's husband before her marriage. He didn't think kissing her was the best decision he'd ever made, but unless he was imagining things, she'd kissed him back. Of course, she could be suffering from loneliness. Clint knew all about that particular emotion.

They ate in silence for several minutes before Clint turned to face her. "Amelia, Mrs. Nelson told me you hadn't been married long when you lost your husband."

She was surprised Mrs. Nelson told him about her marriage. "That's true. Richard had serious injuries when he came home from the war."

"Mrs. Nelson also said he was your sister's husband and the girls are your nieces."

"That's true."

Clint set aside his plate and picked up his coffee. He silently considered his next question. It really wasn't any of his business, but he wanted to know—he had to know. "Did you love him?"

Amelia didn't need to think over her answer. She gave him a truthful response. "I loved him like a brother. I was crazy about the girls, and I wanted them to stay with my family. My sister and I discussed the possibility of me marrying Richard before she died. We all wanted to keep the girls with the only family they had ever known." She hesitated, unsure of what she should reveal, but looking into Clint's eyes, she wanted him to know how she felt. She had never been in love, but she thought she was in love now. "Of course I was sad that he died, but I didn't . . . well, I didn't think I could ever love him as a wife should love a husband."

Clint was relieved to hear that she wasn't pining for a lost love. "Your marriage was one of convenience?"

Amelia nodded. "I don't regret making that decision."

She tried to recall bits and pieces of a conversation they'd had one night. "Did you tell me you had never been married?"

Clint smiled. He didn't think she would remember their conversation. "No, I've never been married."

Amelia took a drink of her coffee as she tried to gather the courage to ask her next question. "Have you ever been in love?"

Clint thought about her question. He'd never stayed in one place long enough to develop a meaningful relationship with a woman. Oh, he'd met some nice women, and even shared intimate relationships, but he'd never considered marriage. "No." He wanted to add *not until now*, but he thought it was too soon to voice his feelings. He intended to court her properly before he declared his love. He was curious about the nature of her relationship with Richard. It seemed logical that as man and wife, they would have shared a physical relationship, but Mrs. Nelson had implied that was not the case. She'd admitted that she loved her husband like a brother, but that didn't indicate they'd shared intimacies. Even if they had shared a loving relationship, Clint knew it wouldn't prevent him from wanting her. But he didn't want a brotherly love. He wanted much more.

Chapter 8

The afternoon Clint reined in at his ranch, Amelia's fever spiked again. He carried her inside and put her in his bed. He hurriedly started a fire to get the room warm before he tried to get her to drink some water. He needed to ride to town to see if his mother was with the doctor. If the doctor was well, he'd bring him back to help Amelia, but he wanted to make sure she was resting peacefully before he left. He intended to stop by Amelia's ranch to see if Casey was still there. If so, he would ask him to come sit with her until he returned. Clint was curious to find out what kind of man he was, particularly if Amelia was considering marrying him.

He looked around the house to see if everything was in the same place as the last time he was there. Everything looked exactly the same. After he made some coffee, he carried a cup to Amelia. She seemed to prefer his coffee more than water. He was just about to tell her he was riding to town to see the doctor when he heard what sounded like a buckboard pulling up outside.

Clint ran outside and saw a man helping a woman from the

wagon. When the man moved aside, the woman looked at Clint. "Son!"

Jumping from the porch, Clint ran to his mother and scooped her up in his arms. His emotions were so close to the surface that he couldn't speak for fear of crying like a baby. He couldn't remember being so happy in his entire life.

"Son, I knew you had been home earlier when my Bible was missing!"

"Ma, I thought you had died! That's why I left." His voice quivered as he tightened his arms around her. "It's so good to see you. I'm so sorry I wasn't here when you needed me. I'm sorry I stayed away so long."

Ingrid held Clint's face between her hands and looked into his eyes. "Shush, now. There's no need for you to be sorry about anything. All that is important is you came home. I knew you would come back."

"Where were you when I was here before?" Clint asked.

"Caring for John," Ingrid responded.

"John?"

Ingrid pulled back and pointed to the man standing beside them. "This is Dr. John Sims."

Clint shook his hand. "Doc, I'm so glad to see you. Amelia has the fever. I brought her back with me."

"Oh, no!" Ingrid ran up the stairs and into the house, with Clint and the doctor behind her.

"She's in my room."

The three of them entered Clint's room, and Amelia opened her eyes. Seeing Ingrid, she started to cry. "I knew you were alive. I tried to tell Clint."

Ingrid sat beside Amelia, and the doc walked to the other side of the bed. He placed his hand on her forehead and gave her a gentle smile. "Hi, Amelia."

"I'm so happy you recovered, Dr. Sims," Amelia said as she brushed her tears away.

The doctor turned to Clint and indicated for him to follow him from the room. He asked Clint to tell him about Amelia's symptoms on the way home.

Clint told him about the spikes in her fever and how delirious she'd been on occasion.

"I'm going to get my bag." The doc turned toward the door.

"I'll take care of your horses," Clint offered.

"Would you mind tending the dogs in the back of the buckboard?"

"Dogs?"

"Yes, a stray dog showed up at my office a few weeks ago, and she gave birth to two little pups. No one has claimed them, so I've been watching over them."

Clint smiled wide, thinking he'd just had another prayer answered—his Christmas gift to Annie and Katie. "I'll claim them."

The doc returned his smile. "That's a fine idea."

While Clint and his mother waited for the doctor to examine Amelia, they fed the dog and made a bed for her and her puppies near the fireplace. Clint told Ingrid about his few days at Honey Creek, and how he'd found Amelia. "A lot of the folks from La Grange are panning at Honey Creek. Some of them want to return to La Grange as soon as they can."

"They can come home now if they want to return. Many of the ranchers have already returned, and we haven't had another case of yellow fever since John got sick. He's received word from other towns that they haven't had any new cases. It seems to have ended as quickly as it started."

"Annie and Katie think Amelia is going to return to Honey Creek with me, but I think I should ride to Honey Creek and bring the girls back with me while she recuperates here."

"Son, do you think you can make it back before Christmas?"

Clint reached for her hand and gave it a squeeze. "I'll be

back in time. I promise I will never miss another Christmas. I have plans for a magical Christmas."

Ingrid smiled at him. "Are you ready to settle down on the ranch? If not, that's okay. I can sell the place and move to town."

Clint couldn't imagine his mother living anywhere else. "I'm planning on staying right here."

Ingrid leaned over and kissed his cheek. "That's wonderful. Now, tell me about the families you met and how they are doing."

Clint told her about meeting Whitt, Bo and Boone. "Those two boys are real characters. Whitt wants to come home." He then told her about meeting Tom Nelson and his family. "All of the children are frightened that something will happen to their family. I fear they have lost the joy of childhood. They aren't even looking forward to Christmas. It's sad to see, especially because I remember how you and Pa always made our Christmas special when we were kids. These kids will be lucky to have a decent meal. That's why I want to bring them home."

"This time has been as difficult on the children as it has been the parents. John and I have been trying to help the families who have returned. Mr. Stanton, who owns the mercantile, is helping as much as he can. Sadly, many of the families have lost their land because they couldn't pay the mortgage. I know Whitt's land is in jeopardy. They may not have anything to come home to. We've been trying to talk the bank into delaying some of the foreclosures to see if the families return."

"What about Amelia's ranch? Is it in jeopardy?"

"I'm afraid so. Once her father died, there was only Casey left to work the ranch. Amelia was caring for everyone, and she couldn't handle the ranch with just one person. I'm thankful your father was smart enough to pay off most of our mortgage years ago."

"You'll never have a reason to worry about the ranch." Clint then told his mother about the gold he'd found at Honey Creek. "I'll have enough money to pay the bank for whatever we owe, and for Amelia's mortgage."

"That's wonderful, Son. I hope the other folks are as fortunate finding gold." Ingrid reached over and placed her hand on Clint's forearm. "Do you want to go back and pan for gold?"

"No, everything I want is right here. I found enough gold to be of some help to our neighbors and to give the children a memorable Christmas. That's all I need."

The doctor walked in, took a seat at the table and Ingrid poured him a cup of coffee.

"Will she be okay?" Clint asked.

"Amelia has influenza, not yellow fever." The doc took a sip of his coffee. "Influenza can be dangerous, but she will recuperate. Her fever is up again, but this is to be expected before she fully recovers."

Clint had seen several men die of influenza in the war, so he was aware of the dangers.

"I'm so happy you brought her home," Ingrid said.

The doc studied Clint's face. "You look exhausted. You're not feeling ill, are you?"

"I'm just tired."

The doctor slapped Clint's shoulder. "I would tell you to stay away from Amelia until she's over this, but I have a feeling my words would fall on deaf ears."

"You might as well go talk to that horse out there," Ingrid teased. "Son, go on in and talk to Amelia while I prepare dinner. I've asked John to stay, and now that Amelia is here, he might as well spend the night instead of coming and going from town."

"I appreciate the offer to stay; it is a long ride to town." The doctor glanced at Clint again. "Amelia told me she wants to go to her ranch. She's worried she's caused you too much trouble."

Clint shook his head. "She's not going anywhere." He

headed to the door. "I'll check on the animals one last time before I visit with Amelia."

Once Clint walked out the door, John looked at Ingrid. "I see why you are so proud of him, Ingrid. He's a fine man."

Clint quietly slipped inside his bedroom and sat in the chair beside the bed. Amelia was sleeping, and he watched her for several minutes before he fell asleep. Sometime later, Clint heard his mother in the room, speaking softly to Amelia. When he heard Amelia whisper a response, he eavesdropped on their conversation.

"I know you are so excited to have him home," Amelia whispered.

Holding out another spoonful of soup to Amelia, she replied, "I knew my prayers would be answered."

"He was wonderful taking care of me. I know he didn't get any rest at all." Amelia swallowed the soup Ingrid held out to her.

"I know you thought I was exaggerating about Clint," Ingrid teased. "Though he's my son, I think he is even more handsome than I remembered."

Clint really wanted to hear Amelia's reply, but when her response came he felt somewhat deflated.

Amelia lowered her eyes and smiled shyly. "The girls fell in love with him."

"I'm not surprised. He was always good with children," Ingrid responded.

"Thank you for the soup, but I can't eat another bite."

"You look much better," Ingrid commented.

"I'm still worried that you could catch influenza from being around me. You certainly don't need this after what you've been through."

"Don't worry about me. You didn't even consider you could get yellow fever when you cared for me," Ingrid reminded her.

"I had already been exposed caring for my parents, and I didn't get it."

"Well, I'm not going to get influenza."

"You sound like your son," Amelia murmured.

Ingrid laughed. Her eyes darted to her sleeping son, then whispered, "I'm not surprised. My husband always told me Clint inherited my hard head."

"I'm going to ask Clint to take me to the ranch. I can take care of myself now. Casey can go for the doc if I need him."

Clint wondered exactly how important Casey was to her. He moved in his chair to let them know he was awake. He stretched and opened his eyes.

"Hello, Son," Ingrid said.

"Something smells good." His eyes moved to Amelia. "How are you?"

"Much better. Your mother fed me soup."

"I'm glad you're eating."

Ingrid stood to leave, then collected the tray. "I'm going to put our dinner on the table." She looked at Clint and said, "Amelia is afraid we'll get sick, so she wants to go home."

"I told you she's not going anywhere." His eyes bounced to Amelia. "You're staying put."

Ingrid grinned at him as she left the room. He'd handled the situation just as she knew he would.

"But . . ." Amelia started to protest.

Clint held his hand in the air. "It's settled." He pulled his chair close to the bed and leaned over until he was mere inches from Amelia's face and grinned at her. "So you think I'm wonderful, huh?"

Amelia's eyes widened, realizing he'd been listening to their conversation. "Well . . ."

He arched his brow at her. "How about handsome?"

"I can't believe you were listening to us. Wait until I tell your mother," Amelia teasingly threatened.

Clint laughed. "Do you think she'll be surprised?" He picked up her braid that was draped over her shoulder. "So, do you think I'm wonderful or not?"

"I believe my words were, *you took wonderful care of me*," Amelia responded primly.

"I don't think that is precisely what you said."

Amelia couldn't argue with him because she couldn't remember her exact words. And she did think he was wonderful . . . and handsome.

Clint tugged on her braid until her lips were within kissing distance. "Doc says you should be completely well in a couple of days."

"Yes," she whispered, her eyes on his lips.

Clint really wanted to kiss her again. But he didn't. Instead, he stood and told her he would see her later.

The doctor checked on Amelia after dinner as Clint dried the dishes for his mother.

"Amelia is crazy about you," Ingrid told him.

"What makes you think so?"

"The way her face lights up when she talks about you."

Clint smiled, thinking of how she'd blushed when he was teasing her.

Ingrid handed him a plate and stared at him. "Do you return her feelings?"

Instead of answering her question, Clint asked one of his own. "What do you know about her husband?"

Ingrid told him what she knew about Amelia's marriage to Richard. "Amelia's sister was so in love with Richard, but, sadly, she died after Annie was born. Richard had serious injuries from the war and he knew his time was near. I know Amelia married him so the girls could stay with her and her parents when he died. Of course, no one could have predicted that Amelia's parents would die from the fever. That left Amelia all alone with so many responsibilities on her shoulders."

"What can you tell me about Casey?"

Ingrid dried her hands and turned to face Clint. "He's worked for Amelia's family for a few years. Amelia's mother told me Casey fell in love with Amelia from the start, but I don't think she returned his affection. He told Amelia he would stay at the ranch until she returned."

Clint thought about the few times Amelia had mentioned Casey. He didn't think she had feelings for him, but then again, she hadn't mentioned Casey was in love with her.

After checking on Amelia one last time before he turned in for the night, Clint walked to the front room and found the doctor sitting by the fire. Two glasses were on the table between the two chairs. The doctor pulled a bottle of whiskey from his bag and filled the glasses.

He handed a glass to Clint when he took a seat. "For medicinal purposes."

Clint laughed as he accepted the glass. "I haven't had whiskey in a while. It'll probably knock me out."

"I'm counting on it. You look like you could use a long rest." The doc took a drink of his whiskey, then said, "I'm glad to have this chance to speak with you alone."

Clint gave him a worried look, thinking he may give him bad news about Amelia's condition.

Seeing the concern on Clint's face, John held up his hand. "It's not about Amelia. I think she's going to be just fine. I wanted a chance to tell you that . . . well, I think highly of your mother. I know it's too soon, but next year, after she's had time to recover from her loss, I'm planning on asking her to marry me." He took a deep breath. "I guess what I'm asking is, would I have your blessing? It would mean a lot to me, as I am certain it would be necessary for your mother."

Clint hadn't considered his mother would ever be married to anyone other than his father. But he wanted her to be happy, and if that included the doctor in her life, then he wasn't going to stand in the way. "If you make my mother happy, that's all I care about." He gave the doctor a stern look. "Don't ever give me a reason to regret giving my blessing."

The doctor looked him in the eye. "Neither one of you will ever have reason for regret. We're both alone now, and I think we'd like to have someone to share what future we have left. If I've learned anything while caring for folks through this illness it's that we never know what tomorrow may bring. We should all grab as much happiness as we can today."

Clint thought the doc sounded very much like his mother. "You sound like Ma."

"I take that as a compliment." He extended his hand. "I'll make her happy, Clint."

Leaning toward the doc, Clint shook his hand. "She's going to need some time, but I will support her decision. I want her to be happy."

John pointed to the blanket Clint had tossed on the floor. "Are you sleeping there?"

"I can hear Amelia from here if she needs anything."

"She's a fine young woman."

"Yes, she is."

John glanced at the dogs on a pallet beside Clint's blanket. "They look as though they've already adapted to their new home."

"It'll be nice having some dogs around again," Clint replied. "Amelia's girls wanted a puppy for Christmas, so I want Ma to keep them out of sight when I get back. I want to surprise the girls on Christmas morning."

"That will be great fun. There's nothing better than watching the excitement of children on Christmas morning."

Clint leaned forward and braced his elbows on his knees. "Now, Doc, can you tell me where I can find a goat?"

The men drank their whiskey as they planned Christmas surprises before they said goodnight. The doc walked to the extra bedroom where he was sleeping, and Clint stretched out on his blanket by the fire. Within seconds he was sleeping soundly.

Chapter 9

"Ingrid, how much chloral hydrate did you add to his glass last night?" John asked as he leaned over Clint to make certain he was still breathing.

"Just a dash, like you told me," Ingrid replied, kneeling beside her son and placing her hand on his chest. "He needed some rest. He told me he hadn't slept much since he left Santa Fe. From the looks of him, he couldn't go on that way or he would be the next one to get sick. I think he was planning on riding out again today if Amelia decides to stay in La Grange." She looked up at John. "Is he going to be okay?"

John nodded. "He'll be fine. Now don't worry. I wouldn't have agreed if he didn't look like he was ready to drop from exhaustion. Maybe we can talk him into leaving tomorrow. But you want him back by Christmas, so he needs to leave soon." John stood and walked to the door. "While you take Amelia some breakfast, I'll see to the animals."

"Did Clint leave?" Amelia asked Ingrid when she entered the bedroom.

"No, he's still sleeping." Ingrid placed the tray on the table while she propped up pillows behind Amelia.

"I'm sure he's worn-out. He never slept on our way back. Every time I woke up, he was watching over me."

"He was very worried about you." Ingrid placed the tray on her lap.

"Ingrid, he was heartbroken when he thought you had died. He rode all of the way to Honey Creek grieving for his family, with no one to share his heartache."

"I know. Clint has always been a solitary man, not one to share what's on his mind. But I think he's learned he can't run from his grief; it always rides with him."

"He has so much love to give. I saw that when he was with the girls," Amelia reflected.

Ingrid smiled. "Clint loves deeply. Sometimes I think he has loved too deeply. He refused to accept the fact that he couldn't always protect the ones he loved from the evils in the world."

Amelia nodded. "He looks after everyone, like a mother hen."

Laughing, Ingrid said, "I think you have him pegged, but you'd better not let him hear you compare him to a mother hen. More like a protective lion."

Amelia smiled. "I suppose that is a more apt description of him. He is fierce when provoked." Amelia told her about the three men who came into their camp on the way home.

"I'm surprised Clint didn't shoot all three of them if they threatened you. He was a sharpshooter in the war."

"I didn't know that, but he made a very accurate shot that night."

Pointing to the tray, Ingrid asked, "Do you need help today?"

"No, I think I'm strong enough to hold a fork." She looked at the tray of food. "This looks delicious. Please don't be upset if I can't eat all of it, though."

"Eat what you can." Ingrid sat in the chair and drank a cup

of coffee while they talked. "Folks are moving back now. I was wondering if you wanted to come back."

"I would like to, but I'm not sure I can keep the ranch. The Nelsons were kind enough to offer us a place with them wherever they decide to go."

"You and the girls are welcome to stay here as long as you like."

"Ingrid, you and your son have already done too much for me."

Hours later, Clint awoke feeling confused. He was still on the floor in front of the fire with the dogs cuddled up next to him, but he had no idea what time it was. He could tell by the sun shining through the window that it was well past dawn. He jumped up and ran to Amelia's bedroom.

"Good morning." Ingrid motioned him into the room. "Amelia and I were just talking about what's been happening in town since she left."

"What time is it?" Clint asked, still groggy.

"It's nearly two o'clock. I was just about to prepare lunch." Ingrid headed to the kitchen, leaving Clint alone with Amelia.

He walked to the chair his mother had vacated and sat down. "I can't believe I slept so long."

"You look better," Amelia told him.

Scratching his two-, or was it a three-day-old beard, Clint was surprised he didn't scare her to death. He needed to see to his grooming. "How are you feeling?"

"Very well. Doc Sims says I'm on the mend."

Clint leaned back in the chair, feeling more relaxed than he had in days. "That's good news."

"Your mother told me many families are returning home. The doc thinks the fever has run its course in La Grange."

"I know." Clint paused for a moment, debating whether he should tell her what was on his mind. He decided he needed to get his thoughts in order before having that discussion. "Do you need anything?"

"No, your mother has taken good care of me. I'm afraid I've been a burden to you both."

"You're not a burden." He stood and walked to the door. "I need to get cleaned up. I'll see you later."

Clint walked into the kitchen and poured himself a cup of coffee. He told his mother that he would be riding to town for some supplies. "Make a list of what you need and I will bring it back with me."

By the time Clint returned from town, it was dinnertime. He walked through the front door with his arms loaded down with packages wrapped in brown paper tied with twine. He piled the packages on the table.

Ingrid turned from the stove, brushed her hands over her apron and pointed to the packages. "What is this?"

Clint pointed to one large sack. "Those are the supplies you needed." He handed her a large bundle. "This is a present."

Ingrid stared at it, thinking she hadn't had a present in a long time.

Smiling at her reaction, Clint said, "Open it."

Giggling like a young girl, Ingrid untied the twine and eagerly pushed the paper aside. When she saw the bolts of expensive material, she gasped. Reverently running her hands over the silks and satins, she exclaimed, "Oh my! It's been such a long time since I've seen such beautiful material."

"Do you think it will make pretty dresses?"

Admiring the pink and cream silk fabrics, she replied, "Son, this is much too fine for dresses."

Clint frowned. "Mrs. Stanton at the mercantile told me it would be perfect."

Ingrid's eyes widened. "She did? I'm surprised. This material is meant for ball gowns, not everyday dresses."

"Perfect. I told her I wanted something very special. Can you make dresses for you, Amelia and the girls?"

"Of course I can. Are we going to a party?"

Clint shrugged. "Can you have them done by Christmas?"

Ingrid nodded.

"Can you also make a fancy dress for Lucy?"

Ingrid gave him a quizzical look. "Annie's doll?"

"Yep."

"I'll make her doll look like a princess."

Clint smiled at her excitement. "I want to see you wearing your new dress on Christmas Day." He saw that she was about to object, so he added, "No mourning clothes on Christmas."

Ingrid gave him a wistful look. "No, your father wouldn't have wanted us to mourn on Christmas."

Pointing to the other packages, he added, "These are all of the other things you ladies wear. I told Mrs. Stanton to put whatever you need in there." He walked to the stove to see what his mother was cooking. "What's for dinner? I'm starving."

"Fried chicken, mashed potatoes, beans and cornbread. I thought we would eat in the bedroom tonight, with Amelia. She's already had a full day; John carried the tub to the bedroom so she could have a bath. She looks better, but I think just that little exertion tired her out."

"It's a relief to know she's on the mend."

"John's talking to her now. We told her it was safe to come home, but she's worried she can't keep the ranch. I told her she was welcome to stay with us."

Clint pulled a piece of paper from his back pocket and held it for his mother to see. "She won't have to worry about her ranch now. I was going to tell her later."

Ingrid saw the note Clint held was from the bank. Once she read the paper, she gave Clint a hug. "Son, this is wonderful."

"I'm going to tell Amelia that I'll leave in the morning for Honey Creek and bring the girls home. I know Whitt will come back with me, and I'll tell the other families it's safe to return if they want to join us."

"I hope they all want to come home. We had some lovely neighbors."

"I want to tell you what I planned with Mr. and Mrs. Stanton for Christmas. They are going to need your help while I'm gone, and I don't want Amelia to know." While his mother finished cooking dinner, Clint shared his plans for Christmas.

Dinner ended, but Clint remained in the room with Amelia so he could tell her he was leaving in the morning for Honey Creek. He told her about his trip into town and that many people were returning to their homes.

"I'm not certain the Nelsons will want to come back yet."

"Do you want to stay with them?" Clint asked.

"That was our original plan. I told your mother earlier that I'm not certain I can keep the ranch. I don't know how I can support the girls if I stay here."

"Ma told me your concern about the ranch." Clint pulled the bank note from his back pocket and laid it on top of her blanket.

Amelia picked up the paper and arched her brow at him. "What's this?"

"Read it."

Unfolding the paper, the first thing Amelia saw were the three words every property owner wanted to see: PAID IN FULL. Her eyes filled with tears as they met his. "Did you do this?"

"There's no reason for you to worry about staying here if this is where you want to be."

"But I can't let you pay off my ranch." Amelia wiped away her tears.

"Of course you can. You saw how much gold I found. It's more than I'll ever need," Clint replied.

"But how can I ever repay you?"

Clint wanted to tell her he was crazy about her, but he didn't want her to feel obligated to him. "You don't have to repay me. That's not why I did it."

They stared at each other for a few moments before she asked, "Why did you do it?"

"You needed help, and you helped my mother in her time of need. I wanted to do something for you and the girls."

Lowering her eyes to the paper, Amelia was thankful beyond measure, but she had hoped he might say he cared about her. She knew he cared about the girls, but she had dreams that he might develop deeper feelings for her. Casey had told her he would take care of her and the girls, but she wasn't in love with Casey. She didn't know exactly when it had happened, but she'd fallen in love with this tall, handsome cowboy. "This is very generous of you, but I want to pay you back when I get on my feet."

All day Clint had planned on professing his feelings for her. He'd even practiced what he wanted to say, but now that he was alone with her, he couldn't remember a word. "We won't worry about that right now. Now that you no longer need to concern yourself about the mortgage, and you're not dependent on the Nelsons; do you want to stay here?"

Amelia didn't have to think about her response. "Yes, the girls and I love it here. Your mother said Casey is still at the ranch, so I'll have some help."

Clint bristled, hearing her mention Casey again. "Then it's settled. I'll leave in the morning to bring the girls home, and any of the other families who want to return."

"I think I should go with you. The girls may not believe that I survived."

Clint shook his head. "I don't think you're up to making the trip. They'll believe me."

"I should probably go home, then. I told your mother if I need the doctor, Casey can fetch him."

Casey again. Clint wanted to ask what Casey meant to her. He figured Casey was waiting for her to return before he asked her to marry him. Nothing else made sense. If a man wasn't in love, he would have moved on and found employment elsewhere when Amelia left La Grange. "How long have you known Casey?"

"He's worked for my family for several years."

"If you want to see Casey, I can go get him, but I think you should stay here. At least, until I return from Honey Creek."

"It's not that I want to see Casey, although I probably need to see if he will want to continue working on the ranch. And I've imposed on your hospitality long enough."

"Why did Casey stay when everyone left?"

"He told me people would come back once the worst was over. I told him he should leave, but he wouldn't listen. He stayed to care for what few cattle we had left."

"Do you have an understanding with Casey?"

Amelia furrowed her brow. "An understanding?"

Clint leveled his eyes on hers. "Does he want to marry you?"

Plucking at a thread on the blanket covering her, she responded honestly. "He told Mrs. Nelson he wanted to marry me."

"He's never asked you?" Clint wondered why Casey would tell other people he wanted to marry her if he hadn't asked her first.

"He told me he would care for me and the girls when Richard died."

"Are you interested in that proposal?"

"Mrs. Nelson told me I couldn't afford to turn down any proposal, considering I may never have another."

Clint noticed she hadn't given him a yes-or-no response. He thought he should give her time to open up to him about what she really wanted. He wouldn't push her. Leaving his chair, he held up one finger. "I'll be back in a minute." He walked to the front room and scooped up the two puppies and told their mother to come with him. Returning to Amelia's bedroom, he held out the pups for her to see. "The girls asked for a puppy for Christmas. Now they get two. I can keep their mother."

Amelia's eyes lit up and she held out her hands to hold one. "Where did you get them?"

"Doc said their ma showed up on his doorstep and she surprised him with two pups. He's been looking after them."

Clint sat on the side of the bed holding one puppy and petting their mother's head with his free hand. "She's a good mother. We need to give her a name."

"She's beautiful, the color of honey. What about Honey?"

Clint nodded. "I like that." He stoked Honey's blond fur. "Do you like that, Honey?"

Honey licked his hand in response. "She approves."

Amelia laughed. "They're adorable. The girls will love them, and we can keep Honey if you don't have time to care for her."

Clint wanted to say she and the girls could move to his ranch and keep all the dogs together. He grew quiet, thinking about her in his home with the girls and the dogs. In his mind, that would be the next best thing to heaven. "What do you think about . . ."

Ingrid walked into the room and, judging by the look on her son's face, she thought she had just interrupted something important. Her eyes bounced from Clint to Amelia. "Amelia, Casey is here to see you."

Clint could hardly believe the man they were just discussing was in his home. He glanced at Amelia to gauge her reaction. Looking down at the nightgown she was wearing, Clint wasn't particularly thrilled at having a man seeing her in her night-clothes.

Amelia glanced at Clint. Seeing his eyes were on her nightgown, she pulled the blanket up to her neck. "I guess . . . I need to talk to him."

Ingrid left the room, and Clint stood to leave. "I'll give you some privacy." He knew it was going to take all the willpower he could muster to walk out of that room and leave her alone with Casey. Glancing down at Honey, he said, "Come."

"You don't have to leave. I want to introduce you."

Still holding one puppy, Clint sat back down in the chair closest to the bed, leaving the one at the foot of the bed the only place for Casey to sit. Honey sat next to Clint.

Ingrid led Casey into the room and introduced him to Clint. Casey nodded in Clint's direction, and though Ingrid invited him to have a seat, he headed to Amelia's bedside.

"I came as soon as I heard you were back."

Amelia's eyes darted to Clint. "Clint brought me back when I got sick."

"Where are the girls?" Casey asked.

"With Tom Nelson."

"You mean you traveled back alone with him?" Casey jabbed his hat in Clint's direction with a disapproving frown on his face.

"Yes. I was ill, and we couldn't risk the girls coming with us."

"Not very proper if you ask me," Casey grumbled.

"We didn't ask you," Clint stated testily, glaring at Casey. In his estimation, the man should have been more concerned with Amelia's welfare. He hadn't even asked her how she was feeling.

Casey briefly glanced Clint's way, then looked at Amelia. "Did the doc tell you that folks are coming back home? It's safe now, so I guess I can go get the girls."

"Clint is leaving in the morning to bring the girls home," Amelia responded. "He will tell all the families who want to return that they can travel with him."

"The girls know me," Casey commented.

Clint stared hard at Casey. "The girls know me and I'm going to get them."

Amelia thought the men were having a staring contest. "Casey, the girls know Clint, and they trust him. He knows exactly where they are camping."

Casey wasn't pleased, but he acquiesced. "If that's what you want. I'll pick you up tomorrow in the buckboard."

Clint couldn't help himself; he refused to allow this man to dictate what Amelia was going to do. He stood, placed the puppy on top of Amelia's lap beside the other one and prepared to show Casey to the door—under his own steam or with help, he didn't care. "She's going to recuperate right here until I get back."

Turning his attention on Clint again, Casey said, "That's kind of your mother to look after her, but it's not necessary."

Hoping to change the direction of the conversation, Amelia held up one puppy for Casey to see. "Look at what Clint is giving the girls for Christmas. They'll each have their own puppy."

Clint noticed Casey barely spared a glance at the puppies. "You can't afford to feed those dogs."

Amelia clutched both puppies to her chest. "It doesn't take much to feed two puppies, and the girls will love them."

"They grow up," Casey said. "Then what?"

Clint told himself not to interfere, but he couldn't help himself. "It's my gift to the girls, so I will pay for their food."

Casey looked over at Clint. "I'd like to speak to Amelia alone, if you don't mind."

Clint did mind, but before he voiced that thought, Ingrid walked into the room, accompanied by the doctor. "Gentlemen, I hate to interrupt, but Amelia needs her rest and the doctor needs to examine her. If you'll come to the kitchen, I just made some fresh coffee."

Clint leaned over to take the pups from Amelia. "I'll be leaving at dawn. When I get back, I expect to see you completely recovered."

Amelia reached out and grabbed his hand. "When will you be back?"

"It'll probably be Christmas Eve."

Squeezing his fingers, Amelia whispered, "Promise me you will be careful."

Clint winked at her. "I'll be careful." He noticed she didn't seem to want to release his hand, and he felt Casey's eyes on them. "Don't worry. I'll bring your girls back to you safe and sound."

She wanted to tell him that she wanted him to come back to her too, but Casey was standing there listening to their every word. "I trust you."

Clint briefly considered giving her a kiss that would give Casey something else to think was inappropriate. With both pups in his hands, Clint motioned for Casey to precede him through the door.

Chapter 10

Clint didn't like the fact that while he was gone, Casey would have a lot of time to visit Amelia and press his case for her to commit to him. He thought Casey might have the advantage, having worked for Amelia's family for a few years. The girls probably considered him part of their family. But in Clint's estimation, Casey should have already been working to help Amelia save her ranch. If he hadn't found the gold, he would have still found a way to help her. On the other hand, who was he to judge? He hadn't been around when his family needed him the most. Maybe neither of them were worthy of Amelia and the girls.

Once they left the bedroom, Casey declined the cup of coffee, saying he needed to get back to the ranch. Clint walked him to the door, and Casey turned to face him. "You should know I'm going to marry Amelia."

Clint stared hard at him as he opened the door. "Does Amelia have something to say about that?"

"She knows. I told her I would stay at the ranch until she returned. We both knew where we were headed when the time was right."

Clint didn't like what Casey was insinuating. "Amelia and I have had a lot of conversations, and never once has she mentioned marrying you."

"I was just letting you know how things are." Casey settled his hat on his head and walked out the door.

"I think I can figure things out on my own." Clint closed the door behind him and turned to see Ingrid standing a few feet away, holding a cup of coffee.

"What was that about?"

"You heard enough to know that he thinks Amelia is going to marry him."

Ingrid handed him the coffee. "Do you have other plans?"

"I think it depends on what Amelia wants. I have a feeling you will be seeing a lot of Casey while I'm gone."

"You could have let him go get the girls," Ingrid replied.

"I told the girls I would come back. A promise is a promise." Clint's eyes shifted to the door. "Besides, I don't know if he could handle trouble."

"Son, I know you think highly of Amelia. Maybe you should tell her how you feel before you leave."

"We'll see how things look when I get back. Now, I have a favor to ask of you while I'm gone." He started to take a drink of the coffee, then hesitated. "Did you or the doc add anything to this coffee?"

Clint left the house the next morning while everyone slept. He was tempted to wake Amelia to tell her how he felt about her as his mother suggested, but he decided to give her time to think. She'd faced so many changes over the last several months, she needed to recover before she made any hasty decisions.

On the way back to Honey Creek, Clint had nothing but time to think about what he wanted. The very first night on the trail, he realized how much he enjoyed having Amelia with him. That was a first for him. He'd always been a man who traveled alone. There were times he was lonely, but never before had he contemplated marriage.

Reaching the campsite at Honey Creek, Clint had just set the brake on the wagon when the girls ran to him. He jumped from the wagon and swept them both up in his arms. "I'm happy to see you, girls."

Both Katie and Annie started talking at the same time, making it difficult for Clint to understand what they were saying, but he was able to hear enough to know someone had rode into their camp and scared them. "Slow down, one at a time."

"Some men came and stole our gold," Annie told him breathlessly.

"They didn't take our gold, but they stole Mr. Newcombe's and Mr. Nelson's," Katie corrected. "Bo and Boone said those men didn't think the kids had any gold."

"I'm scared they'll come back." Annie's chin started to quiver.

Clint hugged them tighter. "You don't have to be afraid now. I'm here."

"But they had big guns like yours," Annie told him as tears slid down her cheeks.

"Don't cry, honey. I'm here. No one is going to hurt you," Clint promised.

"I'm glad you came back," Annie whispered in his ear.

"But where's Ma? In the wagon?" Katie asked.

"I'm taking you home to her. She's much better and she's resting at the ranch with my ma. Folks are going back home now and your ma wanted me to bring you home."

"Are you sure she's better?" Annie asked.

"I promise, and she can't wait to see you."

"You wouldn't just say that so we won't cry, would you?" Katie asked.

Clint reached in his pocket and pulled out a small velvet pouch. "I brought this with me so you could give it to her for Christmas."

Katie took the pouch and pulled out the locket her mother had seen in the mercantile. She held it for Annie to see. "It's the Christmas present we wanted to buy Ma."

Annie wiped her tears away and examined the locket. "It's so pretty. Ma will love that."

They wrapped their arms around Clint's neck, giving him the best hug he had ever received.

"Thank you. Ma will be so excited," Katie said.

"I bet she will wear it every day," Annie added.

"Is Miss Ingrid okay?" Katie asked Clint.

"Yes, she's just fine, and she's looking forward to seeing you two. Now, let's go talk to Whitt and the boys and tell them the news."

Clint and Whitt panned for more gold until darkness descended. Fortunately, they both found several more nuggets.

"I think you're a good luck charm," Whitt told Clint. "I didn't find this much gold the whole time you were gone."

Clint chuckled. "That's the first time anyone ever called me a good luck charm."

Whitt arched his brow. "I don't know about that, I'd say Amelia thinks you are her lucky charm."

Clint hoped Whitt was right about that. He wanted to be more than her good luck charm.

Whitt looked at the gold in his hand. "At least I replaced some of what those men stole. I was going to pay on my mortgage to prevent the bank from foreclosing on my land. If those men hadn't threatened to harm the children, I would have put up a fight. They were the same three men who rode into camp that night before you left."

Clint knew if he had been there, the situation would have been different. "You couldn't take a chance with the children. One day the odds will not be in their favor." Clint figured he had a score to settle with those men for scaring the girls.

Later that night, after the women and children were asleep, Whitt, Tom Nelson, Ben Wilburn and Clint sat around the fire, discussing returning to La Grange. After everyone agreed to go back home, Clint told them about his run-in with the three robbers on the way to La Grange. "I shot one of them in the hand, and Amelia shot one in the foot."

Whitt laughed. "I noticed one of those varmints had his hand wrapped, and one was limping. I'd like to run into them one day when the women and children aren't with us."

The next morning the wagons were loaded by daybreak and they were on their way to La Grange. The children were so excited to be going home that they asked dozens of times when they would arrive.

"I'm planning to get there by Christmas Eve," Clint told them when he rode next to the wagon. Whitt and the boys were riding by his side. "Everyone can spend Christmas Eve with us and have dinner. On Christmas morning we'll all go to church, and then we'll go to the hotel to have dinner with all the folks in town."

"That'll be like a party," Annie exclaimed.

"That does sound like a nice way to celebrate Christmas." Whitt looked at his boys. "Don't you two think that sounds like fun?"

Bo and Boone both nodded their agreement.

"Will we have a real Christmas dinner?" Bo asked.

"Son, your mind is always on food," Whitt teased.

Clint laughed, thinking about the first night he met the boys. Bo had asked him for food then. "We'll have a big dinner."

The first night they made camp, Clint was talking with the girls when Katie asked him if Casey was still at their ranch.

"I met Casey when he came to the ranch to visit your ma. I imagine you'll be happy to see him again."

"I guess." Katie cast a quick glance at Annie.

"Casey told me I was too old to have Lucy."

Clint frowned. "I'm sure he was teasing."

Annie shook her head back and forth. "No, he wasn't."

"I don't think Casey likes kids too much. He never talks to us," Katie added. "Grandpa hired Casey because he needed help on the farm."

Annie touched his arm. "If you married our ma, we would have you all the time."

Most nights, the girls fell asleep in Clint's arms chatting away about Christmas, and how they couldn't wait to give Amelia her gift. After they would drift off to sleep, Clint would lie awake thinking about what Annie said about him marrying Amelia. He figured Casey was visiting Amelia while he was gone; possibly he'd even asked for her hand. Like the girls, Clint couldn't wait to get home.

Days later, on Christmas Eve, they arrived at Clint's ranch as the sun was dipping below the horizon.

Ingrid, Amelia and John walked to the front porch to greet them. Clint lifted Katie and Annie from the wagon and they ran to Amelia. Clint hugged his mother and shook hands with the doc.

Amelia released the girls, ran to Clint and threw her arms around his neck. "Thank you for bringing them home."

Clint held her for a few minutes, enjoying the feel of her in his arms and appreciating her greeting. "They were anxious to get home to you." When she released him, he looked her up and down, thinking she looked more beautiful than ever. "You look like you've fully recovered."

She gave him a smile. "I feel wonderful. And your mother and I have been busy cooking. It's been so nice spending time with her."

Clint wanted to ask how many times Casey had visited, but the girls were listening to their conversation.

Ingrid welcomed the guests and shared their plans for the evening. "Children, after dinner I want all of you to help decorate the Christmas tree."

"Are we going to pop some corn to string?" Boone asked.

"Ma wouldn't have a tree without corn." Clint kissed the top of his mother's head. "I'll get the horses settled before dinner."

Dinner ended, and the children helped decorate the Christmas tree the doctor had chopped down the day before. When the tree was finished, sleeping arrangements were made for the night. Before they retired, Ingrid told them the plans for Christmas Day. "Everyone, get some sleep. We will have a quick breakfast in the morning, and then we'll ride to town for church service. Afterward, we'll have a big dinner at the hotel. Everyone is bringing a dish because they only have one cook at the hotel right now. Amelia and I have cooked several dishes to take for all of us."

Clint said he had an errand to run, and the doc offered to go with him, knowing what he was going to do. Three hours later, when they returned to the ranch, everyone was asleep. They shared another whiskey by the fire before the doc fell asleep in a chair. While the doc was snoring softly, Clint poured himself another whiskey and thought about his future. Now that he was home again, he couldn't bear the thought of being far from his mother, or Amelia and the girls. He knew his presence brought comfort to the girls, particularly after the encounter with those men who'd stolen the gold. Before he'd left the ranch tonight, the girls had told him good night, and he'd overheard Annie ask Amelia why he couldn't sleep with them like he did on the trail. He couldn't help but chuckle when he heard Amelia try to explain why that particular sleeping arrangement would be inappropriate here.

"But Mr. Mitchum let us sleep beside him on the way home. He held us so we wouldn't be scared," Annie retorted.

Amelia smiled at the thought of Clint holding the girls at night and patiently answering all their questions. "Well, that's different."

"Why?" Annie pressed.

"Annie, a lady must be married before a man can stay in her room," Katie explained to her sister.

"Why?" Annie asked.

"That's just what's proper," Katie replied.

"That's silly," Annie informed her.

Clint had to agree with Annie on that point.

Chapter 11

Ingrid and Amelia prepared a simple breakfast of apple cinnamon rolls with milk for the children and coffee for the men. After the men ate, they hurried to the stable to ready the wagons and buckboards for the trip to town. Clint hooked a team to his buckboard, planning to take Amelia and the girls with him.

While waiting for the women, Clint and Whitt were standing by the porch talking when Clint suddenly stopped in midsentence. Amelia and Ingrid walked from the house wearing their new dresses. Clint walked closer and removed his hat. "Ma, I've never seen such beautiful dresses, or two more stunning ladies."

Smiling, Ingrid placed a kiss on his cheek. "You chose the lovely material."

"Yes, thank you. Your mother is a talented seamstress. I've never owned anything so fine," Amelia added.

Clint held out his hands to help them down the stairs. "I'll be fighting every man in town over you two."

As soon as Annie and Katie walked outside, they ran straight to Clint.

"Look what Miss Ingrid made for us!" Annie exclaimed, holding out the skirt of her new dress.

"You girls look so pretty."

Annie thrust her doll at him. "Look at Lucy! She got a new dress, too."

Clint took Lucy and examined her new dress and her new eyes, which greatly improved the little doll's appearance. His mother had put Lucy back together. "She looks real pretty."

The doctor took Ingrid's hand in his and led her to the stable, where he'd left his buckboard. Honey and the puppies were hidden in the buckboard, and they didn't want the girls to see them. The doc's buckboard was at the back of the group as they made their way down the lane leaving Clint's ranch.

Reaching the dirt road that led to La Grange, they rode for another quarter of a mile until a huge banner draped across the road came into view. CHRISTMAS ROAD was written in big, bold letters. Clint heard the excited chatter not only from the children, but from the adults.

Pulling the buckboard to a halt, Clint jumped down and helped Amelia and the girls to the ground. As if timed perfectly, Mr. and Mrs. Stanton rode in from the opposite direction, followed by several buckboards filled with the families from town.

Whitt and the boys jumped from his wagon and joined Clint and Amelia. "Clint, what's all this?" Whitt asked.

Clint clapped Whitt on the back. "You'll see." He turned to see the excitement on the faces of the children. "There are presents hanging from the trees for the ladies and children. Now, everyone go find the present with your name on it." He motioned for Whitt, Tom and Ben, saying, "I want to talk to you in private for a minute."

By the time the adults were on the ground, all of the children, except Annie and Katie, were running to the trees looking for their names on the presents. Fortunately for Clint, he'd picked out gifts for all the children he'd met at Honey Creek. Mr. and Mrs. Stanton had selected gifts for the families who had remained in La Grange, and Mrs. Stanton had wrapped the presents. After Mr. Stanton delivered them to the ranch, Ingrid hid them in the stable until Clint returned. When Mr. and Mrs. Stanton told the town about the surprise Clint had planned for the children on Christmas morning, they decided to rename the road leading to La Grange to Christmas Road. Mr. Stanton and the doc had hung the banner for the families to see when they returned to their homes.

"This was the errand you had to do last night?" Whitt asked.

"Yep. The doc and I hung all the presents last night. Early this morning I left the house to go pick up Bo and Boone's presents."

Whitt gave Clint a puzzled look just as Bo called out to him, "Pa, look at our goats!"

Whitt looked at Clint with watery eyes and said, "I don't know how you did this, but thank you."

Clint motioned for the men surrounding him to move a few steps away, where they could talk in private. "I know you men were worried about your ranches being foreclosed on. I talked to the banker, and he agreed to push back the dates where he could." He handed each of them paperwork from the bank, reflecting the now-current mortgages.

Whitt studied the paperwork. "But you paid the portion that was due."

"It wasn't much, and that's a Christmas gift," Clint responded.

All the men choked back tears as they shook Clint's hand, thanking him for his generosity.

"Now, go see what your children are so excited about."

Clint walked back to Amelia and the girls. Annie slipped her hand in Clint's. "Thank you for our dresses."

"We love them," Katie added.

"I'm glad. Now, let's walk back to Doc's buckboard."

When they reached the buckboard, Clint lifted Honey from the back.

"Is that your dog, Mr. Mitchum?" Annie asked as she petted Honey.

"I reckon she is, and your mother named her Honey. What do you think of her?"

"She's so pretty," Katie replied.

Clint put Honey on the ground before he picked up the two puppies. "Honey told me these two were for you. But their ma has to stay with them for a while because they're so young."

Both girls started to cry.

"We've always wanted a puppy," Annie sobbed.

Clint held out a puppy to each girl. "Your ma agreed you can each have one, but you have to promise to take good care of them."

They both looked at Amelia. "Really? We get both of them?"

Amelia smiled through her own tears. "Yes, but you should thank Mr. Mitchum."

"Thank you!" They hugged the puppies, promising to take good care of them.

Clint kneeled down in front of them. "You're welcome, but why are you crying?"

"These are happy tears," Amelia told him.

Clint shook his head. "I have a lot to learn."

"Casey always said we couldn't afford puppies," Katie reminded her mother.

"Casey has no say in the matter. He won't be working at the ranch anymore," Amelia replied, her eyes on Clint.

Clint looked at her and arched his brow.

"He visited me while you were away and I told him we would never marry."

Clint grinned, pulled her closer and whispered in her ear, "Now that's a nice Christmas present."

"What are their names?" Katie asked, totally ignoring the conversation about Casey.

"You have to name them; they belong to you." Clint pointed

to the puppy Katie was holding. "That one is a boy, and the one Annie is holding is a girl."

"We'll think of good names," Annie promised.

Clint glanced up to see his mother and John approaching. "There's a present with your name on it, Ma."

"For me?" Ingrid questioned.

"Yes, ma'am, but you have to find it," Clint replied.

Ingrid and the doc walked to the trees to find her present.

Annie pulled at Amelia's skirt. "Ma, we have a present for you."

"Miss Ingrid helped us wrap it." Katie pulled the small package from her pocket.

Taking the gift in her hands, Amelia admired the wrapping. "This is so pretty. But how did you girls manage to get me a present?"

"Didn't I tell you about the magic of Christmas?" Clint asked.

The girls smiled up at Clint conspiratorially.

Carefully unwrapping the present, Amelia gasped when she saw the locket she'd seen months before in Stanton's mercantile. "It's the locket we saw that day."

Annie and Katie grinned at her. "We remembered."

"You certainly did. It's lovely." Amelia immediately tied the black ribbon holding the locket around her neck.

"It looks real pretty on you," Katie said.

Amelia kissed the girls. "I shall wear it always. Thank you, girls."

Clint took Amelia's hand. "All of you, come with me."

When Clint passed his mother, he asked, "Did you find your present?"

"Here it is." Ingrid pulled the small package from the tree and pulled off the paper. Her eyes widened in surprise when she saw the gold star locket brooch, designed with a large opal surrounded by seed pearls. "Son, it's beautiful." She turned to him, wrapped her arms around his neck and pressed a kiss to his cheek. "It's the most beautiful present I've ever received, and I'm going to put your photograph inside."

"It's not as beautiful as you are, Ma."

"You know I already gave you your Christmas present, don't you?" Ingrid whispered in his ear.

"Yes, ma'am, I do, and in the process you put me back together, just like Annie's doll." He glanced at Amelia. "And I need to ask Amelia something right now. We'll be back in a minute."

"What present did you give him?" the doc asked Ingrid when Clint walked away.

"Amelia."

Reaching the tree where he had hung a small box tied with a blue ribbon, Clint plucked it from the branch and took hold of Amelia's hand. "Amelia, I'd like to know . . ." His throat went dry. He wanted the moment to be perfect—a moment they would remember when they were old and gray, telling this story to their grandchildren. He removed his hat and started again. "Amelia, would you do me the honor of becoming my wife?" He looked at the girls standing beside Amelia, their eyes wide in surprise. "I'd like to know if you girls would do me the honor of becoming my daughters."

The girls quickly exclaimed, "Yes!"

Clint grinned at them, feeling more confident by their eager response. The girls wanted him as a father, but did Amelia want him as a husband? He turned his dark eyes on Amelia. "I can't be one without the other."

Tears started to flow down Amelia's cheeks. "This is the best Christmas of my life," she whispered.

Smiling at her response, Clint asked, "Are those happy tears?"

Amelia nodded.

Clint thought if he could judge his success by tears, then he'd succeeded in giving Amelia and the girls a wonderful Christmas. He opened the small box, plucked out the sapphire and diamond ring and gazed into her eyes. He arched his brow at her.

"Yes!" Amelia threw herself in his arms. "I can't believe this is happening."

Clint reached for her hand and slipped the ring on her finger. "The magic of Christmas," he whispered in her ear before he kissed her. He kissed her for so long that he forgot all about the people around them until he heard Annie ask, "Does that mean Mr. Mitchum can sleep with us now?"

Pulling his lips from Amelia's, Clint answered Annie's question. "Yes, it does."

"Can we call you Pa now?" Katie asked.

This time it was Clint who started to get teary-eyed. "Nothing would make me happier."

Everyone had gathered around Clint and Amelia, including Mr. and Mrs. Stanton. After everyone offered their congratulations, Clint thanked Mr. and Mrs. Stanton, his ma and the doc for their help with the Christmas surprise.

Mr. Stanton had a request of his own. "Clint, can you come over to our buckboard for a minute? I need to show you something."

With his arms around Amelia and the girls, Clint followed Mr. Stanton to the back of his buckboard, with all the other folks trailing close behind.

Clint looked inside the buckboard. Seeing nothing but a blanket, he looked at Mr. Stanton. "What's wrong?"

"Move the blanket aside," Mrs. Stanton instructed.

Tossing the blanket aside, Clint stared at the contents. He glanced up at the faces gathered around the buckboard. They were all smiling at him. "What's this?"

"The magic of Christmas!" Katie replied.

"It's your nightingales, Pa," Annie exclaimed.

Wishing you a magical Christmas!